MESRRA'S

POWER

EMMA K BLACKER

2QT Limited (Publishing)

First Edition published 2020 by

2QT Limited (Publishing)
Settle
North Yorkshire
BD24 9BZ

Cover design:Robbie Associates Ltd.
Cover images: shutterstock.com

Printed in the UK by Lightning Source

A CIP catalogue record for this book is available
from the British Library

ISBN 978-1-9130-71-47-9

Titles in the Lismarian Series

Hannoki's Will
Lovoa's Challenge
Mesrra's Power

Prologue

'CAPTAIN Wilhelm, thank you for joining us. Please take a seat,' Admiral Simon Johnson said as Captain Alex Wilhelm came into the room.

Alex looked around him and saw, as well as Admiral Johnson, his uncle Admiral Gareth Yoland and also another person he did not know. Judging by her uniform, she was a member of the Admiralty.

Alex sat opposite the admirals; as he did so, the third person was introduced to him as Admiral Natalie Webb. He knew the name but nothing else about her.

When he had brought Brelsa to Cornucopia from Lismar, Alex had known that he had breached numerous laws and at some point he would have to answer for his actions. Knowing what his grandfather David Wilhelm had fought for, and having read what had happened in the past, he was willing to take the punishment.

The pathological need for secrecy to protect reputations had left Alex not knowing who to trust. This time the message about what had been happening to the Lismarians had to be loud and public. If people knew the clothes that they desired so much came from living beings, there would be a moral outcry. He had been right.

Alex knew this would only stop the overt aspect of the trade; the wings had been taken as well, and he did not know where they had gone. He only wished he had been able to take Brelsa back home before this meeting; he just hoped the Federation of Worlds and its Navy, the FWN, would not stop her return to her home planet.

'I think everyone here agrees that this is a unique situation, Captain.' Admiral Johnson said.

'Your actions in bringing an alien here breach many laws and protocols, which are in place to protect both of our species from any viruses or bacteria foreign to us. Also, they protect Brelsa from learning too much about our technology and harming the Lismarians' natural development. The punishment for your actions could be severe. Do you understand?' Admiral Webb added.

'Yes, sir, ma'am. Though Brelsa refused a detailed examination, she was routinely scanned on boarding the *London* and nothing was detected.'

Alex could have added that when the ship's doctor spoke to her with Conner, Brelsa had no concept of disease. He trusted Admirals Johnson and Yoland, but he did not know Admiral Webb and he did not want to reveal that amazing fact just yet in case it put the Lismarians in more danger.

'Brelsa and her leaders are aware of the risks of sickness and, rightly or wrongly, they accepted them. In terms of technology and knowledge of other races, the attacks on their people have already exposed these. Brelsa coming here would only improve her people's perspective that not all aliens exist to kill them. Their knowledge of technology is so limited that the only thing we can do is show them what is possible. Respectfully, I have to say that this is not normal procedure for a disciplinary board and I'm not prepared to say more without legal representation.'

'I'm sorry, Captain. Admiral Webb spoke out of turn. This meeting has nothing to do with disciplinary proceedings and what you've just told us will not be used in any investigation without your authority after legal representation,' Admiral Johnson clarified.

He continued. 'We've spoken to Mr Cal Everson and Miss Jane Keyworth about their investigation into the Lismarian skin trade. It will take us some time to go through all the information, so a formal board won't happen for some months. The purpose of today's meeting is to discover if there are any immediate risks to the FWN. We have your initial report. Your ship will have to remain in port so the weapon damage can be examined before repairs are started.'

'Yes, sir. What further information do you require?'

'Our main concerns are why your communications went down before the attack, and the information about the pirate ship that was gained from the fight. Please talk us through what happened from when you encountered the other ship,' Admiral Johnson said.

'We were heading towards the planet Lismar to investigate any travel in the area and to ensure that the people were being left alone to develop in their own time,' Alex explained. 'Once we were in protected space, we detected another ship. We maintained our distance and attempted to gain further information. We couldn't discover much, other than that it was large and dense. We worked on the assumption at that point that it was heavily armoured. We thought that was strange if it was going to Lismar where there is no technology. I decided to keep far enough away to stop them detecting us and watch where the ship was going.'

'Why did you not report in at this time?' Admiral Webb asked.

'Intelligence suggested that ships were travelling through the protected area of space to save time on trading routes. We were assuming it could be heavily armed, but we had no evidence. I didn't feel at the time that I had enough information to hand.'

Admiral Johnson again brought Webb to order. 'This meeting is not to question actions that were or were not taken, it is to assess risk. Please continue.'

Alex resumed his explanation. 'The ship went into orbit around Lismar and immediately started to send shuttles down to the planet surface. They separated, going to the north and south. We started to close the distance so we could open fire on them, but before we could take action there was a large surge of energy from the planet and some of the shuttles were destroyed. When a second energy build-up didn't occur, I ordered the rest of the shuttles to be fired upon. This was when I ordered an emergency transmission to be sent.'

'Your report said that the communications were down. Do you know why?' Admiral Yoland asked.

'I don't. I believe that the other ship was able to disrupt them.'

'Why do you think it was that and not the energy surge from the planet?'

'The energy was not focused up at us but at the shuttles, which had broken through the atmosphere. Also, there would have been evidence of damage, which there wasn't.'

'Thank you. Please continue,' Admiral Yoland said.

'Having fired on the shuttles, we revealed our position and came under attack from the ship. Their weaponry and shielding were greatly advanced over ours and our sensors didn't recognise the weapons they were using. We would have been destroyed if the Lismarians hadn't intervened by focusing their energy onto the enemy vessel.'

'Thank you, Captain. We are still waiting for ships to arrive into Lismar's orbit, so we don't have a report from them yet. What level of damage did they do to the ship?' Admiral Johnson asked.

'They reduced it to debris.'

'You said before that the Lismarians had no technology. How were they able to blow up a ship in orbit?'

'They have a unique ability to manipulate the energy they gain from the suns. I have tried to detail it in full but it's truly something that needs to be seen to be believed.'

'Why did they delay and not attack the second set of shuttles?'

'They needed time to absorb more energy.'

'Will the Lismarians be a danger to us? Will they attack the ship in orbit, or the ships when they arrive?'

'No, sir,' Alex stated. 'They are telepaths. They attacked

when they picked up the mental intent to kill them, and they attacked the pirate ship when they felt its intent to kill us. If all we are planning on doing is securing the orbit, they will leave us alone.'

'What is your opinion of the ship that was destroyed?' Admiral Johnson questioned.

'That it's not one of ours. What little we were able to detect was technology unknown to us. The Lismarians said that it was not just their skins that were taken but their wings as well. From what my father told me, it was the wings that were of most value and were used in technological advances. We don't know where the wings went. I think others outside the FWN are involved. Based on reports I've read, I believe it might be the Urigans.'

'Do you have any evidence of this?' The question was sharp, and all three admirals had tensed up.

'No, sir, it's based solely on how advanced the weaponry was and intelligence that the Urigans are developing their technology quickly. Our industry exploded more than seventy years ago due to the Lismarian wings. When the trade stopped, the industry came to a halt and many new innovations – mainly those of Theron Gallo and Petro Diaz – suddenly ceased, creating the great economic depression.'

'That is not in any report I have read,' Admiral Webb stated.

'No, ma'am, it's not a formal report. It was what my grandfather believed. He originally discovered and stopped the trade.'

'Do you have his accounts of this?' she wanted to know.

'No, my grandfather died before I was born. He passed his knowledge to his children and my father told me everything he knew. My grandfather was very distrustful. He's been described by those who knew him well as being paranoid. Unfortunately, all I know is what I was told. There are no written records that I know of.' He did not mention the file that Jane had created.

'That could cause us a few issues. You do understand that, don't you, Captain?' Admiral Webb said.

'Yes, ma'am.'

'Be that as it may, as previously stated this meeting is not to establish blame. Is there anything else you want to add?' Admiral Yoland cut in.

Admiral Webb looked at her colleague with frustration and Alex wondered if she was about to ask him what he knew about his father-in-law. She seemed to decide against it. 'No, sir.'

'We thank you for your assistance, Captain Wilhelm. Do you have any questions for us?'

'Are you going to let Brelsa go home?'

'That has yet to be decided but we'll keep you informed. If there is nothing else, thank you for your time.' Admiral Johnson dismissed him.

❋

'Well, Gareth, you forced your way into the meeting. What are your thoughts?' Simon Johnson asked his friend after Admiral Webb had left. She had been reluctant to go and had tried to draw Admiral Johnson away from Admiral Yoland, but both had made it clear they had other business to attend to and refused to be drawn away.

'Thank you for letting me take part. I got the impression that Natalie was not happy.'

'You're right, she wasn't. She didn't believe you'd be impartial, due to your connections to the Wilhelm family.'

'If it had been a disciplinary board I'd agree, but on a fact-finding interview it's irrelevant. I'd also argue that Natalie is not impartial herself, not after her brother's suicide. I'd have expected her to take some time off.'

'I agree. I find it difficult to understand her brother's actions. Do you think there was more to it other than he blamed himself for missing the skin trade?'

'I don't know – it's too early in the investigation into his death. Who knows what will come out of it? That aside, why am I thinking that you know more about this than I do?'

'Because I do,' Gareth said. 'I know you sent Alex Wilhelm to Lismar, but I don't know how that came about or how much you know about the history of the planet.'

'Only what Cal and then Alex told me. Cal had connected the planet to his father's death; he contacted me to help him because I knew his father very well. As a result of my enquires, Alex found out what I was looking at and contacted me. He told me about how the Lismarian population had been killed for their skins and wings. They thought it had started again, which is why I sent Alex, at his insistence, to the planet to investigate. He knew more about the history than I did and he had a personal interest in going. I know your family and the Wilhelms are very close. It didn't occur to me then that this was anything more than a family legend. I should have contacted you sooner. I'm sorry. I hope you plan to trust me with what you know.'

'I don't know how much David told his children but Alex Wilhelm was not entirely correct when he called his grandfather paranoid. There were attempts to stop him looking into the trade of Lismarian skins and wings by arresting him for minor infractions. He had the advantage of being a very powerful telepath with the backing of the United Telepathic Association and a wealthy and politically influential father. His connections got him released quickly and he fled back to Lismar. As a result, the trade was revealed. It never sat well with him that those responsible were never hunted down and found. If Elen, his partner, had not become pregnant I believe he would have left the FWN and not returned until he'd found them. But his fear for his child outweighed the need for justice – it was something he struggled with for the rest of his life.'

'How sure are you of this? I know the Wilhelm and Yoland families are close, but how close?' Simon asked.

'My father was an excellent friend of David Wilhelm

from before he discovered the trade. They remained close until he died. Our families remain very close – my ex-wife Mary was his daughter.'

'Do you or your father have anything officially recorded about this?'

'No. I checked before this meeting and every report my father made was sealed and isn't accessible. Whoever was behind this was careful in clearing their tracks. The only place they went wrong was not leaving enough time. If they'd waited another generation, they might have got away with it.'

'Could David have left information anywhere that could not be easily accessible? It appears he was very cautious. He also sounds like someone who would want to leave his knowledge behind, just in case.'

'I can ask my father. Maybe he knows something I don't.'

'Thank you,' Simon Johnson said. He hoped that if there were records then they could be shared with the FWN; that would help them learn more about what was happening and who was attacking the Lismarians. 'What are your thoughts about the enhanced weaponry Alex described? Do you think the Urigans could be involved?'

'We can't rule them out. I know the two main conspirators, Petro Diaz and Theron Gallo, were able to use their connections to flee our space and were never found. The Urigans are not that far away, but we weren't looking in that area of space.'

'You're wondering if Petro and Theron could have sold out the Lismarians to them?'

'Their money and connections wouldn't have helped them outside the Federation; they would have needed to make other allegiances. Sharing what they knew about the Lismarians would not be outside the realms of possibility. But they must still have connections here for the ships to travel through our space. I'm wondering if the skins were a payoff for this.'

'Still, the timing seems strange. If Petro and Theron are

responsible, would they still be alive?'

'Why not? My father is, and he's the same age as them,' Gareth said. 'They also both had families. I don't know how much they were investigated at the time, but I doubt anyone has been watching them for some time.'

'I'll make discreet inquiries as to what they are doing now. Are you able to get more information from your father and ex-wife?' Simon asked.

'I will certainly be asking them.'

'We still have one immediate problem, though. What do we do with Brelsa?'

'I don't see any reason why she can't go home if we can be sure she's not carrying any viruses that will infect her people,' Gareth replied. 'As Alex said, the Lismarians have known for generations about space travel. This will give them a different perspective. My daughter, Amber, captains a deep-space ship. Using her would keep Brelsa close to those we know we can trust.'

'Where is Amber at the moment?'

'On shore leave at Europa.'

'She's not going to be happy about being recalled.'

'I know, but she'll obey orders and will understand when she knows why.'

Chapter 1

A few days after his meeting with Simon Johnson, Gareth Yoland left Cornucopia and travelled to Europa to talk to his father, Mark. On arrival at his parents' home, he had to argue with his father's staff, who had apparently been given orders that Mark was not to be disturbed under any circumstances – and the staff always followed orders. They had tried to show Gareth the door, but he did not care what his father wanted. As far as he was concerned, after they had spoken he would leave his father alone.

'I know you want to get rid of me because you're following orders. I understand that,' he said to the staff member who confronted him. 'You know as well as I do that I'd normally respect his privacy. But this is not a social visit, this is work and it's urgent.'

'We can try. It doesn't mean he will talk to you.'

'Thank you. I know he can be very cantankerous at times, but if you get me through the door, I can guarantee he'll want to hear what I have to say.'

Gareth went to the study and waited while the member of staff knocked on the door and opened it at the murmured response. Gareth pushed into the room and saw his father hunched over his desk with an old-style computer in front of him, a type Gareth had only seen before in old recordings and pictures. Mark Yoland was scrolling through something on the screen. He might now be over a hundred years old, but he never let anything stop him, not even age.

'I thought I told you I did not want to be disturbed,' he snapped without looking up.

'I'm sorry, Father, but I have an important matter to

discuss with you.'

'Gareth, it's good to see you but I'm too busy to talk to you now. You need to come back another time.'

'I'm sorry, Father, but this is about the Cornucopia fashion show. I don't know if you saw the media coverage.'

'Thank you, you may go,' his father said to the member of staff. Once the door was closed, he turned to his son. 'So what do you know?'

'I know we are going to be honest with each other. I'll tell you what I know, and you will fill in the blanks. This is you and me. Anything said here will be between just us. We'll sort out the rest as we need to.'

'Agreed. Take a seat,' Mark ordered.

Gareth settled himself and recounted the events as he had been told them: the murder of the head chairman; the renewed attacks on Lismar; the ship that had been sent to Lismar; the discovery of what had been happening there, and the events at Cornucopia.

'You were involved with all of this when it started. From what I've been able to find out, only a handful of people knew about what had happened. Of those, David Wilhelm died in a shuttle accident and his wife predeceased him. As far as I'm aware, the only person left who was in any way involved and is still alive is you.'

'You know a lot,' Mark said. 'What is said stays in this room?'

'Of course.'

'David did not die in a shuttle accident. I'm assuming he died on Lismar.'

'I spoke to Alex, his grandson. He didn't mention that, and the Lismarians said nothing. How did that happen?' Gareth asked, shocked.

'Alex probably didn't know. As for the Lismarians, I don't know,' his father admitted. 'David was very secretive about his work. The FWN closed the investigation shortly after Admiral Mathers committed suicide. Diaz and Gallo fled and could not be found. It was believed they had left FWN space and their names were placed on a watchlist. The investigation would re-open if they ever returned. David was never convinced the matter was correctly investigated because everyone was afraid of people discovering the truth. Those believed to be responsible were either dead or had fled and the area of space around Lismar was restricted, so no ships could go near the planet. As far as the FWN was concerned, the matter was closed and the Lismarians were safe. David was not satisfied with this and continued to investigate. He was never able to find where Diaz and Gallo went and it angered and frustrated him.

'When his wife Elen died, he had already exhausted all lines of investigation here, so he decided to go back to Lismar. He was worried that, because the FWN had buried the trade, it would happen again. He knew how the wings had been used, the advances that had been available and then suddenly lost. All the companies involved suddenly stopped operating and went into liquidation when the Lismarian trade was discovered. David always believed that greed would overrule morality. He went back because he wanted to make sure the Lismarians were as prepared as they could be.'

'How do you know he returned to Lismar when his family don't?'

'I took him and left him there, then faked the shuttle accident. David considered telling his children what he'd planned but at the last minute decided against it. He didn't want them coming after him.'

'I can't believe you allowed that,' Gareth exclaimed.

'Why? He'd already spent months there before the trade was discovered. What more damage could he do in a few months that had not already been done?'

'I'm sorry, you're not making much sense. You say David went back to help them prepare should the trade start again, then you said there is little he could do and implied he would die soon. Was he sick?'

'Not then. I don't know how much you know about Lismar but it's a very hot planet with little food and water. David only had two environmental suits and six months' worth of supplies. Once the suits failed and the supplies ran out, he wouldn't have survived for long.'

'You have no way of knowing that for sure.'

'When David originally crashed onto Lismar, he had his shuttle for shelter and a water supply, but that was not enough. When he returned to FWN space, he was severely dehydrated, malnourished and suffering from skin cancer. The doctors believed he wouldn't have survived another month on the planet.'

'That sounds like an awful way to die,' Gareth said.

'It would have been.'

'What could he offer those people that was worth it?'

'He hoped to improve the machine he'd built and advise on how best to use it to improve the planet's defences.'

'What machine?'

'Alex didn't mention that?'

'No, I've only spoken to him during an informal interview. There was another admiral present who he didn't know.'

'Alex, if I remember correctly, is a telepath,' Mark stated. 'If you trusted the other admiral, he would have too.'

'Exactly.'

'Ah,' Mark said, understanding his son. Whoever this admiral was, he had concerns about them but commented no further.

'Tell me more about this machine,' Gareth said.

'After David returned to FWN space, he used the information he'd gained to come up with various plans for a machine. When he recovered, he snuck out of FWN space back to Lismar and built a machine that increased the Lismarians' natural ability to expand the energy they absorb from their suns.'

'Do you think that's how they were able to destroy the ship in orbit?'

'I'd have thought so. They could easily destroy shuttles

coming down to the surface. As far as I know, they had never before tried to destroy anything in orbit.'

'How was that allowed?'

'It wasn't. The FWN was never told about it.'

'I think there's a much bigger story here, which I'd really like to know about,' Gareth said thoughtfully. 'But for now, the Lismarians have a machine that has allowed them to defend themselves. This is something I'll have to investigate. There would be serious questions if they used it against a FWN ship.'

'That wouldn't happen. Though the Lismarians are telepaths, they only sense us if our attention is directed towards them, and they can tell if the interest is hostile or not.'

'I just hope you're right about that,' Gareth said. 'It's a shame David didn't leave you the details of his investigation before he hurried back to Lismar.'

'He did. Why do you think I have this old thing out?'

'How were these files never found?'

'This computer isn't connected to any networks, so no amount of searching would have found them.' Mark smiled.

'How detailed was the investigation?' Gareth asked.

'Very. David had looked extensively at Gallo and Diaz and their families. He'd also looked at Admiral Mathers and his associates, as well as other companies he believed profited from the Lismarians. However, he could never prove anything. I'm still going through everything – you're welcome to help me.'

A knock on the door broke their concentration. 'I said I didn't want to be disturbed,' Mark shouted.

The door opened to reveal his very annoyed-looking wife. 'I don't care what you ordered. It's late and you need to eat. You'll get no sympathy from me if you make yourself ill. And how much work do you think you'll get done then?' They stared at each other until Mark blinked.

'Fine.'

'It's good to see you, Gareth. You're staying for food, I

assume?'

'Of course he is. We have too much work to do,' Mark growled.

'I'll have it sent in to you.' His wife turned and left. A few minutes later the food arrived.

'We'll need to find out if anyone kept track of Gallo and Diaz's families after David left,' Mark said.

'No, they didn't. A year after the original attacks, the FWN stopped investigating the families. Once David left, no one paid any attention to them. After being briefed by Alex, I made some enquiries. The families have moved. I've started a discreet investigation to track them down so we can see what they know.'

'Who have you asked? Can you trust them?' Mark asked, worried.

'Don't worry, I've asked Cal and his partner Jane to look into it. They were responsible for uncovering the trade starting again and bringing it to light. Their only aim is to get to the bottom of this.'

'Sounds ridiculous. Why are they so interested if they don't have their own agenda?'

'They do. Cal is the son of the recently deceased head chairman, who was murdered because he discovered the link between the skins going on sale and the old trade,' Gareth explained.

'You mean Cal Everson?'

'Do you know him?'

'Only by reputation. His company holds the contract for all FWN buildings' security. He is also an expert in shielding technology. I can't imagine he took his father's death well. Will you keep me updated?'

'Of course. There's a lot of personal information here on the family members. It will help Cal and Jane with the searches. Can I share it with them?'

'Just the personal family information for now. I'll download it for you – tell them to keep it offline. How do you plan to get it to them? I'm not overly happy with others knowing about this,' Mark warned.

'I could give it to Alex to pass on if you're worried. I just won't tell him what it is.'

'Alex is a telepath and connected to this. He's going to know it came from me.'

Gareth grinned. 'He might guess, but he's not a powerful telepath. And having been married to Mary, I've learnt some very valuable skills. I can block him out. But would it be so bad if he knew?'

'It's not that I don't trust him, it's not knowing who else is involved. For now, I want to keep this as close as possible,' his father said. 'Do you know what will happen to the Lismarian who came here?'

'Amber is going to take her back home.'

'Good. Amber will make sure she gets back safely.' Mark paused before continuing, knowing that his son wouldn't like what he was about to suggest. 'It might be worth talking to Mary. I can't believe that David didn't make sure someone else knew everything in case something happened to me before I could pass it on.'

Gareth's heart sank. Just what he needed: a visit to his ex-wife who had never forgiven him for their daughter's choices. 'Mary was always very close to her father and an extremely strong telepath like him. Please tell me she didn't know about this?'

'I don't know, David never said either way. I did tell him he needed to talk to someone other than me. If he told anyone else, you know as well as I do that it would have been her.'

❀

After leaving his father, Gareth made his way to the United Telepathic Association. He had spent his entire working life in the FWN; he should have been used to cold, official buildings, but this place still unnerved him.

The whole structure was shielded against telepathic communication. Gareth had always assumed they made the public areas as inhospitable as possible to put visitors at a disadvantage. Now he was second-guessing his decision not to make an appointment with his ex-wife. Would she even receive him? This place was very much her territory.

'I'm here to see Mary Wilhelm. Can you let her know?' he told the receptionist. The UTA was traditional and always had someone to meet visitors; what they could not detect mentally, they would pick up by assessing body language. Though there were automated systems which claimed they could do the same, the UTA still trusted human instinct over a computer program.

'Do you have an appointment?'

'No, but it's important that I meet with her as soon as possible.'

'Of course, I'll see if she is available. Who shall I say wants to speak to her?'

'Her ex-husband.' Gareth saw a slight hesitation.

'One moment, sir,' the receptionist said and put the message through. 'Would you like to take a seat while I await a response?'

'Thank you.' Gareth tried to make himself comfortable, wondering how long Mary would make him wait. He did not think she would be pleased to see him.

Gareth was not a telepath but he could read the uncomfortable expression on the receptionist's face. He bet he was wondering how mad his boss would be that her ex-partner was here. Gareth had seen the facial recognition software when he entered, which accounted for him not being asked to confirm who he was. They already knew.

Being here brought back many memories. Gareth knew that he and Mary had got together too young. They had seen a lot of each other growing up; their parents had been best friends. Mary had initially been keen to join the FWN once her training in the UTA had been completed. She had her father's powerful telepathic gift but was determined to do what her father had never been allowed to do and join the FWN. Her parents had been so proud of her the day she was sworn in – the day both Gareth and Mary were sworn in, having married a few days earlier. Together they had thought themselves unstoppable.

Mary had hated the FWN and resigned after her first tour, returning to the UTA. She and Gareth had been supportive of each other's decisions and he had been so happy when she became pregnant with Amber. He was glad then that his wife had left the FWN and could offer stability to their newborn baby.

Their relationship had slowly broken apart due to it always being long distance and their different priorities. Both recognised that; both accepted it. They had remained friends until Amber turned her back on the UTA. Their beautiful, talented daughter, whose telepathic strength rivalled her mother's, had chosen the FWN; she had picked Gareth over Mary.

'Gareth, it's been a long time.' He looked towards the voice and smiled, relieved that his ex-wife had not rejected him and surprised that she had come down to meet him herself.

'Mary, you look stunning as always.' Even as he said it, he knew the truth of it.

She ignored the compliment. 'Please follow me.' She turned abruptly, expecting him to obey. They walked together in silence until they entered an office and the doors closed behind them. Without talking, Mary pressed her palm on a security pad, only lifting it when the lights flashed around her hand.

'What's that?'

'Just activating the room's additional security.'

'What extra level of security? I thought you couldn't read my mind here.'

'I can't, and I'd have been upset if you didn't know the answer to that. I thought I'd taught you to detect and block a mind read.'

'I'm sorry, my comment was out of order.'

'It's fine. I was making assumptions about why you're here. It's the first time in years you've wanted to meet. Bearing in mind the events at Cornucopia, I thought you'd want to talk as privately as possible.'

'You're right,' Gareth said. 'I've spoken to Alex, who was at Cornucopia, and my father about his knowledge of past events. But there are still gaps. I came here to see if your father told you anything about the Lismarians.'

'He did more than tell me, he shared all his memories with me,' she admitted.

'You didn't think about sharing this information?'

'While the Lismarians were unknown, what was the point? I planned to pass the information on if needed. I was going to call you to explain, but you showed up here first.'

'Why didn't you get in touch before? Why keep it secret?'

'I promised my father I'd keep it to myself unless I saw any indication of the trade restarting.'

'I'm sick and tired of our fathers' secrecy over this.'

'My father couldn't talk about it – he'd have been arrested if he'd done so. He did the best he could to make sure a few people knew so they could pass it on, as I will do now with you. And when I next see Amber, I'll share my memories with her.'

'Thank you.'

'If you have the time now, we can go through all that I know.'

Chapter 2

WHEN Amber received her orders that shore leave had been cancelled, to say she was annoyed was an understatement. They had been patrolling space for over two years. Her crew were mentally and physically exhausted. Those who could were planning to spend as much time with their families and loved ones as possible; she was aware that some families had travelled not just across Europa but from other planets to be together. They had thought they had a month; now that was being cut in half.

All her crew would report back to duty as ordered – that was what was expected when you signed up to the FWN – but it didn't mean that they would like it. She expected to feel their discontent for weeks, months. It was at times like these that she wished her room had mental shielding in place. She could already feel the headache coming on.

The next day she boarded the first shuttle returning to the FWN *Ottawa* along with all but one of her senior crew, who stayed on the planet to supervise the embarking process. On docking, each of her officers went to their respective areas of responsibility to oversee the preparations to leave orbit while she went to the bridge to coordinate everyone's return.

Walking onto the bridge, she was met by an ensign, one of the few who had stayed on board to monitor the ship's systems. He gave her a status report.

It would take a few days to get all the crew back on board. Having been told they had a month before they needed to return, some of them had travelled long distances. The first would return in the next few hours.

Amber could feel the crew's discontent and frustration pounding against her mental shields over the next forty-eight hours. They all resumed their duties without complaining to her or any of her senior officers, but she was sure that a lot was said among themselves.

After the anger and frustration of having to return to duty, the question in all their minds was why. It was a question she could not answer; she would receive her orders when she arrived at Cornucopia.

Amber had seen the media reports and knew that her cousin was involved in revealing to the public an unknown trade in alien skins in the federation space. She had no idea how he had become involved. The only reason she could think of for the recall was that the Admiralty thought she knew something about it, that Alex might have given her confidential information. She sincerely hoped that was not the case. Amber didn't know anything about the events her cousin was involved in; even if she did, the FWN should have recalled her and not penalised her crew.

'Captain, everyone has reported back for duty and the last shuttle has docked,' an ensign informed her, breaking her train of thought.

'Thank you,' she said. 'FWN *Ottawa* requesting permission to leave Europa.'

'Stand by *Ottawa*, a request has just come through from Admiral Yoland to join you on your departure. He is waiting at Port 5 for collection.'

'Understood. Sending a shuttle down now.' Amber gave the relevant orders. She had not realised her father was on the planet. Maybe he could brief her on what was going on.

Amber made her way to the shuttle bay to await his arrival. She did not have long to wait. She watched as the hatch opened and Gareth walked out. She had not seen him in years and now realised how much she'd missed him. Whatever reason he had for being on her ship, Amber was glad to see him. She could not stop a smile tugging at the corners of her mouth as she saluted him.

'So formal, Amber! No hug for your father?'

She laughed and walked up to him happily, wrapping her arms around him, protocol forgotten. 'It's good to see you,' she said. 'Do you want to want to come to the bridge, or do you want to be shown to your quarters?'

'I'll come to the bridge then, after we're underway, we can talk.'

Once they were en-route to Cornucopia, Amber and her father went into the meeting room next to the bridge.

'Though it is good to see you, Father, I do feel that this isn't a coincidence.'

'I'm sorry. Your being recalled was by my order but it was a decision I didn't take lightly. I needed someone I could trust completely. It was luck that you hadn't left so I could return to Cornucopia with you.'

'I have so many questions, I struggle to know where to start.'

'What do you know about what happened at Cornucopia and the events surrounding it?' Gareth asked.

'Only what I've seen and heard on the news.'

'Then let me explain what happened, and about a race of aliens called the Lismarians.'

Once he'd finished, Amber looked at him in disbelief. 'How was it possible for these attacks to take place?'

'I don't know. That's why I need you. We need to keep everything about this as close as possible – that's why I recalled you and your crew.'

'But I didn't know anything about this.'

'I know, but you're family and this is very much a family matter.'

'What do you mean by that? What more are you not telling me?'

'A lot, but it would not be appropriate to tell you before I get the chance to brief Admiral Johnson,' Gareth explained. 'Alex will have his own story to tell as well. I know you think I'm not being fair, Amber.'

'My job is to follow orders, not to question the reason

behind them,' she said. 'If anything, I'm annoyed because you pulled rank and made this personal. And other than giving me a few extra details to what is being reported on the news, I'm still very much in the dark about what's going on.'

'I know. I'll make it up to your crew for this recall.'

'You'd better. They were gone a long time and they needed to reconnect with their families.'

'I'm sorry.' It did not escape him that she had mentioned her crew reconnecting with their families but not herself, though her mother's offices were on Europa.

As if something her father had said had just sunk in, Amber said, 'You keep talking about going back to Cornucopia. Why were you here on Europa?'

'To see your grandfather and mother.'

'Please tell me they're not involved in this.'

'Very much so. When this assignment is over, please get in touch with your mother. She's told me what I suspect is most of what she knows – what's relevant – but she seems to think that sharing with you on a mental level is just as important.' When Amber made no reply, her father continued. 'I know things have been bad between you for a long time, but maybe this will help you talk again.'

'Fine. I'll see what she has to say.'

❈

They docked at Cornucopia a few days later. The crew were given a forty-eight-hour pass and a bonus payment to use at their discretion. Amber disembarked with her father and headed to the control centre to receive her orders.

As she walked into the conference room, she was surprised and relieved to see her cousin Alex. She felt a wave of reassurance from him. She saw another admiral, whom she knew as Admiral Johnson, as well as a lieutenant commander she did not know.

'I'm sorry for the disruption to your shore leave, Captain. I believe Admiral Yoland has filled you in about the events here,' Admiral Johnson stated.

'Yes, sir, though I still have many questions.'

'As do we all, Captain. At this time not much more is known, but an investigation has already started. The alien, Brelsa, travelled here from Lismar to reveal to us that the clothes our rich people were desperate to buy came from living, sentient beings. What we need now is a captain and crew we trust to get Brelsa home again. We don't consider this a high-risk assignment, but we thought it best to keep it in the family. If you know what I mean.'

Amber was only just starting to.

'I thought you knew about them,' Alex said, reading her mental agitation.

'I had no idea. It's a long time since something has taken me so unawares.'

'I'm sorry you didn't know, but Brelsa needs our help. Please help me get her home safely. Be careful what you say – Admiral Johnson can be trusted, but not everyone in this room.'

Amber did not need it spelt out to her who he was referring to. *'Understood. Who is he?'*

'He is representing Admiral Webb. Her brother, Stuart Webb, the deputy head chairman, committed suicide after the Lismarian trade was exposed. I'm not sure of her motives.'

'You think that there are some in the FWN who supported the trade?'

'How else could they have succeeded? If our suspicions are correct, they would have had an admiral and politician in their pockets.'

'I'll help get Brelsa back to Lismar safely but if I don't get answers to my questions, I will be really annoyed.'

'Thank you.'

'Captain, is there a problem?' the unknown lieutenant commander asked Amber.

'No, sir, I'm just trying to take everything in,' Amber replied. 'Brelsa will be the first alien I've met; it will be an honour to take her home.'

This officer was not telepathic. That was a strange choice when dealing with telepaths. Amber would easily detect an attempt at a mental intrusion, but would not necessarily be aware of her telepathic conversation with her cousin being overheard.

'We will inform Brelsa she is to return with you. Your formal orders and risk assessment will be sent to you. If you've any further questions, please come back to me. Is that understood?' Admiral Johnson said.

'Yes, sir.'

'Then you are dismissed.'

Amber stood up. As she turned to leave, her cousin Alex spoke to her again. *'Thank you. Can I come to your cabin tonight to explain?'*

'You'd better. I always like to know what I'm getting into.'

⚛

After the meeting, Gareth Yoland went to see Alex. He did not stay long; he just handed over a file. 'Give this to Cal and Jane. Make sure they don't look at it while connected to a network. Hopefully it will help with their investigation into Diaz and Gallo.'

Alex knew better than to ask any questions.

⚛

'Where did you get this from?' Jane asked Cal as he handed her a storage file.

'It appears Alex has a lot of connections. He was given it to pass to us. I don't know how much use it'll be, though. It's clearly old tech.'

'I won't know until I look at it.'

'We were told to look at it offline. Is it possible?'

'Yes, but not on this computer,' Jane said, getting up, going to a cupboard and pulling out another one. It was not like any system Cal had seen before. Jane placed it on the desk, logged on and plugged in the file, loading it up.

'That looks old and basic,' Cal said.

'It's not. It looks that way because when I built it I wasn't interested in how it looked, only what I required it to do. I'm not going to spend time I don't have making it pretty.' When Cal just looked at her in surprise, she continued. 'Seriously, you write a backdoor hack into your programs, and you know what I can do. Did you honestly think I didn't have multiple-access systems, including ones that run offline?'

'You just get hotter and hotter.'

'Seriously?' Jane asked, and Cal sent her a wicked smile in response. Jane chose to ignore him or they would not be looking at the file any time soon.

They sat in silence as the file loaded. 'Wherever you got this from, the formatting is definitely old.'

'What does it say?'

'Give me a moment, I need to reformat it to make it readable.' Jane's fingers flew across the keyboard.

Cal could make little sense of the information on the screen, then suddenly it changed into a series of documents.

'Do you plan to read over my shoulder?' Jane asked.

Cal knew that voice and moved away.

Jane started looking through the information, quickly getting the gist of what the files contained. 'It's about the Gallo and Diaz families, their parents, siblings, partners, children. All their tax, accounting, social networking – every possible way to track someone remotely is here. The files are detailed until about fifty years ago, then they stop.'

'That's around the time David Wilhelm died. Do they help you now?'

'They should do. I can trace the information here, pick up where David left off, but it will take me some time.'

'Is there anything I can do?'

'See if you can get the rest of his records – and a cup of coffee,' Jane requested.

'I can't believe I knew nothing about this,' Amber said when Alex came by later that day. She'd been lucky and, at an extortionate price, had secured a shielded room to stay in overnight which allowed them to talk freely.

Alex had given her his account of what had happened and everything he knew about the Lismarians; a lot she already knew from what her father had told her on the voyage from Europa.

'My father told me everything that he knew,' Alex admitted.

'It would have been nice if mine had done the same. Or my mother. Apparently she knows even more.'

'My father told me everything when he fell ill. Maybe your parents are waiting until they have to pass on the information.'

'Because death is always announced before it happens,' Amber retorted sarcastically. 'Sounds like a poor argument to me. Thank you for telling me what you know. I'll make sure Brelsa gets home safely. Father mentioned that I got recalled to duty to keep it in the family. How much does Admiral Johnson know?'

'Everything your father and I are aware of,' Alex admitted.

'You have to be joking.'

'He discovered the trade had restarted before me. He created my orders to go to Lismar, and forged communication afterwards. That's the only reason why I'm not currently being court-martialled.'

'What about Admiral Webb?'

'She claims she wants to be involved to understand her brother's suicide, to explain that there was no way he could've known what was happening. She wants to clear his name.'

'You don't believe that?'

'No. I don't think she cares about her brother's death. I feel that there's something more, but she can block her mind.'

'You've tried to read her mind? Alex! She could know.'

'She didn't detect it and it was worth the risk.'

'Are you sure? She didn't come today,' Amber pointed out.

'If she was suspicious, she'd have sent one of her telepathic entourage to the meeting,' Alex argued. 'Amber, when you meet the Lismarians, when you see what was done to them, you'll understand the need to do what is necessary to protect them.'

'The FWN know now. They will protect them.'

'Like they did before? Our grandparents failed them, Amber. This should never have happened again.'

'Then stop talking and let me see.' It was a direct challenge. That level of mental intrusion was very uncommon; people had a right to their privacy, especially of their thoughts, feelings and experiences.

'Alright.'

❈

Amber took Brelsa on board that morning. Her cousin, Alex, was given permission to join them while his ship underwent repairs; also joining them was Ensign Conner, with whom Brelsa had made friends, as well as Cal and Jane. As Brelsa knew Alex, it was considered prudent to let him travel back to Lismar to reassure her and her people.

The rest of the crew stayed behind. In terms of the investigation, the Admiralty had stated they had all the information they needed from Alex. Amber wondered how much of this was dictated by Admirals Yoland and Johnson.

When Brelsa boarded, she went straight back to the hydroponics but stopped short when she saw it. A section of it was clear and gave an excellent view of space.

'I'm sorry, we should have warned you. Are you going to alright here?' Ensign Conner asked. She and Brelsa had travelled together on the shuttle to the ship.

'Why is this here?'

'Most exploration ships have a viewing area. Some people like to see space, it can help with feelings of claustrophobia. But the FWN thought it took up unnecessary space, so they tried incorporating it into the hydroponics area. They thought being around plants would also be beneficial.'

'So all new ships have these now?' Brelsa asked.

'No. They forgot that an equal number of people hate looking out into space because it gives them vertigo, a feeling of falling. The ships that have these viewing areas will keep them, but in the others they have reverted to the original plan. Do you think this will be a problem for you?'

'I don't know. It is very beautiful, and I have no problem with falling.'

'Please let me know if it worries you once we start travelling in space.'

⚛

'How is our guest doing?' Captain Amber Yoland asked as she sat in the conference room with Alex.

'Same as before. She sits in the hydroponics, talks to others when spoken to, but otherwise she keeps to herself.'

'She isn't trying to integrate with the crew? Was she asked not to because of her circumstances?'

'No,' Alex replied. 'She obviously knows she's only here for a short time, and your crew were warned about what they could discuss with her. As before, she doesn't even acknowledge the officers when they come and work around her. The only person she makes any effort with is Ensign Conner.'

'Do you know why?'

'Conner is my strongest telepath. She connected to Brelsa's leaders, the First Protectors Solvan and Lovoa, when we first arrived at Lismar. She talked Brelsa through everything when she came on board. The Lismarians seem to communicate much more by telepathy – maybe Brelsa feels better being around people she can talk to mentally.'

'Did you get that from her?'

'No, from Conner. Though they don't understand each other on a mental level, where possible Brelsa likes to use images to reinforce the spoken word.'

'Why don't you see if she opens up to you?' Amber suggested. 'She knows you better than me.'

'I could, but Conner struggles as a Level 5 and I'm only a measly Level 3 telepath. What level are you again?' Alex asked innocently.

'Fine. I'll get your Conner to introduce me properly. I met Brelsa when she came on board, but it was brief. While on the topic of guests, what about the other two?' Amber asked, referring to Cal and Jane.

'Glued to their computers and going through the information I provided. I'm confused as to why they wanted to come with us.'

'Leave them to it. Maybe they just liked the idea of going on a trip.'

'Those two always have their own agenda. They wanted to come for a reason.'

'Should I be concerned?'

'No, they are very much on our side.'

⚛

Amber walked into the hydroponics with Conner. She loved coming in here, seeing the stars flash by; it was one of the reasons she'd fought to keep hold of this command. But now her attention was not on what was outside but what was right in front of her.

Brelsa sat with her eyes closed and face raised towards the solar lamps, paying no attention to anything around her.

'Brelsa,' Ensign Conner called. On hearing her name, Brelsa turned her head and looked towards them but remained where she was, waiting for them to come to her. 'The captain has come to see how you are doing.'

'Why?'

'It's important to me that you are as comfortable as possible during the trip back to your planet,' Amber replied.

'Thank you. This is a nicer ship than the last one.'

'I'm glad you like it. Would you like to see the rest of it?'

'Not at the moment,' Brelsa replied.

Amber could understand why none of the crew had tried very hard to make the Lismarian feel welcome. 'We will arrive back at Lismar in a few days. I haven't been there before. Can you let me know what to expect when I get there?'

'Why can't the others tell you?'

'They were only on the planet for a short time and they still don't know anything about your people's customs. I want to make sure the correct respect is paid to your First Protectors when we return this time.'

'You could not give the First Protectors the reassurances they would need. We value honesty and, though we won't pry into each other's minds without consent, it is rare to withhold it.'

'Is it because I'm human that our telepathic abilities are not compatible?'

'No it's...' Brelsa started to say.

Amber felt a mental push against her mind. *'Yes, I can feel you,'* she said and felt Brelsa withdraw but not before she sensed something that worried her.

'I can't understand you mentally. I'm sorry. When speaking I'm told your translators make it possible that we can talk, but mentally it doesn't work,' Brelsa said.

'It's fine, I just acknowledged you.'

'You are much stronger than Ann.' Brelsa looked towards Ensign Conner.

'When our minds touched, I felt that you were very cold.'

'It's fine. I can't cover my markings – I won't take in any energy otherwise.'

'We could get you blankets,' Amber offered. 'If the solar lamps are directed to your front, then the blankets can cover your back and help keep you warm.'

'Thank you, that would be nice.'

Amber put in the request for blankets to be brought to the hydroponics, as well as gloves and socks, having noticed the lack of patterning on Brelsa's hands and feet.

When the items arrived, Brelsa burst out laughing at the sight of the socks and gloves but was willing to try them if they would help to keep her warm. Amber realised that whoever had taken the order had thought to include a hat. It was not long before Brelsa was sitting there with the hat, gloves and socks on, the blanket hooked behind her wings and covering her back. She looked very odd, but Amber could tell that she felt a lot warmer.

⚛

'It's been interesting being captain of your ship for the last few days,' Alex joked, meeting up with Amber for dinner as they approached Lismar.

'Thanks for taking over. Brelsa has been very forthcoming about her culture and she's been teaching me her language. It's difficult to know if any of what she's telling me about her people will be relevant, but we may never have another chance.'

'It's fine. I prefer captaining your ship to taking orders from you.'

Amber laughed but understood; it would drive her mad to take orders from her cousin. 'There's one thing I'm curious about. Ann Conner – you refer to her by surname but Brelsa by her first name. Why is that?'

'When she came on board, she introduced herself as Conner – so Conner she's always been. I hadn't realised Brelsa called her by her first name.'

Chapter 3

AS the FWN *Ottawa* arrived into Lismar's orbit, they opened communication with the FWN *Cairo* which had stayed behind to protect the planet.

'It's all been quiet here since the pirate ship was destroyed,' the captain said.

'That's good to know. Has there been any communication with the planet?' asked Amber.

'None, but there are no strong telepaths on my ship. I'm just glad that they didn't consider us a threat and left us alone.'

'They are certainly an impressive race. Hopefully we'll be going down to the planet soon to return Brelsa home. Would you like to send a crew member as well?' Amber asked.

'That may be a good idea. I know who I'd want to send. Please let me know when you plan to go down so I can arrange their transport.'

'I will do.' Amber ended the communication before turning to her cousin. 'What are your thoughts?'

'I think we should ask Brelsa to contact her First Protectors, let them know we've brought her back and want to come down to meet them again. I'd advise against going down uninvited.'

'Agreed.'

Amber made her way to the hydroponics. She had thought about asking Ensign Conner to make the request, but she had to admit she was fascinated by Brelsa and relished any excuse to talk to her. As she entered, she saw Brelsa looking out at the stars. There was something about her stance that screamed frustration.

'Are you alright Brelsa?'

'I know I'm nearly home. I can feel the suns, but I can't see them.'

'They are there but we like to maintain as much distance as possible.' Amber knew that a slight alteration of the ship's course would bring one of the suns in view. She did not believe that Brelsa could feel the sun; it was more psychological. Brelsa knew that the sun gave her power; she knew it was near.

Brelsa turned to face Amber. 'Is there something I can help you with?'

'Can you contact your First Protectors, let them know you're back and that we would like to come down to the planet to meet them?'

'When can I return to Lismar?'

'That depends on your people,' Amber replied. 'We're happy to return you when your First Protectors allow us to bring you down to the surface.'

Brelsa made no reply. Amber could hear nothing mentally but she suspected that the Lismarian was communicating with someone. That was confirmed a moment later.

'You are welcome whenever it is convenient,' Brelsa said. 'The suns have just risen.'

'We will leave in an hour,' Amber informed her.

'I will let them know.'

⚛

'You can't go down,' Alex argued when Amber let him know her intentions.

'Why not?' Amber challenged.

'You're the captain; your place is here on the ship. You know that.'

'Normally yes, but you're here. And didn't you joke about how you like having control of my ship?'

'I'm here as a guest, not as a captain, regardless of what I said before.' When Amber made no reply, he continued, 'Why is this so important to you?'

'I don't know. I just feel a connection to Brelsa and want to explore it. This will probably be my only chance.'

'Amber—' Alex said, thinking about their grandfather and his obsession with this race.

'Please, Alex, I can't explain it. I just need to go down there. And with you here, there's no reason why I can't.'

He could not deny the truth of her statement. A ship only needed one captain and, though he was a guest, he could take control of the *Ottawa* if required. He was concerned about her determination to go down to the planet. Alex knew Amber had been unaware of the family history; what she did know had come from him and her father over the last few days. She was not happy at having been kept in the dark. All he could assume was that her need to go to the planet was driven by her telepathic talent. He felt that if he explained to her the reason why he objected, she would just want to go more.

'You're right, there isn't one,' he conceded.

⚛

Brelsa was excited to be going home, and she was impatient as she sat and waited on the shuttle to be taken back down to the surface. When Amber had asked her to contact Solvan and Lovoa earlier that day, Brelsa had doubted she could reach them but she had easily. She was surprised by how much she had missed a familiar mental voice.

As soon as she was informed that the shuttle had landed, Brelsa fumbled with the safety harness, irritated at its restriction. Conner, who was sitting next to her, reached over and released it. Brelsa stood and waited for the hatch to open, but it was not immediately released as Conner and Amber were putting on their environmental suits.

As the hatch descended, the light from the two suns started to penetrate the shuttle's confines and Brelsa felt her skin tingle with anticipation. She was so glad to get back to Lismar and she walked quickly out of the shuttle, into the full power of the two suns. For the first time since she had left, she was not cold. She felt a rush of energy that made her gasp in surprise.

Though Brelsa had volunteered to go to Cornucopia to prove where the skins were coming from, she had been terrified, not knowing how she would cope without the suns. She had grown up with the horror tales of her father's lightless cells. The strange lamps they had on the ship where they grew produce had helped, but she had felt vulnerable, knowing that she would be limited in her ability to defend herself if need be. It occurred to her that she had been reduced to the capability of the majority of her people.

While on Cornucopia, Brelsa had tried some of their food, much to the horror of the doctors assigned to keep an eye on her. They mentioned words like anaphylactic shock and described what an allergic reaction could do to a human. They persisted in wanting to run tests; she continued in refusing. She had no idea what an allergic reaction was and, as far as she was concerned, it was her risk, her choice. The food helped her regain some physical energy and strength. She had even enjoyed trying different things, not always successfully. Any reactions to the food healed quickly if she stayed in the sunlight, fascinating the doctor who was with her at the time and renewing his requests for a complete medical exam. There had been threats of what they called a court order but, whatever discussions ensued, the doctors left her alone.

'Are you alright, Brelsa?' Lovoa asked as she walked towards her. Solvan was close behind.

'I'm fine, I have just missed the suns,' Brelsa replied. She opened her eyes to look at the First Protector. 'I see congratulations are in order.'

'Thank you,' Lovoa said. Her hands went to her stomach, protectively covering the baby that could be seen moving around inside her. Solvan wrapped his arm around her waist, pulling her close as the rest of the crew walked off the shuttle.

Lovoa recognised the mind of Ensign Conner; the rest were unknown to her.

'Welcome to Lismar; I'm First Protector Solvan. This is my mate, Lovoa. Ensign Conner, it is good to see you again.'

'Thank you; I'm glad to come back. Please let me introduce you to Captain Amber Yoland, and Lieutenant Jayson who is from the FWN *Cairo,* the ship which has been in orbit since Brelsa left. The pilot is staying on the shuttle.'

'You have no security officer this time,' Lovoa stated.

'I didn't feel it was necessary,' Amber replied. 'We are here to return Brelsa and explain what has happened since she left.'

'Then please come inside.'

'Would it not be better to talk out here?' Amber asked.

'It would, but it would not be good for you,' Lovoa replied. Amber was surprised at their understanding of human frailty after such brief contact.

'With these suits on, it makes no difference to us. Let us talk out here,' Amber said.

Brelsa's relief was evident as they settled themselves on the stone seats.

Amber explained everything that had happened at Cornucopia. The horror and disgust that had resonated through the human community meant that the FWN would be proactive in preventing any further attacks.

Lovoa should have been relieved; however, she picked up a real fear. The humans had no concern about their people committing new acts of violence, but the captain was scared for them. Lovoa was frustrated that she could only understand the spoken word, but she recognised the verbal reassurances that Lismar would be protected. She could only feel an uncertainty from the humans; there was something that they feared. She did not say anything but instead she waited. It was the captain Lovoa thought that she needed to talk to – alone.

Amber said that a lot of the coats made from Lismarian skins had been handed in, not just at Cornucopia but in the weeks before they left. These coats were on board the *Ottawa*; she had not wanted to bring them down for the first meeting, not knowing what the First Protectors' thoughts were about them.

As Brelsa had predicted, they wanted the coats. Amber sent the shuttle back to retrieve them.

'Are you not going back with them?' Lovoa asked her.

'It will not take them long to return with your people's skins. I was hoping I could stay here until they return.'

'Of course.' Lovoa wondered if Amber felt her need to talk to her. They stood together in silence as the shuttle took off.

'Until Cornucopia, I had never heard about you or your people,' Amber told Lovoa. 'I found out that my grandfather was here and built the machine that you used to destroy the ship in space.' She chose her words carefully. 'That he came back here to die.'

'When your people came down before, there was one male – Cal, I think his name was – who examined our machine. He said his kind – your kind – had been here before.'

'Did he take the machine back with him?'

'No, it is still here, but it doesn't work any more.'

Suddenly Amber suspected why Cal had wanted to come here: he wanted the machine, whatever it was. He had wanted to come down with them, but she had refused.

'Why didn't we take it back with us?' Amber asked, another bit of the puzzle that had been missed.

'They did not want to,' Lovoa said simply.

'How many other Lismarians know about the machine?'

'None, as far as I know. Only a few of our people can read, so our written records are limited. We normally share information mentally. Before Solvan's parents took over, the previous First Protectors died before they could pass on what they knew. What written records there were described how the machine was used and some of its history, but nothing further. The records did not say where it came from.'

'My grandfather was here recently, in the last fifty years. I believe he built the machine.' Amber knew she probably should not say so much, but what damage could it do now? She was curious to learn more about her grandfather and the people he had left his family for.

'Fifty years means nothing to me.'

Amber was about to explain the concept behind a year but realised that Lismar had two suns and she did not know the effect it would have on the seasons of the planet. She decided to make it as simple as possible. 'Brelsa has been gone for what we call a month, or four weeks. A year is twelve months.'

'That is a very long time,' Lovoa said.

'Would anyone still be alive who would remember my grandfather?'

'No, we do not live as long as you have described. I'm sorry.'

'How long do you live for?' Amber asked curiously.

'I'm not sure. I don't know how to work it out.'

'I can help you,' Amber said.

Amber was shocked to discover that, from the timescales she was able to establish, the Lismarians only lived for about twelve to fifteen Lismarian years. After seventy-five years, even with all their technology and ability to record events, so much had been lost. For a race that was so short-lived, and who were very limited as to those who could read and write, it was not surprising that they had forgotten so much; it was amazing that anything was remembered at all. It was a shame; she would have loved to know what had happened to David.

'I'm sorry I can't tell you anything about your grandfather,' Lovoa said.

'It's alright. I never knew him – he came back here before

I was born. Your people meant a great deal to him.'

'Do you think we are still in danger?' Lovoa asked.

'Not from humans,' Amber answered honestly.

'But possibly from someone else?'

'It's too early to know for sure, but we'll do everything we can to keep you safe.' Amber did not say any more as the shuttle returned, turning the mood sombre.

Brelsa, Solvan and his parents, Bahia and Essac, came out to meet the shuttle as Ensign Conner walked off it.

'Captain,' Conner said. 'We have brought everything.' She didn't know how to phrase it in front of the Lismarians.

'How would you like to proceed?' Amber asked the First Protectors.

'We don't want to go onto the shuttle. Can you bring the skins out and put them inside?' Lovoa said, indicating their home.

'We can, but are you sure you want them in there?'

'Where else should we place them? We can't leave them on the plateau, the winds will blow them away.'

Amber picked up the Lismarians' uncertainty. She knew they wanted the coats, the skins of their people, but they were not sure how they would feel when they saw them, or how they would deal with them.

Amber went onto the shuttle with Conner behind her. It was full of coats. On the *Ottawa,* there did not look to be so many but in the smaller confines of the shuttle it was a different matter. And she knew these represented just a fraction of the number of Lismarians that had been killed.

Amber picked up the first few skins and carried them past the watching Lismarians. She could feel their emotions but did not know what they were thinking; she was not sure if she wanted to know.

Once all the skins had been carried off the shuttle, Amber stood before the First Protectors and Brelsa, and felt the weight of the blood that had been spilt.

'Thank you for bringing them back to us,' Lovoa said.

'I fear that there are many more still to be returned.'

'We will gladly receive them back.'

'I will make sure that they are brought here.' Amber's mind was screaming in anger and frustration. She wanted to beg forgiveness that this had happened but she could not. The admirals of the FWN had made it clear that no blame was to be attributed to them.

'Thank you for your help – and we understand. Whoever is to blame, this is not your guilt to hold,' Lovoa said.

Amber was glad to hear her reassurances but she knew there must be a lot of guilt among the FWN. The investigation was still fresh and could take years to unravel.

The Lismarians asked what had happened to the wings that had been taken. Amber did not know; there had been no mention of wings, and she had no idea why they had been taken. All she could say was that it was being investigated. Knowing that Lovoa and Solvan would probably have died of old age by the time the investigation had finished just made her feel worse.

It had been agreed that an FWN ship would remain in orbit for the foreseeable future to make sure the planet was defended against any further attacks. Amber knew that the Lismarians had a lot of questions to ask but she politely rebuffed them. She hoped that one day they would get all the answers.

As there were limited telepaths on the FWN *Cairo*, the FWN *Ottawa* would remain in orbit for a few days to allow the Lismarians to communicate their concerns before a replacement ship arrived.

Chapter 4

BRELSA thought she would be so happy to be home but, as she stood and watched the shuttle take off, she felt a longing to go with it that surprised her. She pushed the feelings away, thinking that all she needed was time among her people.

She did not immediately go back to see her family but spent a few days with the First Protectors after the humans had left, talking over everything she had seen and experienced. Both Lovoa and Solvan, as well as their parents, had a lot of questions. They wanted to make sure they had everything they needed before the FWN *Ottawa* left orbit.

Amber had said that they only expected to remain for a few days but she would signal down to let them know when they were due to leave. As the days on Lismar passed and they heard nothing, however, Brelsa assumed Amber had forgotten to let them know of her departure. She thought about checking but decided against it.

'Go home, Brelsa,' Lovoa advised, as she joined her on the plateau. 'I think you need to try and reconnect with your family.'

'I know. I'm just worried I won't find it home any more.'

'It has changed, as have you, but you won't know if it is still home until you go there.'

It was with a heavy heart that Brelsa returned home to her family the next day. She had not realised how important that final farewell would be. Before she left, she was warned that there had been a lot of changes in her family's collective. She considered asking for more information but decided against it, preferring to see for herself.

⚛

Lovoa watched as Brelsa flew down the peak. Once she was sure she would not return, the First Protector called up to Amber to let her know. It was not long before she was watching the shuttle land.

Lovoa was looking forward to meeting the captain again. Amber's mind intrigued her; she had a strength the other humans did not have.

Amber and three others, all of whom were familiar to Lovoa, walked off in their strange suits. Lovoa knew from Brelsa that they liked the temperature a lot colder and the heat of Lismar was too much for them.

'Thank you for letting me know when Brelsa left and allowing us to come back,' Amber said.

'You're welcome. Brelsa has been struggling with everything she has seen. Being here when you returned would make it harder.'

'I'm sorry to hear that. I hope she will be alright,' Amber said, worried. Although a lot of consideration had been given should something happen while Brelsa was with them, no one had considered the effect the trip would have had on her once she had returned to Lismar. The Lismarians had only encountered a few alien races before, all of them at the same level of advancement. What must humans seem like to these people?

'I hope so. She has gone back to spend time with her family.'

'That is good to hear.' Amber felt doubt from Lovoa, who did not think being home would help Brelsa. 'If there is anything we can do to assist Brelsa, you must let me know. But, for now, I believe you met Cal Everton and Jane Keyworth previously. They've come to look at your machine.'

'They are welcome. But you are welcome to take it with you, as it no longer works.'

'We'll need to arrange its removal at some time, but our leaders don't know it is here and we don't want them to know just yet. But we do need to know how it works in case we need to build more.'

'Then welcome, and please do what you need to with it,' Lovoa said, showing them where the machine was hidden.

⚛

As Brelsa flew near home, she had feelings of dread. She had contacted her brother, Isslac, and let him know she was returning. Though she had felt his excitement at seeing her there was something else she could not identify. As she approached her home, she saw a male standing on the battlements. For a moment she did not recognise him and wondered where her brother was. Had this stranger taken over the collective? He had more markings.

She was tempted to circle before landing to see if there was anyone else but decided against it as the male was waving at her in welcome. As she landed, she recognised his face and took in the full details of the pattern on his skin and saw the similarities to her own, Brelsa finally recognised her brother a moment before she felt his familiar mental touch.

Her brother had mated and grown in strength. Who had he mated with, she wondered, as he embraced her in welcome.

'I'm so happy you are safely back,' Isslac said.

'So am I. But a lot has changed here while I have been away by the looks of it,' she replied, indicating the change in his patterning. 'Anything else I need to know?'

'Quite a bit,' he admitted. Brelsa wondered if she should have asked for more information from the First Protectors before coming back. 'Come, I will explain everything and introduce you to my mate,' Isslac said as he led her inside.

Brelsa listened as her brother explained what had happened since she had left. How, once he had been released from the lightless cell, Ovato and Welra had tried to regain control of the collective but, with the help of Gilcan and Essac, they had failed. They were now restricted to the same rooms Gilcan had been in previously. They had learnt quickly that the guards supported Isslac.

To secure his position, Isslac had mated. As he and his mate were stronger than their parents, the collective went to them; it also gave them the support of his mate's family.

'Do I know her?' Brelsa asked. She did not recognise the new markings.

'I don't think so, but let me introduce you to my mate, Erle.'

Brelsa turned as a female walked into the room. She stood up to meet her new sister. 'I'm very pleased to meet you,' she said, but got a cold reception from Erle. Awkwardly, they both sat down.

A ping of regret went through Brelsa. If she had stayed here, there were males she could have mated with that would have allowed her to take over her family's collective. She could have been a Protector here. She still could be, but not in her home now that her brother was established. Had she made the right decision to leave Lismar?

❈

Over the next few days, Brelsa explored her home. Her brother showed her all the improvements they had made since she had left, but these all seemed insufficient compared to what she had seen with the humans. She tried to settle but could not. Her brother and Erle, with the help of Gilcan, were running the collective as they saw fit; though they were willing to make a place for her, they did not need her.

Though the mating had given her brother the extra strength he needed to formally take control from his parents, it had given his personality a colder edge that Brelsa did not like. After a few days, she tried her best to avoid Erle whose character grated on her like fingernails running down stone.

Brelsa stood on the battlements looking out over the fields. Life had seemed simple before; she had known her place and accepted it, not knowing any better. Now she was not so sure. She had seen what the humans were capable of, more than her people could ever possibly imagine. She still worried when the humans said that the threat was gone and the Lismarians were now safe. She had seen how big the human community was, and she knew there would be times no one would be looking at Lismar. Another attack could happen.

Brelsa remembered the pain of the attacks as her people were skinned alive. She knew that Lovoa and Solvan had destroyed the trader's ship in orbit before it had destroyed the FWN ship. Brelsa knew the humans were worried, that there was more than they were saying. She had been so frustrated that she could not read their minds. Spoken language was fine, as their language was stored into what they called translators, but mentally it was just a jumble.

Her experiences had given her a glimpse of what was out there and she realised she would no longer be satisfied with home, no longer satisfied with what was expected of her. Her brother was so happy with what they had achieved and, if she had not known any better, she would have been amazed at the changes they had made in such a short period. But she knew they could all be for nothing.

Her future here would be to mate, to run a collective and to have children who would become Protectors, not for happiness. It was not enough and hopelessness filled her.

She was sure the humans had gone by now. In desperation, she reached up her mind, hoping to touch the ship she had been told would remain in orbit. She was surprised when she recognised Amber's mind. So Amber had not left without saying goodbye after all; she was still here.

Now that it was a possibility again, the question arose in Brelsa's mind: what if the humans let her go with them? She knew it would be hard, especially when there were so many risks, but she was still tempted to leave with them. There was so much that she could learn; with them she could experience more than she could yet imagine.

Brelsa said goodbye to her brother and Erle. She did not tell them why she was returning to Hannoki's Peak, just that she had something important to discuss with Lovoa and Solvan. As she flew back up the mountain range, she came to a decision about what she wanted to do. But first she needed to talk to the First Protectors and she didn't know if that was possible or not.

As she landed, Lovoa was waiting for her on the plateau. 'We did not expect to see you again so soon, Brelsa. Are you alright?' Lovoa asked as she led her inside.

'Did you know that the FWN *Ottawa* is still in orbit?'

'We do. Their departure was delayed. Why?'

'Is there any chance I can leave here on an FWN ship?' Brelsa asked.

Both Lovoa and Solvan were stunned into silence.

'I find that I don't fit in here,' Brelsa said. 'I want to discover more.'

'Are you looking for our permission?' Solvan asked.

'Nearly. I know what I want, I just don't know if it is possible. I want to leave here. I want to go back into space with the humans. I need to know if they will let me.'

'I can ask for you but the decision won't be ours, it will be theirs,' Lovoa said. 'If the humans agree, have you thought about what you will be giving up?'

'I only ever cared for my brother and since he mated he is not the same. I look at what he has – at what I might have if I mate for power. That power is nothing compared to what I have seen.'

Lovoa had her own views about Erle so she remained quiet. 'You said you were weak the whole time you were away. Could you manage just being able to absorb enough energy on the ship to keep going?'

'I was adapting by the time we left. I wasn't as cold, and I could balance and maintain my power levels. It was a shock at first but I was coping.'

'You would be the only one of our kind out there and you could find it lonely.' As Lovoa spoke, she ran her hand over her stomach where her baby could be seen moving around.

Brelsa took a deep breath. She knew what Lovoa was suggesting; if she left, Brelsa would never have her own family.

'You and Solvan are lucky, you are a good match. Many Protectors mate for power and most of the time they are miserable. I don't want that. Out of the males I know, there are several whom I would consider if strength were the only thing that was important – but I have not met anyone I want to mate with. I want to see what else there is. I have considered what I would be giving up. The unknown holds more sway.'

'We will communicate with Amber and let her know we want to talk,' Lovoa said. 'But there is no guarantee the humans will take you.'

⚛

A shuttle came down and landed on the plateau. One person in an environmental suit disembarked and met with the First Protectors for a short while before returning. The shuttle left.

⚛

A scream ripped through the air, shrill, piercing and full of anger and frustration.

'It's alright little one, you are loved and safe,' Lovoa said as she held her newborn baby girl in her arms and mentally tried to reassure the squirming bundle.

'She is as strong-willed as her mother,' Solvan said, running a finger gently over his daughter's cheek. He laughed as a tiny hand grabbed hold of his finger and held on tight, then he ran his thumb slowly over the back of the small hand, reinforcing the mental message Lovoa was giving. Slowly the baby stopped crying and settled peacefully in her mother's arms under the two suns.

Lovoa and Solvan sat and watched as her markings became visible under the suns' light. It was already evident that when they had fully emerged, those markings would cover her whole body as they did with her parents. She would be as strong as them.

Solvan knew his parents were waiting nearby for news of their first grandchild. He could feel them desperately wanting to come but holding back to give him and Lovoa this time together.

'I wish my mother were here,' Lovoa said suddenly.

'She would have been so proud of you.'

'Can we name her for my mother?'

'Of course,' Solvan agreed. 'Welcome to the world, Mesrra.'

'Are we going to invite your parents? I don't know how much longer Brelsa can restrain them,' Lovoa said after they had sat for a while in silence marvelling at the life they had made.

Solvan laughed and kissed her before mentally telling his parents to come in. With the speed that they arrived, it was evident that they had been waiting just out of sight. Gently Lovoa handed her baby over to Bahia and smiled as she longingly took her granddaughter into her arms.

⚛

Brelsa walked out onto the plateau to join Lovoa and Solvan as they cradled their baby in the full power of both the suns.

'Thank you for joining us, Brelsa.' Solvan said as she approached.

'Of course. I take it you have news.'

'We do. Amber came down at our request just before Mesrra was born. She made it clear the FWN would normally never agree to take someone from a planet with no technology. However, she promised to make a case in your favour to see if they are willing to make an exception for you as you have already travelled on a spaceship. If you are still considering leaving, she will come down and explain what is involved,' Lovoa said.

'She implied that if the FWN agree to take you, it would mean that you could not come back. You will never get to see your brother or his family again and you will never get to have your own family,' Solvan added.

'They did not have that concern before. I could have told my brother everything,' Brelsa objected.

'Many people were very displeased that you went to Cornucopia. They allowed you to return in what they called a "calculated risk". Though you saw a lot, the trip was a short one and confirmed what we knew, that the humans can travel in space and come from another planet. If you were to live among them, you would start to learn about their technology, how they make things, which is what they are worried about.'

'I can never come back?'

'That is what they implied. But, as I said, Amber needs to ask permission. If her people agree, these are the conditions she thinks they will set. She will let us know when she has an answer from her superiors. They will need your decision quickly. Remember that if you go, you can never mate. You can never have your own children. Think carefully about what you really want and what is a reaction to your recent experiences and your brother's mating.'

'I will. Thank you.'

❀

A shuttle arrived the next day with Amber on board. The FWN had agreed that Brelsa could leave on the *Ottawa*. Conditions had been set; as Amber had assumed, Brelsa would not be allowed to return home.

'You don't have long to make a decision, Brelsa. We've had our orders to leave here.'

'How much time do I have?'

'We leave today.'

Brelsa had a hundred questions but only going with the humans would answer them. She was not sure of the life ahead of her, but she knew that she did not want the life expected of her. She was willing to take the chance and hope for the best.

Chapter 5

'SO what are we supposed to do with an alien who could easily die on us and has no knowledge of technology?' Admiral Simon Johnson asked, frustrated. Admiral Natalie Webb had just told him that Brelsa was returning on the FWN *Ottawa* with Amber. He wondered why Admiral Yoland had not informed him himself.

'She and her leaders are aware of the risks and have accepted them. And if Brelsa is with us, it means she can't influence her people about what she has seen,' Natalie said, as if the rationale were simple.

'Brelsa has no technical understanding. What she saw would only show what is possible. Neither she nor any of her people could even begin to replicate it. I'm surprised that this was agreed to – and so quickly – bearing in mind the risk involved to Brelsa.'

'Don't take your frustration out on me. Captain Yoland received the request which she passed on to the Admiral of the Fleet. The authority was given by them,' Natalie snapped back. 'Maybe it was thought that having a Lismarian live with us would help rebuild our reputation.'

'In my opinion that's a cheap shot when someone's life is at risk,' Simon retorted. 'I bet the Board of Chief Physicians was not even consulted.'

'They were and they were in favour of Brelsa returning to FWN space.'

'How could they condone her leaving her home world when we know nothing of Lismarian biology? Their doctors won't be able to help her if she falls ill.' When no reply was forthcoming, he found it himself. 'They hope she'll agree to tests. And if she doesn't, they want her body when she dies. What makes them think they'll get her remains, that she won't be returned home?'

'The condition of her leaving Lismar is that she can't return. Her people don't expect to see her again.'

'I'm sorry, but when Brelsa dies her body will be treated as she chooses. If she has to live with us and obey our laws, she'll be protected by them as well. The doctors shouldn't get hold of her unless she agrees.'

'Of course,' Natalie said, but Simon was not convinced.

After Natalie left, Simon sat for some time thinking about the conversation. He couldn't help but feel Natalie had her own agenda in all of this. His first reaction was to contact Gareth and ask for further information but he stopped himself. If his friend knew anything, he would have told him. Instead, Simon decided to wait until dinner. He and Gareth had a standing arrangement while on Cornucopia. Nothing would happen in the next few hours that could not be changed.

⚛

'I had a visit from Natalie Webb today. It looks like your daughter is bringing the Lismarian, Brelsa, back into FWN space,' Simon Johnson said as he joined his friend at the bar for a drink before dinner.

'Why? Amber was sent to Lismar to take her home. We fought hard to allow Brelsa to return to her people,' Gareth said, surprised.

'Amber didn't tell you anything?'

'No, but she wouldn't. She would have forwarded the request to FWN headquarters as per protocol, not to me.'

'She wouldn't have given you the heads up?'

'No, Amber can be very by the book, especially about things like this where there's a lot of intrusive supervision. Do you know what the FWN plan to do with Brelsa?'

'Natalie didn't say. I'm not sure the Admiral of the Fleet has thought that far ahead. From what Natalie said, I believe the Board of Chief Physicians may have swayed their decision for their own purposes.'

'They're determined to find out how the Lismarians' ability to absorb and use energy works,' Gareth said. 'They tried to get a court warrant to force Brelsa to submit to an examination before she was returned home. It wasn't granted.'

'Do you think they'll cross the ethical line?' Simon asked, worried.

'I hope not. But if Brelsa is in FWN space, they'll have more opportunities to pressure her and maybe she will eventually agree, especially if she starts to feel unwell.'

'I don't like where this could lead us. We need to make sure that Brelsa is placed with people that we can trust.'

'Ideally she would stay with Amber but she's being posted to patrol near Urigan space,' Gareth responded. 'Alex's ship won't be operational again for some months, and his crew are being reassigned. I'm not sure who else I trust.'

'Do we have to put her on a ship?'

'No. What are you thinking of?'

'On a ship Brelsa is isolated,' Simon explained. 'If we place her on a planet or spacebase, then she becomes known to that location. That could offer her a level of security.'

'A planet would be better, as she would have direct access to sunlight. But while a ship is very isolated, a planet is the opposite and she could get lost in the population.'

'A spacebase? There wouldn't be enough permanent personnel to get to know her well and it would be easier to adapt living quarters to her needs.'

'I like it.' Gareth smiled grimly. 'Now we just have to sell it to the Admiral of the Fleet.'

❊

Admiral Yoland had hoped that he would have a chance to speak with his daughter when she returned to FWN space, but the ship did not break orbit. A shuttle returned Cal and Jane to Cornucopia before the *Ottawa* left for Europa, where Brelsa would stay until the doctors were happy that she could cope long term on a spacebase and adjustments had been made to her living area.

⚛

Walking into their quarters, Cal saw a message blinking on the screen. He was surprised, as all messages could have been forwarded to him on the *Ottawa*. He opened it and saw that is was a request for him to go to Gareth Yoland's office. The auto-forward had been removed. He acknowledged the message and responded that he would be there in the hour then headed for the shower.

Jane was waiting for him as he came out. 'Why does he want to see just you?'

'I don't know,' Cal said. 'But I'm sure I'll find out very soon.'

'Take this.' She handed him a small data chip. 'It contains what I've found out so far. I'll keep him updated with anything else I find.'

⚛

'Thank you for coming, Cal. I appreciate you've not long returned and you probably have a lot to catch up on,' Admiral Yoland said as he invited Cal into his office.

'I have to confess I'm curious what it is you want to talk about,' Cal said, sitting down. 'Jane is leading the investigation into Diaz and Gallo. She hasn't found anything significant yet but she asked me to give this to you.' He put the data chip on the table.

Gareth picked it up and placed it in his pocket. 'That's not why I wanted to talk to you. The Admiral of the Fleet has asked me to approach you on behalf of the FWN. We'd like you to work with us against the Urigans.'

'I feel I shouldn't have to ask this, but who are the Urigans?' Cal asked.

'A race that has recently come to our attention. At

present we don't know too much about them, other than that their ships and weaponry are more advanced than ours. We have reason to believe that they've been working with criminal elements in our society and have benefited from the attacks on Lismar. Since we've put a stop to the trade, we've seen an increase of Urigan activity. We think that they may increase the rate of attacks against us as a result.'

Cal stood up, ready to leave. 'I'm sorry, Admiral. I don't build weapons.'

'We know. That's not what we want from you – we have other people who are experts in that field. What we want is your defensive technology. You were there on Alex's ship in Lismar's orbit, you know how quickly our shields crumpled under the attack from the unknown ship. We want you to help improve them. Help protect our ships.'

'Do you think the ship was Urigan?'

'That is yet to be determined, but the analysis of the sensor scans is similar to information recorded during previous encounters.'

'What have the other captains said?'

'Captain Wilhelm is the first to survive,' Gareth said. 'We only have the data that was recorded and could be retrieved from those previous encounters.'

'It doesn't sound like you have much. I'll need to see everything you've got to have a chance of building something effective.'

Chapter 6

MESRRA stood on the plateau of Hannoki's Peak. She had watched her parents fly down the mountain many times and it had always seemed so much fun. She wanted to see what it felt like, to know what was of so much interest at the bottom. She knew that she could do it – how difficult could it be?

Looking around to make sure no one was watching, Mesrra pushed a mental image of herself happily playing outside so no one would suspect what she planned. Then she spread her wings and plunged off the side of the mountain.

She screamed. She had only ever flown around the plateau; it had not prepared her for the winds that battered at her now as she plummeted to the ground.

Hearing the scream, Solvan ran outside. He did not need to search the plateau for his daughter; he knew where she was through her fear. He looked down but already Mesrra was out of sight.

He shouted to Lovoa, who ran to join him, before jumping off the side of the mountain in pursuit of his daughter. He prayed to Hannoki that he would reach her before she crashed to her death.

⚜

For the first few heartbeats, Mesrra panicked. Had she jumped to her death? She didn't want to die – she was not going to die, at least not without a fight. She stopped fighting the winds that battered and tossed her around and started to angle her wings into them. Her descent slowed. As she experimented, she dipped and rose on the currents, controlling her descent. Though somewhat clumsy, she now had some control.

She saw her father approach. She knew she was in so much trouble.

Solvan made to grab her but stopped as he realised Mesrra was gliding on the current. 'You have control of this,' he said. 'I am here if you need me.'

Mesrra flashed her father a massive smile as she worked her way down the mountain.

'I am with her, she is fine,' Solvan let Lovoa know. He knew his mate was about to jump off the side and go after them. He felt her acknowledgement.

Every time Mesrra lost the current and dipped, she felt her father prepare to grab her. That just increased her resolve to fly without help.

Solvan followed her closely all the way down. It was not a graceful descent but Mesrra made it on her own. She just wished she'd landed on her feet instead of on her stomach. She picked herself up as her father landed lightly next to her and extended his hand. Mesrra swallowed her pride, took it and let him pull her to her feet.

'I have to admit that was the worst descent I have ever seen,' Solvan said. Mesrra lowered her head in embarrassment. 'However, I don't think anyone has decided to jump off the side of Hannoki's Peak before without knowing what they were doing.' Mesrra smiled up at him. 'No, don't take that as praise,' her father chastised her. 'You were foolish and reckless.'

'But you didn't stop me,' she dared to answer back.

'Maybe I should have. Do not think for one minute that I agree with your actions just because I didn't carry you down the mountain. You were lucky. The conditions today are mild. You thought this descent was difficult – most days you would have been slammed against the mountain by the winds. You do not try this again until you fully understand the risks.'

'Yes, Father. How do we get back?' Mesrra said, somewhat

daunted as she looked up at the mountain.

'The same way, of course.' Mesrra looked at him in horror. 'You thought you were good enough to fly down, now you have to get yourself home. How else were you planning to get there?' When she didn't reply, he continued. 'You did not think that far ahead?'

'No,' Mesrra admitted, embarrassed.

'You need to consider that your actions will have consequences. Getting down is easy in comparison to flying up.'

Mesrra looked up again and worry turned to resolve. Solvan saw and felt the change in her. The girl nodded her head, mentally accepting the challenge her father had set. Without saying anything further, she launched herself into the air. Smiling, her father followed her.

It got harder and harder as Mesrra battled her way up. Her wings started to shake with stress and exhaustion. Her parents had made it seem so easy. Solvan stayed close in case she faltered. It did not reassure her, it just made her more determined to prove she could do it.

Solvan felt his daughter weakening but at the same time her determination increased. He was not going to offer his help but he was ready to catch her should her wings fail.

As they neared the top, Mesrra slowed. The currents pushed her around but she did not give in. She fought every step of the way, so much her mother's daughter. As the peak neared the winds got stronger; Solvan thought she would fall, but she always regained control at the last moment.

Mesrra saw the peak with relief. Controlling the flight down was difficult but it was nothing compared to the return trip. She was tempted more than once to ask her father for help but she knew this was a test and she did not want to be carried like a baby. He was trying to prove a point. So was she. She would make it on her own.

As she got to the plateau, she collapsed, exhausted.

'Mesrra,' Solvan called. She barely acknowledged him

before falling into an exhausted sleep. After reassuring himself that she was just drained, her father left her sleeping in the full sunlight. She would recover quickly.

He went back to talk to his very worried and angry mate. 'What was she thinking?' Lovoa was not really expecting an answer. Only Mesrra would know why she had tried such a dangerous flight.

'Lovoa, she's fine, just exhausted.'

'Then she is doing better than me. We were lucky – she could have killed herself.'

'I know,' Solvan said, taking her in his arms. 'I'm sorry, it never occurred to me that she would try the flight down on her own.'

'Nor to me. I assumed that she would wait to try it with one of us the first time, like you did with your parents.'

'So did I. When she wakes up, we will have to set rules about what she is allowed to try. With her abilities, we can't assume anything.'

'I know.' Lovoa sighed. 'I wish your parents were still with us.' Bahia and Essac's ability to absorb sunlight had recently failed and they had passed away before the birth of their second grandchild, Kelvic.

'So do I.'

Chapter 7

'CAL,' Jane said in a coaxing tone. He did not respond, too engrossed with the data in front of him. 'Cal!' she said more loudly.

Finally, she got his attention. 'Did you find out anything?' he asked. They had returned to Europa several days ago from Cornucopia, where they both had better access to equipment.

'No, and it's frustrating me that there doesn't seem to be anything when I know there should be. Could you help me out?'

'Of course.'

'You know how easily you got into that warehouse where your father's car was?' Jane said.

'Yes,' Cal replied, suspicious of where this conversation was going.

'Any chance you can get me into Stuart Webb's office and home address? I know I'm missing something. I can't find any digital footprint, so I want to see if there's any physical evidence.'

'It won't be as easy.' Cal frowned. 'The warehouse wasn't sitting in the middle of a high-security complex.'

'Can you do it?'

'Webb's office is in the central government building. I know I can't get in there because I looked at the possibilities of getting into my father's office when he was killed.'

'I thought you saw his office.'

'I did, but only after I was invited to do so. Officials had already removed everything connected to his work. I imagine that by now they'll have done the same for the deputy head chairman.'

'Damn,' Jane swore.

'On the upside, the chances are we wouldn't find anything in his official office. There are so many security measures in place that an unauthorised or unknown device would set off a security alert,' Cal pointed out.

'What about his home address?' Jane knew that Cal's company had the security contract; he would know what was in place there.

'That is a possibility,' he admitted.

Jane stood anxiously next to Cal as he bypassed security. He had reassured her it would be fine. Stuart's home was an imposing mansion, not far from where Cal's father had lived. Jane was not surprised Cal had one of his 'back door' accesses.

It was not long before the door swung open. Excited, Jane rushed forward, convinced that this was where she would find the answers. As she entered the house, she saw nothing in the hallway. She made her way into the first main room; again there was nothing: no furniture, no pictures, no anything. Jane went from room to room, and it was all the same. The address had been stripped; a scan showed that there was no technology present other than the security alarm.

She stood, shocked and frustrated. Stuart had not been dead for long, yet it looked like his life had been erased.

Both Cal and Jane searched the whole address thoroughly but there was nothing. 'Can you look at who has been here?' Jane asked.

'Yes, but I doubt it will be much help,' Cal replied.

'Unfortunately, Admiral Yoland, Jane and I didn't uncover anything about Gallo and Diaz and what happened to them after they fled FWN space,' Cal said. He and Jane had gone to meet Gareth at his offices on Europa to update him on what they had – or more to the point had not – found out.

'Were you able to discover anything at all?' Gareth asked.

'Gallo and Diaz left quickly after the Lismarian trade was exposed. Money was transferred into various accounts. When the government moved in and started to take control of the families' assets, a lot was seized but a fortune remained hidden,' Jane explained.

'I assume the families used this to fund Gallo and Diaz's exile.'

'That's what I thought originally,' Jane continued. 'But there were no withdrawals. Even after the investigation ended, the funds weren't touched.'

'Is there an account you missed?'

'I don't think so. I've been able to track all the money, so unless they hid money before all of this started, everything is accounted for.' Jane's frustration was evident.

'What do you think happened? You must have a theory,' Gareth pushed.

'I think they fled quickly, taking just what they needed, expecting their families to keep them supplied in the long term. But they didn't. They cut them off and worked instead at rebuilding their lives away from the scandal.'

'Why would they do that?'

'Both Gallo and Diaz, though wealthy, married their wives for their political and social connections. They also both had young children. Their families would want to protect their own interests and Gallo and Diaz would be a liability. They would want to distance themselves as much as possible. The wives showed themselves as victims, unaware of what their husbands were doing, and threw themselves on the mercy of their parents for financial help and security.'

'Do you think the families were innocent?'

'I think they were politically savvy,' Jane countered.

Gareth knew what that meant. If the families knew anything, there was no record of it. 'Did you find out anything about Diaz and Gallo after they left?'

'No, there's nothing at all. They were either very good at covering their tracks, left FWN space, or died soon afterwards.'

'I appreciate you looking.'

'There's one other thing that I discovered that doesn't sit well with me,' Jane said. 'Deputy Head Chairman Webb – he's the man that took over after Cal's father was killed who later committed suicide – and Admiral Natalie Webb are Diaz's grandchildren. Their mother was his daughter. They changed their names before entering the FWN.'

'We would have known if that was the case.'

'You do know. They declared it on joining, and asked for anonymity due to their family connection. That was granted. As a result, the records were sealed.'

'If the records were sealed, I'm not going to ask how you know,' Gareth retorted. 'Is there anything about their activities I should be aware of?'

'Not that I can discover. But if they're in contact with the Urigans, it's likely to be with a technology that we're not aware of.'

'Thank you. Can you monitor Admiral Webb and let me know if you pick up anything of concern?'

'Of course. But if she is involved, she's been cautious so far,' Jane said.

'I'm sorry we couldn't find out more for you,' Cal apologised.

'It's strange,' Gareth mused. 'In some ways I'm reassured. If you can't find anything then we didn't miss blatant corruption. On the other hand, how did they do it? What weaknesses did they exploit?'

'We'll keep looking into it,' Cal reassured him.

'Not you, Cal. I want you focused on the shielding technology from now on. The Urigans are getting braver and have attacked another one of our ships. I fear we'll soon be suffering heavy casualties.'

Chapter 8

One human year later

BRELSA was trying to contain her emotions. She was in the hydroponic bay of the FWN *Berlin* as it approached Lismar, a place she had never thought she would see again. That was one of the conditions set when the humans had agreed to take her with them.

Though the FWN had kept a ship patrolling near Lismar, communication was prohibited. The FWN were only allowed to attempt it if there was a threat to the planet. They wanted to give the Lismarians a chance to develop without their interference.

For the humans it had only been a year, no time at all, but Brelsa was sure that she would see a lot of changes when she got back home. When she'd first left to expose the trade, she had only been gone a month yet her brother had changed so much she had no longer recognised him.

Shortly after arriving back into FWN space Brelsa, had gone to live on a starbase. It had a hydroponics bay, the same as a ship, and she was given a room specially equipped with solar lamps. Slowly she had started to learn to talk to people, hesitantly at first without the mental reinforcement. How did she know she could trust them? Then she realised that this doubt did not stop the humans communicating. Why should it stop her?

She had been asked to return to Lismar because the humans wanted to go down to the surface to talk to the First Protectors. They needed Brelsa to facilitate the request to land and to make introductions. The FWN had not explained why they wanted to talk to her people again, other to review their progress. Out of respect for the First Protectors, anything further would be discussed with them first. But Brelsa had been promised that the visit was nothing that would be detrimental to her people.

'Lovoa, Solvan, can you hear me?' Brelsa had been asking that for the last few hours, ever since the bridge had said they were near Lismar's orbit. There had been no reply and she was worried. The last time she had returned it had been so easy.

When she expressed her concern to the captain, she was told not to worry and to keep trying, as they didn't know the minimum range for communication with Lismar. Brelsa assumed Amber must have got closer to the planet on the previous return. But then Amber had a better understanding of telepaths.

Suddenly there was a response. *'Brelsa? Are you alright?'* The slight echo indicated that Lovoa and Solvan were merging their minds.

'Yes, I am fine. I am on a ship approaching you. They want permission to come into your orbit and to land a shuttle.'

'Are there any concerns?'

'No, it is a review about how you are progressing since the attacks. They do not want anyone but you to be aware of their presence, and they want advice on how far to maintain their distance.'

'Where you are now would be best. You are just within our range. If the ship needs to get closer for the shuttle, then come to their maxim range and let us know.'

'I will inform the captain and update you on when we will be landing.'

'It will be good to see you again,' Lovoa and Solvan both said before the connection was withdrawn.

Brelsa sat for a few minutes, surprised how alien her own kind now seemed. It was the first time she had spoken her language since she'd left Lismar. She worried about how she would feel once she was back in her own world.

Taking a deep breath, she called the bridge to inform the captain that she was in communication range and what the First Protectors had said so the captain could make a decision on how much closer they needed to go. The arrangements did not take long; those who were going down to the planet had already been selected and the shuttle was stocked with provisions to make the stay more comfortable in the heat. All Brelsa had to do was tell Lovoa and Solvan that they were ready to come down and confirm that they were still allowed to land on the plateau before joining the crew in the shuttle bay.

The *Berlin's* security chief was leading the trip, which included a diplomat trained in first contact and two anthropologists to assess how the impact of an advanced culture had affected Lismarian development. Brelsa wasn't sure how Lovoa and Solvan were going to react to the visit or the questions they would be asked. She knew that they had been relieved when contact with the FWN had ceased, and that they had been very unhappy with her decision to leave. Ironically, her own family had not shown much interest in her choice.

Climbing on board the shuttle, Brelsa sat near the hatch and strapped herself in. She had spent hours teaching the visitors about her culture and planet so they were prepared, but she did not consider any of them to be her friends. Right now, she wished one of them was, just in case her return home did not go well.

Brelsa missed her friends on the starbase and Ann Conner. Conner had been reassigned to the FWN *Ottawa* under Amber Yoland, a ship they did not want Brelsa on.

As everyone settled on board, she looked around. Most of them were excited at the chance to meet and examine such an alien culture.

'Shouldn't you be wearing your environmental suits?' Brelsa asked.

'We are at maxim range for a return trip,' the security officer replied. 'It will take us some time to get there. We can suit up on arrival if we need to.'

Brelsa realised that no amount of data they'd been shown had helped them to accept how hostile the environment was for them. The data said that humans could survive a limited time without adverse effects and that a whole species thrived on the planet, so they thought that they could also cope. Yes, the last time she'd gone down on a shuttle the crew had suited after landing but the shuttle was not as full as it was this time. Getting the suits on this time would be interesting for them. She was just glad that the humans were not so arrogant that they had not bothered to pack the suits at all!

Deciding that she had nothing more to say, Brelsa closed her eyes and sent her mind towards her planet. As the shuttle left the ship, she felt it get closer and closer. She knew they had landed before the pilot informed them, and she knew that Solvan and Lovoa were waiting just outside. During the trip down, she had told them who was with her but not gone into any details.

When the pilot gave the command, the passengers started undoing their safety harnesses and getting their things together. They were determined to go outside without the environmental suits on to begin with; they had brought an environmental tent that they felt they could erect quickly enough.

Brelsa smiled when the hatch was released. She tried hard not to laugh as the heat rushed in and everyone gasped in shock as reality hit them.

As soon as she walked out through the hatch, it started to close behind her.

'Brelsa, it is so good to see you again,' Lovoa said, hugging her.

'It's good to be back.'

'Are the others going to leave the shuttle?'

'They are just putting on their environmental suits. They should be out shortly.'

'Are you back to stay?'

'No,' Brelsa said, knowing the humans would not allow it even if she wished to.

'Then why are you all here?' Solvan asked.

'They wanted to see how you were and check that there had been no further attacks.'

'Is that all?' Solvan asked.

'I don't understand what they hope to find out that you could not tell them,' Lovoa added.

'I could not tell them what has been happening here for the last year,' Brelsa pointed out.

The shuttle hatch opened again and the passengers walked out. The conversation changed to introductions. As Brelsa listened, she saw two little heads poking around a corner watching them. They had the same markings as Lovoa and Solvan. Her previous thought that one year meant a lot more to Lismarians than humans was brought home forcefully to her.

❁

The humans had retreated back to their shuttle. With the permission of the First Protectors, they put up the tent that allowed them more room out of the suns. While they did this, it gave Brelsa and Lovoa time to talk.

Brelsa was revelling in the chance to absorb the suns' rays. Though the special UV panels that had been fitted to her room allowed her to cope with space travel, she was weak because they did not have the capacity of one sun, let alone two.

'How do you cope away from the suns? I remember being locked in a lightless cell and I thought I was going to die,' Lovoa said.

'It is not easy but the humans can replicate the suns' rays. It is nowhere near as good, but it does mean that I can survive. Whenever possible, I go down to a planet and absorb as much sun as possible. When you do not expend it, the lamps allow me to manage on stored energy for a surprisingly long time. The more I have had to do it, the easier it has become.'

'I don't think I could be away from the suns,' Lovoa confessed.

'I doubted I could at first but, as you know, it was our best chance of stopping the traders. And then knowing that I could survive made me want to see as much as I could.'

'Do you regret going?' Lovoa asked.

'I didn't until I got home and saw what I have missed. I know that congratulations are in order. I saw your children watching us when we arrived.'

'Thank you. They were warned to keep out of sight but Mesrra was so curious, and her brother follows where she goes.'

'I was surprised when I saw them. Mesrra was a baby when I left. And your son?'

'Kelvic. I will introduce you to both of them tomorrow. They are desperate to meet you.'

'I'd like that,' Brelsa said, then laughed. 'I cannot believe you and Solvan have two children.'

'I know, especially when I think back to the first time we met.'

'I was so ashamed of my parents.'

'You should visit your family's collective while you are here. A lot has changed there as well.'

'I don't know, I...' Brelsa started to say, knowing the humans would not allow it. Before she could explain, she noticed a small figure approaching them slowly, as if she were unsure of her welcome. 'I think someone could not wait until tomorrow.'

'Mesrra,' Lovoa said, exasperated.

Chapter 9

LOOKING up at the sky, as she had done every morning since Brelsa left, Mesrra finally accepted that she was not returning.

Kelvic had recently become heavily involved with the collectives; he often returned home excited and talked for ages to their parents. Mesrra had struggled to understand his passion but then she had never spent time on a collective. Was she wrong for failing to do so? She was more likely to take over as First Protector than her brother, yet she knew little about how the people lived.

If she became a First Protector, it would be part of her role to ensure the other Protectors did not abuse their power as her father and grandparents had. Accepting that she needed to know more, and wanting to understand what Kelvic was so excited about, Mesrra jumped off the plateau and flew down the side of the mountain at speeds that would have infuriated and worried her parents.

Landing softly, she walked among the workers on Isslac's collective. She knew that Brelsa's brother was trying new ways to improve the farming techniques and the standard of living for the workers. Her own brother was fast becoming fascinated, as well.

Mesrra did not announce her arrival to Isslac and Erle; she wanted to see with her own eyes, not be shown what others wanted her to see. She landed on the farms that looked as if they were the furthest from the Protectors' residence. The crops were limited and sparse. A few people were toiling away, their markings so limited that she wondered how they coped. She watched them for a while until her presence started to draw attention, then one of the workers approached her. She wondered if she should leave, if they were unhappy about her watching them.

'Can I help you, Protector?'

'I am sorry, I didn't mean to disturb you,' Mesrra said.

'You didn't. I just wanted to make sure you didn't need anything. I do not think you are from here.'

'I am not, I was,' she paused, wondering how to explain her presence, 'I was just looking around,' she ended weakly. As the male nodded and started to turn away, she asked, 'How many types of crop do you grow?'

'Three, but not at the same time. What we grow depends on the time of the year. But there is always something growing.'

Mesrra wanted to ask more, but knowing so little about farming she couldn't frame the right questions so she thanked the male and flew away. She did not go far. She felt uncomfortable being watched as she left, especially as she wanted to take a quick look at where they lived.

At first she thought that the cabins were in a state of disrepair but, as she looked closely, she realised this was not the case. Some had been repaired; others were newer; all were basic and small.

Was this the sort of place her mother had grown up in? Mesrra could not imagine it. She had never asked her mother to share any personal memories. She had been shown everything about the traders at an early age as both her parents were determined that their knowledge would be passed on and did not die with them.

Her father's parents had known nothing about what was coming when they had taken over after the death of the previous First Protectors. They had had to learn everything for themselves. Luckily there had been a few written records. Being children of Protectors, and expected to have their own collective one day, meant that they could read. Most of the people could not and would never need to.

Mesrra decided to talk to her mother when she got back. How could you solve a problem if you did not fully understand it?

Leaving the habitations behind, she made her way out to the fields on the other side where no one seemed to be working at the moment. Crouching down, she ran her fingers through the soil. It was so dry that it passed cleanly through her fingers. The ground at the base of Hannoki was always wet; there were pools of water linked together by streams. Lots of things grew, but nothing that could be eaten. She wondered if anyone had ever tried to plant food crops there.

Mesrra returned to Hannoki's Peak without visiting Isslac or Erle. What she had seen had raised a lot of questions and she thought she would get more honest answers from her mother, who had no agenda where collectives were concerned.

She landed on the plateau and went in search of Lovoa. She did not have to look far; she found her parents together, working on some papers.

'Are you alright, Mesrra?' Lovoa asked as she joined them.

'Yes. When you are free, can we talk?'

'I can talk now.' As if on cue, Solvan made his excuses and left them alone. 'What is troubling you, Mesrra?'

'I went down to see a collective today, to see what Kelvic is so interested in. I did not expect what I found. I had so many questions but I felt I should have already known the answers.'

'Did you talk to the Protectors?'

'No. I was aware of my lack of knowledge. I feared they might only tell me what they wanted me to know,' Mesrra said. Then she added tentatively, 'I hoped you would be willing to share your memories with me.'

'I never worked on a collective. My parents were independent farmers.'

'I know, but you are familiar with the basics about

harvests and general conditions. You would still know what is acceptable and what is not.'

'I do not know if I have the answers you want, but I will show you what I know.' And Lovoa did.

Mesrra broke the connection, disappointed. She had hoped to get answers from her mother but she had got nothing. Her parents had tried growing crops near the forest, where the ground was moist, but they had failed. The work and living conditions were far worse than anything she had seen.

What she had hoped to achieve to make things better now seemed irrelevant. Life was already better; the Protectors were doing what they could. Any influence from her would be insignificant.

Mesrra left her mother. She would explore further but she felt there was little value she could add. The Protectors, under her parents, were driving change. Her brother was happy to help, to be their voice. But Mesrra kept thinking there was more that could be done. What, she had no idea, but she knew it was time to stop dreaming and accept the responsibilities that one day would be hers.

Chapter 10

MESRRA was in her room looking at the star chart Brelsa had helped her to create when she had visited so long ago. They had taken some of the precious paper that her parents had stored. Solvan had not been pleased; how paper was made was one of those pieces of knowledge that had been lost.

She wondered where Brelsa was now. Mesrra was very young when Brelsa had visited and had been fascinated by everything she represented. Brelsa had taken the time to talk to the child, telling her stories of what she had done and seen. Mesrra smiled at the memories; she had taken every moment and kept it close. Her younger brother, Kelvic, could not understand her fascination with the humans; he had been nervous of them and happy to keep his distance.

As she grew older, Mesrra started to resent the restrictions on her life. She became even more obsessed with all that Brelsa had told her. Kelvic dismissed his sister's interests; he could not see anything beyond Lismar and protecting his home. Mesrra couldn't fault him for that, and part of her was relieved by his passion because it meant that it didn't have to be hers.

For a long time after Brelsa's visit, Mesrra dreamed that she would return and take her away. In reality, it was not known when Brelsa would return, if ever. Slowly the dreams died, reality started to creep in and Mesrra realised that, like her brother, she had a responsibility to Lismar. Soon all she had left was the star chart. But that did not mean that she was happy with the situation.

'*Mesrra, Askran is coming here to see you,*' her mother

called.

Sighing, Mesrra stood up and went out to meet him. Her duty.

'Askran, a pleasure as always,' Mesrra said as she walked onto the plateau where he was waiting for her.

He was a good match, or so she was told. He was not as strong as her – but no male was, as far as she knew. Mesrra had always known that she would lose power on mating but with Askran the loss would be minimal. However, she felt nothing for him and resented giving away any of her strength to him. She knew the closeness her parents shared was rare; they had been lucky as they had hardly known each other when they mated.

Askran was keen to mate, to gain Mesrra's strength and the status it would lead to, but she kept putting him off, asking for more time to get to know him better. She could feel his frustration but the more frustrated he got, the more she held him at arm's length. As much as he was keen to increase his abilities, she did not want to lose hers.

Mesrra had never used her full power and she had been told that she would not notice the difference after she mated. She did not care; she would know. Unless she mated with Askran, she could not be First Protector, so the mating would bring both personal loss and many advantages.

Their meetings were getting more awkward, neither knowing what to talk about without addressing the topic of mating which invariably led to an argument.

Askran left again, unsatisfied.

⚛

Mesrra's parents said nothing to her as they watched Askran fly off. Both Lovoa and Solvan understood their daughter's reluctance to mate, but they were worried what would happen to her if she did not do so. Unmated, she wouldn't have any authority; did Mesrra fully understand what this would mean? Askran might not be the perfect match but he was good and strong. Their mating would eventually make them First Protectors, since Kelvic was not as strong as Mesrra.

Lovoa sighed in frustration; she hoped her daughter would make the right decision in time.

'Are you going to talk to her?' Solvan asked.

'No, she needs to make the decision on her own. She is too strong-willed. I fear any attempt to persuade her towards Askran will turn her further against him.'

'Askran is ambitious – he won't wait much longer. I hope she realises that.'

'I think she does. I just hope she realises that what she wants isn't possible.'

Later that day colours tinged the sky, drawing the First Protectors' attention. They went onto the plateau to watch.

'Whose mating flight do you think that is?' Lovoa asked. 'I hadn't realised that any of the Protectors' children had paired off.'

'It could be anyone. Think of your parents,' Solvan reminded her.

'No, I feel no surprise. This couple knew what to expect.'

'I can think of one instance where we wouldn't have been told,' Solvan said, hoping his suspicions would not be confirmed.

'Askran? Surely he would have told us if he'd planned this,' Lovoa said, picking up on her mate's thoughts,

'Not necessarily. Mesrra has been cold towards him. If he has received another offer, he may have decided to accept it and guarantee his place as a Protector.'

'If Askran had told Mesrra there was another offer, it might have pushed her into deciding to mate.'

'Possibly – or she would have become more stubborn and made the situation worse.'

'Do we tell her?' Lovoa asked.

'Not until we know for sure that it is Askran. It could be one of his siblings or the child of another Protector. If it is him, we'll know soon enough. We can deal with it then.'

'Well, I guess that answers the question,' Solvan whispered to Lovoa as they stood on Hannoki's mountain peak and watched Askran land on the plateau in front of them. They had received his official request to visit that morning, something he had not done for some time. Now, as he stood in front of them, their suspicions were confirmed: Askran's patterning had changed. He had mated.

'Askran, it is good to see you.' Lovoa said. She could feel Solvan's anger as he stood next to her. *'Mesrra rejected him. Listen to what he has to say first,'* she advised. She felt Solvan accept her words, though he still considered Askran's mating to be a slight to his daughter.

'Even in these circumstances?' Askran asked, indicating his changed markings.

'You have the right to decide who to mate with. Did you come to see us or did you wish to see Mesrra.'

'To see you both and explain. I could not wait for Mesrra any longer. I was given another option and decided to take it.'

'She is on the west balcony,' Lovoa said.

'You do not want to know why?'

'She deserves to hear it first.'

'Thank you,' Askran said. He walked past them, wondering if they had done him a favour or not.

'Are you going to warn Mesrra?' Solvan asked.

'No,' Lovoa replied. 'They need to have this conversation. And with the mood she has been in recently I don't trust her not to jump off the side of the mountain and fly away.'

'I cannot believe she would be so rude.'

Lovoa choked on her reply.

※

Askran saw Mesrra standing on her own. Her back was to him as she looked over the mountains; he knew she was aware of him but she did not acknowledge him.

'Mesrra,' he said as he came to stand next to her.

'When did you know you were going to mate with someone other than me?'

'Your parents warned you,' he stated.

'No, I have not spoken to them. I know you well enough that I felt it when the mating started. You certainly did not light up the skies did you?' she said cruelly.

'That is not fair or appropriate.'

'Maybe, but neither was coming here yesterday and promising to give me time to make a decision, then leaving and mating with someone else. You should have told me.'

'Would it have made a difference to you if you had known?'

'I don't know. But I know that it hurts that you did this.'

'I am sorry, I didn't have a choice. When I got home, my parents had collapsed. Both my mated siblings were arguing over who would take over the collective. I had run out of time. Fasla is an old friend of similar strength to me. With her, I could take control of the collective when my parents died.'

'If Fasla was willing to mate with you, then why come to me?' When Askran did not reply immediately, Mesrra realised she knew the answer. 'You really liked her. If that was the case why come here?'

'You are a lot stronger than her.'

'And you wanted my strength,' Mesrra finished for him.

'Can you blame me?'

'Why did you come here today?'

'I felt you deserved an explanation.'

'You hoped your pathetic story would keep me on your side.' When Askran said nothing, Mesrra continued, 'Please leave.'

He did not say anything else and extended his wings, intending to fly off the balcony.

'I am not against mating,' Mesrra said. 'I did not want to lose my strength but that was not the only thing holding me back. I always knew you were hiding things from me, not being honest. I could have broken through your mental shields and found out for myself, but I wanted you to tell me, to be honest with me, and not leave it until after the mating to reveal your secrets. That is what held me back.'

'I was not ready for you to be in my head,' Askran admitted.

'I would have been the moment we were mated.'

'By then it would have been too late.'

She knew what he meant: he loved Fasla but he wanted Mesrra's strength.

'Then this is for the best,' she said.

Askran took to the sky without saying anything else and Mesrra turned her back on him.

Chapter 11

Two years later

BRELSA was happy to be in orbit around Lismar again, though she expected it would be for the last time. When she was last here, an FWN ship had still been in orbit, though not in communication with the planet. They had taken the opportunity to install a sensor net around Lismar that would send notifications if anyone came close. No one had, but the FWN wanted to run diagnostics to make sure it was operating as expected. The net had been created by Cal and was the first of its kind.

During the last FWN visit, Solvan and Lovoa were informed that the net was going to be installed so they would not be concerned when they sensed the orbiting ships. The FWN had asked the First Protectors not to tell anyone else.

This current visit was planned to be the final one unless some new problem arose.

Not knowing how sensitive the Lismarians would be to their arrival, the telepaths on board had been trying to reach the surface. The ship was now at a distance from which Brelsa could easily talk to the First Protectors, but she had received no response from the planet. The FWN wanted to see how near they could get to the planet without the First Protectors knowing, in case they needed to return to perform maintenance on the sensor network. They wanted to leave the Lismarians alone unless absolutely necessary.

❀

When Lovoa and Solvan received Brelsa's request to enter the planet's orbit, they were surprised and worried. It had been so long since they had last heard from her, they thought she would never return. What did her arrival now mean?

Brelsa reassured them that the visit was routine; for the humans it had not been long. As before, they wanted to make sure the Lismarians had no issues that needed to be addressed.

But that was not Lovoa and Solvan's only concern. What effect would Brelsa's visit have on Mesrra? They were aware of how fascinated their daughter was with the humans. They had been relieved when Mesrra had started to follow her brother's interest in the collectives and farming.

'Why do they need to keep coming back?' Solvan asked, frustrated. They had given permission for the shuttle to land and the humans were expected shortly.

'At least this means they are keeping watch over us,' Lovoa pointed out.

'They are to blame for the traders.'

'Some of them were, most were not. They are here to make sure we are still safe.'

'If we were being attacked, these visits would not help them or us.'

'We don't know what is going on with the humans and we can't judge them all as one,' Lovoa said.

'I know, but it is difficult to move on when they keep returning.'

'We could ask them not to come back.'

'I want to, but where would that leave Brelsa?'

'How do we know these visits are not just as hard on her?'

※

Lovoa and Solvan stood on the plateau and watched as the shuttle door opened. They were relieved that Brelsa was the first to come out. She paused as she exited and seemed to stagger briefly. Solvan went towards her but Lovoa stopped him.

'She is just getting used to the suns again,' Lovoa reminded him. He stood back, giving Brelsa the room she needed to adjust.

It was as if the humans had the same thought. It was not until Brelsa had recovered and walked towards the First Protectors that they walked out of the shuttle.

'Brelsa, it is good to see you again,' Lovoa said. 'I think your companions are the same as last time?'

'It is good to be home and to see you again. I have missed this,' Brelsa said, seeming overwhelmed. After a moment she continued. 'Yes, they thought it would be best for consistency.'

After the meeting with the humans, Lovoa and Solvan were reassured. If the sensor net was working as it should and the Lismarians had no other concerns, this was the last planned return by the humans.

Brelsa would stay on the planet in case communication was needed with the ship but, as before, she had to remain on Hannoki's Peak. She was happy spending her time taking in the suns and was keen to see how much Mesrra had grown. She doubted that Mesrra was still the inquisitive child she had been the last time. Brelsa found it horrifying that human children took so long to grow and become independent. It did not occur to her to ask if her brother had any children.

She did not have long to wait. Brelsa was surprised at the beautiful, strong young woman Mesrra had become.

'Brelsa, it has been so long since I last saw you. I had given up hope that you'd return. Do you remember me?' Mesrra asked, getting straight to the point.

'Of course I do. You kept on asking questions about what I had been doing. I can't believe how much you've grown since I last saw you.'

'It has been a long time. I cannot wait to hear about what

you have seen and done since you were last here.' Mesrra sat next to Brelsa, confident of her welcome.

They talked of general things for a while. Mesrra was getting frustrated by Brelsa's refusal to answer a lot of her questions about humans and how they lived.

In an attempt to change the subject Brelsa asked, 'Is there anyone special you are looking to mate with?'

'That is a touchy subject at the moment,' Mesrra replied after a pause.

'It was with me as well. Not everyone is as lucky as your parents. Do you want to talk about it?'

'There is not much to say. There was sort of someone – Askran. He wanted to mate with me but I was unsure.' Mesrra explained what had happened. 'I was not hurt emotionally, as I implied to him, but I did see any chance for me to mate disappear. There are no males as strong as me and I hate that fact. My brother was able to compromise but I cannot. Askran was my best option and now that has gone. I cannot help wondering what is left for me.'

'It may not seem like it now, but it could have been for the best. I loved my brother but he changed when he mated with Erle for her strength. She was mean and narrow-minded and he did not change for the better.'

'That is a diplomatic way of putting it,' Mesrra said, knowing the couple.

'It is a problem with how we are. Both males and females need to mate for status. I can understand why that was the case when we had to protect ourselves from the traders, but we might see changes in the future.'

'Do humans mate?'

'They do, but not like us. They can have several mates, or partners as they prefer to call each other. And you can be successful if you are on your own or with someone.'

'That would be nice. Are you happy with your life?'

'It has not been easy and there have been times I had regrets. But when I put everything together, no, I do not regret my choices.'

'Can I leave with you?' Mesrra asked Brelsa a few days later, having sought her out on the plateau.

Brelsa stood facing the suns with her wings outspread, taking in as much of the suns' power as she could. At the question, her wings snapped back in and she turned to look at Mesrra. 'Have you spoken to your parents?' she asked, surprised and worried about the request.

'Not yet. I did not want to talk to them until I knew if it was possible.'

'I do not know. I will need to discuss it with the captain, and she would have to get permission from the leaders of her people. But are you sure that this is what you want?' Brelsa asked.

'With everything you have seen and done, how can you ask that? Life is so limited here. And with the threat gone, what else is left for me? To be a farmer like my mother's parents?' Mesrra scoffed.

'There is nothing wrong with being a farmer,' Brelsa challenged her. 'And I seriously doubt your mother would appreciate your attitude. Now the attacks on our people have stopped, our society can change. When the traders started attacking, our people adapted to defend themselves. Now we need to adapt again, to look at ways to improve ourselves. Travelling with humans has shown me what can be achieved. They are always striving to develop and better themselves.'

'It is alright for the humans, they already know so much.'

'That was not always the case. Reading their history, they started off with nothing, less than we have now. We are luckier than them. We know what can be achieved, what is possible. The humans never had that, yet look where they are now.'

'How long did it take them to know, to understand enough?'

'A very long time,' Brelsa admitted. The humans had tried to explain it to her but the span of their history was something she could not comprehend.

'I can see Kelvic making a difference,' Mesrra said. 'He is so patient and always asking questions, wanting to know why things are as they are. I don't know where to start.'

'Then follow his lead and support him.'

'That is the problem. I have tried. I have spent time on the collectives, talking to the farmers and Protectors. I have my mother's memories of her time on a farm, and I am frustrated by them. Even if I could see things as Kelvic does, I want to find my own way. I need to mate to have social standing, but I don't want to. In the same way, I don't want to be subservient to my mated brother. I want to find my place.' When Brelsa did not immediately reply, Mesrra challenged her. 'You don't want me to leave here.'

'I felt like you did. I wanted more than the life I envisioned here. Your parents pointed out what I would be losing but I was determined to go.'

'You said you do not regret leaving.'

'I said I do not regret my choice. I had fewer options than you. I can already see how Lismar has changed under your parents. But it is not easy living with the humans, and there were times I doubted myself. I was prepared for being weak due to the lack of suns. Being able to eat and sleep as much as I wanted helped, as did the solar lamps, but there were times when I felt helpless. You talk about not wanting to mate because you will lose your strength, but if you leave here to travel you will have no strength.'

'But I will have the freedom to be me.'

'You will not have the freedom to decide where you go. The FWN will place you on a starbase or ship, and you will go where they tell you. That is really not so bad because their world is so big. What is bad is how lonely it can get. Though many humans have made me feel welcome, I am the only one of my kind and there are things about me that they do not understand. When I left Lismar I agreed that I would never return. I consider myself lucky I have been able to come back, however briefly. But I cannot leave

Hannoki's Peak, I cannot come home. I have not spoken to my family since I first left. I cannot mate and have a family of my own. When I left, I didn't think I wanted these things but now I am not so sure.'

'What changed?'

'I got older.'

'So you lied! You do regret leaving.'

'No. I have started to grieve the loss of a family I cannot have but that is in conflict with the life I have had. I do not know how I will feel in the end, and that is what worries me. You need to consider not just the here and now but the future. If you promise not to tell the humans, I can show you so you know what you are asking.'

'I would like that.'

❋

Mesrra sat looking out over the mountains. What Brelsa had shown her had given her a lot to think about and she did not have much time to make a decision. Brelsa had contacted the captain and the humans were willing to allow Mesrra to leave with them, but on the same conditions as Brelsa. She would be saying goodbye to her family. The thought of never seeing them again hurt in a way Askran's betrayal never had.

Brelsa and the humans should have left today as the suns set, but they had agreed to stay another day to allow Mesrra to make her choice.

❋

'I'm sorry about Askran,' Kelvic said as he sat next to Mesrra on the edge of the mountain, staring over the landscape.

'Thank you.'

'I know you were not sure of the mating. I knew the moment I met Derla that she was the one for me, the same way our parents knew. The right mate is out there for you. Just be patient.'

'That is the problem – I am not sure he is. I am not sure I want to give a part of myself to anyone else,' Mesrra admitted.

'With the right mate, you are not giving up a part of yourself. You are sharing it.'

'I still don't think I'm ready.'

'Then wait. You are extremely powerful and the daughter of the First Protectors. Don't let society dictate to you. Help me to improve our way of life.'

'That is what Brelsa suggested as well.'

'Then why do you not sound convinced?'

'Because I am not,' Mesrra admitted. 'I have dreamed about travelling space for years, but it never seemed possible until Brelsa came back. Now I have a few hours left to decide whether to stay or leave. Brelsa shared her experiences with me, hoping to change my mind, but I still want to go.'

'Have you spoken to our parents?'

'I want to be sure of my decision first.'

'I think you know what you want, you are just scared of telling Mother and Father,' he teased.

She punched his shoulder. 'Wouldn't you be?' she asked. 'The chances are I will not see them – or you – again. That is the only reason I am hesitating.'

'You cannot let that stop you. Brelsa has returned. They may let you visit. And you do not know what fate holds for us. I would hate to be the reason you live your life with regret.'

⚛

'How long have you been thinking of going?' Lovoa asked her daughter when Mesrra told her she wanted to leave Lismar.

'I have been thinking about it since Brelsa first came here. But it was not a reality to me until she came back,' Mesrra confessed.

'You cannot seriously consider going! There is so much

to do here,' Solvan said.

'And you have Kelvic for that. You do not need me.'

'Of course we need you, Mesrra. How could you not know that?' her mother cried.

'What can I do that you and Kelvic cannot?' Mesrra challenged them.

''There is more to need than the work you can do,' Lovoa said.

'That is not need, that is want. You want me to stay.'

'Of course, we do. We love you.'

''Then please let me go.'

'Has Brelsa explained the disadvantages to leaving?' Lovoa asked.

'She has done more than that, she has shown me.'

'And you still want to go?'

'I want to leave Lismar. Leaving you is the hard part of the decision, but I need to find my way on my own terms.' The determination in Mesrra's voice was clear.

'I will always love you, and you will always be welcome back here,' Lovoa said.

'Thank you, Mother.' Mesrra hugged her parents before leaving to tell Brelsa that she would be going with her. She did not see her mother's skin turn blue in sorrow, or Solvan take Lovoa into his arms in an attempt to console her.

Chapter 12

MESRRA stood looking at the entrance of the shuttle and knew a moment of panic.

'You do not have to do this,' Brelsa said.

'You have our support in whatever decision you make. We will always be proud of you,' Solvan said.

'I want this.' Mesrra walked straight onto the shuttle. She had said her goodbyes to her family a short while ago. She knew they understood. Anything further would be procrastination on her part. She did not see the look of sorrow on her parents' faces as she walked away from them.

Mesrra had never seen anything like the inside of the shuttle. She thought she had been prepared once she had seen Brelsa's mind, but seeing it and experiencing it were two different things.

'I know it is a lot to take in. Are you alright?' Brelsa asked her.

'Yes,' Mesrra said as she sat down. She knew Brelsa was offering her the opportunity to leave but she had made up her mind.

Mesrra was shown how to strap into the chairs for safety and, on command, the shuttle took off. She felt her mental connection with her family disappear as she left Lismar. She hadn't thought she would miss the connection; it had always been there so it had not occurred to her that it would go.

The shuttle docked. With shaking hands, Mesrra unfastened the security belt. As an experiment, she reached out for power but there was nothing.

'Stop trying,' Brelsa said. 'There is no sunlight here. The

solar lamps give us what we need to survive, but we cannot store any power.'

'I remember.'

'I have asked that we stay in orbit for a day. It will give you a chance to change your mind. I know it is not long, but it was the best I could arrange.'

'There is no need,' Mesrra stated.

'Once we leave, it could be years before you return again – if ever. I know a day is limited time, but at least you will have some idea of what it is like to adapt to the restrictions of the solar lamps.'

'I will not change my mind.'

Brelsa saw her own stubbornness in her young friend and hoped that Mesrra did not come to regret it.

Brelsa took Mesrra into the hydroponics section of the ship where she spent most of her time. She took pleasure in her friend's amazement at all the plants that grew there, and fondly remembered the first time she had seen them.

'What is this place? Why do I feel better here?' Mesrra asked.

'They have special lamps that help the plants grow but they do not produce anywhere near as much energy as a sun, let alone the two we have. I find they make space travel manageable but I am unable to expand any power.'

'What is all this green? It's not like the forest at the base of Hannoki's mountain range,' Mesrra said, indicating the plants around them.

'No, all of this can be eaten. It helps to balance the humans' diet.'

'There is so much here,' Mesrra said, looking at it all. 'Can we eat any of it? I did not think to bring any food with me.'

'Yes, humans eat a lot more than we do. I will show you what we can eat – they are called corn and beans. I will also make sure you know what to avoid,' Brelsa explained.

'How did you learn all of this?'

'Trial and error. I tried these foods while on a planet

when the sun could heal any problems I had, some of which were very unpleasant. Avoid what they call fruit at all costs. The planets I have encountered have only one sun. That is enough to heal us but the lamps are not strong enough to make us better, so be careful what you eat. You must take care because these ships could be days away from a planet.'

'I have read your mind, remember? I know what happened.'

'Not just with the fruit. Also the time I cut myself,' Brelsa reminded her.

Mesrra closed her eyes and explored that memory. 'You had a cut. It didn't heal here and they had to take you to a planet.'

'That is how vulnerable we are without the sun.'

'It did not heal but it got no worse. Could you have coped?'

'I do not know. Neither did the doctors. The humans worry about something called infection, something we have never encountered that can kill them. When the cut did not heal, that is what they were concerned about.'

'Are you trying to scare me back home?'

'No, but I want you to fully appreciate the effects that space travel will have on you before it is too late,' Brelsa said. 'When I left originally, I was told I could never return. I count myself lucky for the couple of days I have spent on Lismar during the last two years. I thought I was ready after a short trip to one of their planets. You think you are ready because you have read my mind. I need you to understand that it will be a lot harder to adjust than you think, especially if the humans want us to be in different places. You may never see your family, or me, again.'

'I know. I will miss my parents and brother and I do not know how I will feel about not seeing them every day. Kelvic tried to interest me in his plans to improve how we farm and build, but knowing that there is all of this,' Mesrra looked around her, 'it never seemed enough. I do not want to compromise. If this is a bad decision, I only have myself to blame. But I do not want to regret not trying.'

'I cannot argue with that. You are so much like me at your age.'

❋

Brelsa stayed with her young friend as the ship pulled out of orbit. They sat in the hydroponics bay in silence. Brelsa suspected that Mesrra was still reaching out to her family until the last moment. 'Are you alright?' she asked, and berated herself for the stupid question.

'Yes,' Mesrra said simply, then continued. 'I am so mixed about what I feel. I am both sad and excited. I feel divided.'

'I was never as close to my family as you are to yours but I miss my home and am sad to leave it every time.' Brelsa touched Mesrra's mind. The girl was keeping her emotions well shielded, but Brelsa could feel a hint of her pain. 'I could ask for us to go back. We have not travelled very far. Soon it will be too late.'

'No, I am fine.'

Chapter 13

AS they travelled back into FWN space, Brelsa taught Mesrra everything she knew, using mental sharing where necessary to speed up the process.

Mesrra was hungry for Brelsa's knowledge. The older Lismarian introduced her to the telepaths on the ship and familiarised her with the difference in how their telepathic abilities worked. It was harder than Mesrra had anticipated; she had always taken her telepathic ability for granted and was shocked when she realised she could not use this skill with most humans. Communication was difficult even with telepathic humans, and Mesrra could not understand anything that was said. Translators resolved spoken language issues but not telepathic ones.

Brelsa spent a lot of time teaching Mesrra the humans' language, reinforced with a mind share so she could communicate on a mental level and did not have to rely only on emotions and images.

Brelsa was also there as Mesrra started to panic when her strength began to deplete and a weakness she had never known before affected her. Brelsa reassured her that this was normal; Mesrra was being affected more quickly because she kept on expending energy on everyday actions. She would have to learn how to do things like the humans. Brelsa reassured her that she would get used to the reduced power and she understood her young friend's anger and frustration at the restrictions this placed on her.

Brelsa prayed to Hannoki that Mesrra would adapt but she worried that Mesrra, having lived on the mountain peak, was much more used to the suns.

The crew left them alone; the only people who came into

the hydroponics bay were those who tended the plants. Mesrra started to watch what they did to distract herself then asked Brelsa questions.

'They cut the plants back to help them to grow stronger,' Brelsa told her.

'You know about how to look after all of this?' Mesrra asked.

'Some – but not as much as the people that work here. I'd be happy to explain it to you.'

'Thank you, I would like that.'

Brelsa was surprised at Mesrra's willingness to learn and the questions she asked. Mesrra had been dismissive of farmers and shown no interest in helping her brother, but it turned out that her knowledge of Lismarian farming was better than Brelsa's – and Brelsa had grown up on a collective and not a mountain peak.

Brelsa introduced her to the crew members; they were more than willing to talk about what they were doing and why. Over the next few days, she was relieved that the lessons distracted Mesrra and helped her to cope. She also realised that her young friend's knowledge was excellent; maybe Mesrra's lack of interest in farming and helping her brother was because she understood where the failings were but did not know how to correct them. That inability to fix the problems had frustrated Mesrra and therefore she had shied away from them.

Brelsa's heart sank. What would happen when Mesrra had learnt enough to help her people improve but realised that she could never go back home to share her knowledge?

She was relieved that Mesrra had started to develop friendships with some of the crew by the time they arrived at Starbase Ra. Here they would separate; Brelsa had only left the base to help communicate with the Lismarians. She had learnt the humans' language during her time living with them but they had not mastered hers, though for it to be in the translator meant it was available for anyone in the FWN to learn. For the most part the translators dealt with the spoken word but, when a ship was sent to check how the Lismarians were doing, the humans wanted someone who could communicate with the First Protectors from space so there was no risk of their ship being accidentally blown out of the orbit.

Brelsa had spent her first few weeks travelling in space after being released from Europa, but had then been asked to stay on a base for a while. The request had not been explained but in the end she'd been happy with this arrangement. She had made friends and learned about their various cultures, which made her feel less isolated.

She knew that Mesrra would not be staying with her. Brelsa had been called to the captain's office the previous day to be told that the FWN wanted Mesrra to leave on a ship. When she had asked why, she was told that Mesrra had left her world to travel, so travel she would.

❈

'I'm surprised the FWN let Mesrra leave Lismar. Brelsa caused enough of a political nightmare, but at least we could argue it was for the best as she'd already seen too much of our way of life. But why add to the problem?' Admiral Simon Johnson asked.

'Our telepaths can't sense the Urigans because of their shields. The Lismarians' abilities work differently and Mesrra is strong. We want to see if she can detect them,' Admiral Yoland replied.

'You want to use her as the FWN used your grandfather?' Simon replied, horrified.

'Why not? It worked.'

'David Wilhelm knew what he was getting involved in. You can't send Mesrra out into space without letting her know why. She'll be struggling to cope. If you want to send a Lismarian out on a hunt for those bastards, why not send Brelsa?'

'I thought about it, but Brelsa has not made friends easily and she's now settled on the starbase. Mesrra is also much stronger and, having lived all her life in near isolation on Hannoki's Peak, she may cope better with the isolation of space travel. If she doesn't, we won't make her stay out there. She can return to Ra to be with Brelsa.'

'Do you plan to tell Mesrra – and the captain of the ship she's on, for that matter – what's going on?' Simon demanded.

'No. Mesrra doesn't need to know the details, just to let the bridge crew know if she feels any hostility to the ship. I'll brief the captain.'

'Do you think it's wise not letting Mesrra know?'

'What do you want me to say?' Gareth Yoland asked. 'That a race stronger than us is looking to start a war over the Lismarians because they want to kill them for their wings? How will that help her? The Urigans can attack for longer than we could sustain a defence. We got lucky. In killing the head chairman, they underestimated Cal and his relationship with his father, his connections and how bloody stubborn he is. That won't happen again.'

'The Lismarians will find out soon enough about the Urigans unless something changes soon. We can't hope to win against them,' Simon protested.

'I know. If Mesrra picks up anything, I'd tell them if I thought I could get more of her people onto ships as a result. But until then, I don't propose to worry the Lismarians about things that can't be changed.'

'Which ship are you putting her on?'

'Amber's, of course. I want her with a captain I can trust. And it will be interesting to see if they can make their telepathic abilities work together.'

※

Mesrra stepped off the ship onto the starbase. She looked around, taking in everything. On the trip she had spent most of her time in the hydroponics and the horticulturalists had spent hours talking to her about the plants, helping her get over the panic of not being able to pull in enough energy to expand it should she need to store it or defend herself. By the time they had arrived at Starbase Ra, she had adjusted to the change.

Brelsa and Mesrra spent a considerable amount of time together after arriving at Ra while waiting for the ship Mesrra was to live on for the foreseeable future. Brelsa showed her around the base, explaining that all ships and starbases followed the same structure and that areas were colour-coded, making it easy to know where you are.

Brelsa watched the wonder in her young friend's face as she eagerly absorbed everything. She showed Mesrra where she would live; the humans had installed solar panels into the room, so she had her own space. She made sure Mesrra knew how basic technology such as the communication system worked, hoping it would help her fit in quicker.

Mesrra saw many other vessels come and go during this period and she was curious why she had not been allowed to leave on one of those. The ship she was boarding was a deep space one – but so were a lot of those that had docked at Ra. Brelsa hoped the delay was because the FWN had found a ship that would be more sympathetic to Mesrra's needs.

⚛

Brelsa found parting from Mesrra harder than she'd expected. She was saying goodbye to her last link with home, maybe forever. She doubted the FWN would ever ask her to return to Lismar to facilitate communication with the First Protectors. There was not even a guarantee that she and Mesrra would meet again.

They stood together at the docking port, waiting for a member of the crew to take Mesrra on board. Brelsa was surprised when she saw Amber walk out to greet them. She hadn't seen the captain since she'd arrived at Ra.

'Brelsa, it's good to see you,' Amber said.

'Amber, I did not expect to meet you again.'

'I'm somewhat surprised myself, to be honest,' Amber said.

Mesrra felt pain from the woman. She turned to Brelsa and realised that her friend felt nothing. She did not know the reason behind it, but detected no threat towards them so she said nothing.

Amber turned to her. 'I've come to welcome you on board, Mesrra. You will be travelling with us for a while.'

'Please take care of her,' Brelsa said.

'Of course. She will be part of my crew.'

Pain and fear rolled over Mesrra again and she hesitated. Should she go? Did she have a choice? That was not something she had considered before. She was curious about where the fear came from. Was it fear for her people in general – was there still a threat to them? Or did she fear going on board? But Mesrra had made her decision, so she said her final farewell to Brelsa and accepted the hand of welcome.

Brelsa watched her young friend walk away. She prayed to Hannoki that Mesrra would remain safe and that she would never have to tell the girl's parents that their daughter was dead.

'Brelsa.' She turned around to see who had called her and saw her friends standing there. 'We wondered if you wanted company.' She was surprised; she hadn't thought anyone would understand how difficult this parting was for her.

'Thank you.' And with one last look at the port, she turned away.

Chapter 14

24 hours earlier

AS Amber returned to Ra, she sent a communication to her mother informing her where she would be and when. Mary Wilhelm had left a message two years earlier, wanting to know when Amber would next dock because she wanted them to meet. This was the first time Amber had received such a request since she'd joined the FWN.

She'd only seen her mother three times during those fifteen years, when they happened to be in the same place at the same time. The meetings had been tense.

The message had arrived after Amber had returned with Brelsa but when she had already deployed on a prolonged mission. If she was honest, she wouldn't have bothered now if her father hadn't advised her to talk to her mother again.

The last time she'd seen her mother, the meeting had been strained as the rare occasions when they saw each other always were. They had once been close until Amber decided to follow her brother and cousins into the FWN instead of staying in the UTA with her mother. As far as Mary was concerned, that was a waste of Amber's abilities. Amber could not argue about that – it was rare that her skills were put to use as they would have been in the UTA – but politics and corporate meetings were not the life she wanted. From everything she had been told about her grandfather David Wilhelm, she took straight after him.

The argument that had ensued when she'd told her mother she was joining the FWN was still so clear. 'Why are you dead set against me going?' Amber had asked. 'You were so proud when Adam enrolled in the FWN.'

'I was, but you are not your brother. It was a good fit for him.'

'What do you mean by that?' Though Amber thought she knew the answer.

'Adam takes after your father's side of the family,' Mary had said. 'And though I love him very much, he is not special like you. Your place is here with me at the UTA. Think what you could achieve.'

'I have no interest in politics and I can do just as much, if not more, in the FWN.'

'Rubbish. Telepaths are not as useful as they used to be. Ships are now being equipped with the same shielding technology as at the UTA. With your strengths, you'd be as effective as your brother.'

'I know, but this is what I want and there's nothing you can do about it,' Amber had argued. Her mother had tried to prove her wrong and had gone to the FWN to try and prevent them accepting her daughter. She had failed; the only thing she'd achieved was to drive a wedge further between them.

After her mother made the request for a meeting, Amber was surprised when Mary said she would see her at Ra. She did not believe that her mother was suffering from nostalgia after all these years so, when Amber's ship docked, it was with trepidation that she went to the meeting. She was also surprised her mother had shown up because they were as far as possible from Europa, where Mary lived. That reinforced the fact that this was not a social visit.

Amber entered the hotel and asked for reception to call her mother's room. There was a time such formality was not necessary and Amber would have called her mother mentally, but now she was not comfortable doing that.

'Principal Wilhelm has asked you to go to Room 400, the top-floor suite. The lifts are behind you.'

'Thank you.' The suite did not surprise her; that her

mother wanted to meet in private did.

As Amber walked out of the lift, her mother opened the door. 'Please come in,' she said.

Amber walked into the room. A starbase suite was still basic compared to the luxuries of Europa and other planets in the FWN. It was a small room with two chairs facing an entertainment screen; to the side was a door which led to a small bedroom and bathroom.

'Please take a seat,' Mary said, closing the door and walking past her to take the further of the two chairs.

'I was surprised that you were willing to meet so far from Europa,' Amber said. 'Even more so here and not in one of the eating establishments.'

'There are things I want to discuss with you that I don't want to be overheard,' Mary said. 'It's good to see you again, Amber. It has been too long.'

'It's good to see you too, Mother.'

Mary activated a device and placed it on the table in front of them. 'Can you sense anything, hear other minds?' she asked.

'I could when I first walked in, but not now. What is that?'

'A little something Cal and the UTA created. Everything within a set circumference is mentally shielded. Very useful for important meetings away from government buildings.'

'I can imagine. I have to confess, I'm intrigued about what brought you here and the need for privacy.'

'I know that you're aware of the Lismarians,' Mary said. 'Before you went on your deep space mission you took Brelsa, I believe her name is, back to her home planet of Lismar.'

'I won't say I'm surprised you know. I can guess how. Why is it important? The whole of the FWN must know about her and her people's existence by now. My cousin arranged a very public display.'

'What do you know about Brelsa and her people?'

'Very little. I'm not sure anyone knows much. I know that her kind were being killed for their skins. I know they are telepaths, though when I had Brelsa on the ship I couldn't understand her mentally due to language differences. I couldn't feel her either, unless I deliberately focused on her. Why do you want to know?'

'How much do you know about your grandfather's involvement with the Lismarians?'

'Only what Alex told me on the trip to Lismar. Why? I only just arrived at the starbase and I have a lot of catching up on current affairs to do, but I'd have thought everything I know would be public knowledge by now,' Amber retorted.

'It probably is. In fact, there are probably a lot of people who know more than you do. What is not common knowledge is what your grandfather knew.'

'How can anyone be aware of that? Alex said he left no records before he died in a shuttle accident.'

'He didn't die in a shuttle accident,' Mary said. 'Your grandfather Mark faked David's death, took him back to Lismar and left him there. I assume he died on Lismar.'

'How did you find that out?'

'About how my father died? Your father told me two years so.'

Amber winced over the term 'your father', not 'my husband'.

'Gareth had only just found out himself about David's involvement with the Lismarians,' Mary went on. 'I've known for a long time. It seems David left two accounts behind, a mental one with me and a written one with Mark Yoland.'

'And you waited until now to tell me?'

'It didn't seem important when the Lismarians were unknown. And you were the one who took two years to meet with me.'

'If I'd known why you wanted to meet, I might have been able to delay my deployment,' Amber protested. 'I'd have met you sooner. You had no right to keep your knowledge of the Lismarians to yourself. If people knew about them, it could have saved God knows how many lives.'

'It wouldn't have made a difference. It wouldn't have prevented the deaths. My father didn't know about the Urigans.'

'If we'd known about the Lismarians, there would never have been an attempt to sell their skins as clothes.'

'No. Revealing the murders would have taken longer because the skins wouldn't have come here, and the Urigans would have killed many more of them,' Mary said. 'I haven't kept what I know to myself. I shared everything with your father when we talked two years ago. It wasn't helpful to him, but it might be helpful to you now.'

'If my father knows everything, why did you still want to see me? If the FWN thinks it's necessary, I'd have been told.'

'There are elements of my knowledge that your father, as a non-telepath, couldn't understand. He let me know why you are here and your current orders. I was already en route when you contacted me.'

'I haven't received the details yet. I get my briefing tomorrow. All I know is that I'm here to collect someone.'

'That someone is another Lismarian.'

'You have to be joking me. Who?'

'Better let your father explain about that and about your orders.'

'Fine,' Amber stated. 'Tell me everything you know. It will be interesting to see if it's of any use.'

'I think it would be best if I showed you, rather than told you,' Mary said, holding her hands out to her daughter. Amber paused for a moment before taking them. 'Let's see how much of your training you remember.'

✳

Amber left a few hours later, her mind reeling with everything her mother had shown her. In the mental share, she'd got all of her grandfather's emotions as well as his memories. All she could do was go back to her ship and collapse onto her bunk.

Tomorrow she would get her formal orders. She hoped that by then her brain would have processed the information Mary had given her. Her mother was right – she was really out of practice.

Chapter 15

AMBER had not known what to expect when she went to meet Mesrra; her mind was still processing her mother's disclosures from the night before. Knowing what the Lismarians could be capable of, the image of Hannoki saving her grandfather by killing the human pirates was imprinted on her mind.

Amber knew that they were missing something with the Lismarians; there had to be a way their strength could be harnessed. She knew they needed a sun or two, that ships made them weak, but Amber saw it as a problem to work on.

She'd been told that Mesrra was the daughter of the First Protectors. Though Mesrra was only two years old, due to how the Lismarians aged, she was nearer to twenty in human terms, the age Brelsa had been when she first left Lismar. Amber remembered the First Protectors; Mesrra's markings on her skin were extensive and the same as her parents.

Seeing Brelsa and Mesrra standing together brought Amber a wave of pain for lost friends and colleagues who had died for the Lismarians. That was what the FWN was about: stopping the atrocities that the Urigans would inflict on these people.

Amber was delighted Brelsa looked so well; she had worried how the Lismarian would cope away from her people. She was annoyed with herself at being surprised at how Brelsa looked. It was estimated that the Lismarians only lived for about twelve to fifteen years, so two years was a considerable amount of time for them.

She welcomed Mesrra on board. Inside, Amber was furious at her orders; the risks would be high and Mesrra had the right to know about them. Amber had accepted them – that was her job – but Mesrra was so young and had no understanding of what lay ahead.

Amber had been told to approach Urigan space again. They were not to look for conflict, but to see what she and Mesrra could sense. The thing Amber hated most was that the Admiralty didn't want Mesrra to know the real purpose; she was just to let the bridge know if she sensed hostility.

Amber was disgusted. She'd sent a message to her father telling him precisely what she felt about her orders, the first time she had crossed the line between career and family. Whether he knew about the orders or not was irrelevant; Mesrra had the right to know the danger she could be heading into.

Smiling, Amber reassured Brelsa about her young friend. The Lismarians said their farewells and Amber took Mesrra on board.

'Unfortunately, I need to oversee our deployment from here,' Amber said, as they passed a sealed door where someone else was waiting. 'This is Ensign Conner. She'll make sure that you settle in and show you round the ship. If you have any questions or concerns, please let her know.'

Mesrra watched the captain walk away before turning to Conner. She found that she did not know what to say.

'I'm pleased to meet you, Mesrra,' Conner said. 'You may not know this, but I was on the FWN *London* when we discovered what was happening to your people. I went down to Lismar, spoke with your parents, and have spent time getting to know Brelsa.'

'Are you here because of me?' Mesrra asked.

'I think it's more that you are here because of us. It was thought you'd be happier on a ship where some of the crew have knowledge of your people and where there are numerous telepaths.'

'Thank you, that is considerate. But Brelsa was barely

on a ship, she stayed on the starbase. The only time she left was to return to Lismar. Do you know why I could not stay with her?'

'She was on a different ship for a short while when we were deployed elsewhere. I think now we know more about you, the choice of ship was a bad one. If you hate travelling with us, we'll see what the FWN want to do. It was felt you should be given the opportunity to see how you like exploration.'

'Thank you. What was your mission?'

'Why don't I show you the room that's been assigned to you and the hydroponics bay? I'm happy to answer your questions, but I think we can find somewhere more comfortable than talking in the corridor.'

Conner opened the door behind her, showing Mesrra a small room with a sink and a single bunk with several blankets. 'Brelsa rarely used the room she was assigned when we took her back to Lismar the first time, but it's here if you need it. There are extra blankets – I know you get cold easily when you're away from the solar lamps in the hydroponics bay. If you need more, let me know.'

'You live in rooms like this?'

'More or less,' Conner said, thinking of the large bunk rooms that most of the crew shared. 'As I said, the room is here if you want it. If you're like Brelsa, you'll want to spend most of your time in hydroponics. If you follow me, I'll show you where that is.' She walked away, making sure that Mesrra was following her.

Mesrra took in everything around her, noting her surroundings so she could find her way back if she needed to. She did not ask any more questions. When they got to their destination, Mesrra stopped short as the doors slid open. This was nothing like the hydroponics bay on the ship that had brought her from Lismar, or the one on the starbase. She did not see the plants in front of her at first but the open expanse of space and the mass of stars winking in the dark.

'I'm sorry, Mesrra, I should have warned you about this. I didn't think to do so as we are still docked,' Conner said.

'It's so beautiful. I have never seen anything like it.'

Conner was about to question how that was possible, then she remembered that Lismar had two suns and it probably never got dark enough to see the stars.

'Would you like me to explain what you're seeing?'

'Yes, please.' Together they settled down and Conner took her through the visible constellations.

❋

Conner left the hydroponics bay a few hours later and made her way to the bridge. The FWN *Ottawa* had left the starbase dock a short while earlier. She'd been worried about how Mesrra would react as they moved forward and the stars seemed to stream by them. Not all humans could tolerate the movement but Mesrra was fascinated by it and asked question after question. She was so different from Brelsa, who had wanted more than Lismar had to offer then had stalled and been afraid to reach out to learn and develop herself.

Conner walked onto the bridge and met the captain's eyes. Amber stood up, handed over authority to her second and left. Conner did not need to be told to follow her. They went into the conference room.

'You were longer with Mesrra than I expected. What do you think of her?' Amber asked as the doors closed behind them.

'Mesrra is driven, curious about everything around her. I found her enthusiasm refreshing. Everything is new and she wants to know and understand her surroundings.'

'Do you think she'll be willing to work with you? See if we can improve on Lismarian and human mental communication?'

'I think she'll be willing to try anything you suggest.'

'Good to know. Thank you, Conner. Is there anything else I should be aware of?'

'Mesrra is very curious,' Conner said. 'It won't be long before she starts asking questions that I can't answer. It might be worth deciding what she's allowed to know.'

'Thank you. I will take that under advisement.'

Amber thought over what Conner had told her. Brelsa had been interested in trying various foods, which the FWN had hoped would lead to other developments but it had not. Brelsa had learned what she needed to know but not much else. Amber knew from her grandfather's memories that Hannoki, and later his son Milkoy, had learned their universal language a lot quicker than David had been able to learn theirs.

As Conner turned to leave, Amber added, 'I want you to teach Mesrra our language. Translators are all very well when we're talking, but it will be useful if we can understand each other on a telepathic level as well.'

'Yes, Captain.'

Chapter 16

AMBER awoke suddenly in a cold sweat. It took a moment for her to orientate herself until she knew she was safe in her bunk. She swung her legs over the side and rubbed her face, needing to wake up properly.

She thought she had finally started to lay the ghosts to rest, but bringing Mesrra on board and being sent out to see if she could pick up the Urigan ships had brought back the nightmares.

※

After returning from Lismar the first time, the FWN Ottawa had been posted to patrol areas of space near the Urigan border. The FWN had tasked them to see if they could detect any movement of Urigan ships. They suspected that they were moving through FWN space but they had no evidence. History had proved that it was possible to hide from ships' sensors and, though the FWN was always working to combat this, it remained an ongoing problem. So Amber had taken on additional telepaths to see if they could sense something technology could not.

For months they saw no evidence of Urigan ships. With no results and no end in sight for the current mission, the crew were getting bored and restless.

Then: 'Captain, a Urigan ship has appeared on our sensors. It's right in front of us and in weapons' range.'

'Sound yellow alert,' Amber ordered. 'Do you know where it came from?'

'No, Captain. One minute there was nothing and then it was there.'

'Are the sensors detecting anything about the ship?'

'No, Captain, other than it is small by FWN standards. I can't give you any indication of mass, weaponry or defensive capability.'

'Open communications.' Once she had received the signal they were open, Amber continued, 'Urigan ship, this is the FWN Ottawa. You have entered FWN space. Please respond.'

They waited in silence for a minute. When there was no response, she continued, 'Urigan ship, if you do not acknowledge immediately we'll take action against you.'

'Captain, they're opening fire.'

'Shields to maximum and return fire,' Amber ordered as the first blast hit their shields, the alert changing automatically to red in response.

The Urigans' weapons were more powerful than expected. Amber tried contacting the FWN for assistance to let them know she had found a Urigan ship – or had it found them? But there was nothing. As her cousin Alex had reported when he got into the fight in Lismar's orbit, communications were down.

Both sides fired again and again. Amber was given updates about shield capacity that slowly decreased; she had no idea if they were making an impact on the Urigan ship. She was just debating retreating when: 'Captain, the Urigan shields have collapsed. I'm now getting a limited reading from them.'

'Are we able to communicate with them?'

'Unknown. The FWN frequency is jammed. I don't know if it would include communication with the Urigan ship,' the bridge ensign said.

'Try. Let them know that we'll be boarding them and get a shuttle party together of security, engineers and a medic.'

'Yes, Captain.'

No one had been on a Urigan ship. Not knowing how damaged it was, Amber did not want to risk towing it to a base in case the Urigans were able to reactivate their weapons. The Ottawa's shields were too low to sustain *another attack. She had to make sure that they had control of the ship before they moved further into FWN space.*

As the shuttles pulled up and prepared to dock, the Urigan ship exploded, killing everyone on board and on the shuttles. Amber had felt the moment of shock and fear as they realised that they were going to die. Then, a second later, there was nothing.

❉

Amber got out of bed and went to the bathroom to splash cold water on her face. She had grown up being told how strong she was mentally but she had felt nothing; neither had any of the other telepaths on the ship. The UTA and FWN couldn't say if this was because of their technology or how the Urigans' minds worked. It was hard to accept that there was now a race that was stronger and more advanced than they were.

They only knew the Urigans' name because the sole survivor told them of the attack on her brother's ship. All she could say was, 'It's the Urigans.'

Trying to block out her grief, Amber was about to return to bed when she remembered her cousin Alex telling her how the Lismarians had reduced a Urigan ship to debris. There had been nothing left of it to examine. A race with no technology had done what none of their ships could.

She mentally reached out and found Mesrra, who was awake in the hydroponics. As far as Amber was aware, Mesrra never left there, never went to the room assigned to her. Drying her face, Amber headed in that direction.

She found Mesrra's mind peaceful. Unless Amber actually sought her, she could not sense her, could not read her thoughts. No wonder her grandfather had been intrigued by the Lismarians.

Thanks to her mother, Amber had an excellent understanding of how their abilities worked and she had started learning Lismarian, along with the other telepaths on the ship. If Mesrra was learning the human language so they could communicate on a mental level, it only seemed fair to do the same. But according to Conner, Mesrra was far ahead of them.

Amber expected to see Mesrra as she had been before, looking up at the stars. It was the only thing that Brelsa had ever done. But Mesrra was helping a crew member tend the plants. Amber had received reports from Ensign Conner that the girl was settling in well.

She was about to leave, not wanting to disturb her, when Mesrra turned. She stood up. 'Captain, can I help you?'

'I came to see how you're doing. It looks like you've settled in well.'

'Yes, your horticulturists have been very welcoming and have been teaching me about the plants here. I'm amazed at what you can grow on the ship – and they tell me that this a small amount compared to what grows on planets.'

'It is. We consider this very limited. I've only been to your planet once and then I only saw the First Protectors' home on the mountain peak. Are the plants on Lismar very different?'

'Some are like your beans, but the rest are different to anything I have seen here,' Mesrra explained. 'I did not know you had been to Lismar.'

'Only the once. I took Brelsa back the first time. I went down to your planet and met your parents. Your mother was pregnant with you at the time. I wasn't there long,' Amber admitted.

'My home is very different from the rest of the planet. Most of it is very dry and water is limited. I have never farmed but my mother's family did. We can only grow about half a dozen plants and then not much of them.'

'You weren't tempted to learn from your mother's family?'

'The traders killed my grandparents before I was born.'

'I'm sorry.'

'It's not your fault and they have been stopped now.'

Amber said nothing. Though the illegal trade humans had been involved with had stopped, would the Lismarians distinguish between them and the Urigans? She doubted it. So the question was whether they could hold back the Urigans.

The trade had stopped for now but if the Urigans won, then they would not be as restrained as the rogue humans had been. Amber looked at the young Lismarian; she could not believe that Mesrra was only a few years old.

'How were your parents able to do it? To destroy a ship in orbit so easily?' Amber asked, getting to the point. 'My cousin Alex told me that when he went to your planet to discover what was happening, to see if you were being attacked again, there was another ship there. They got into a firefight and, just before they lost, your parents destroyed it. I could never understand how they could do that when they have no weapons. Did they have something to help them?' She was thinking of the machine, her grandfather David had made, but Amber had no idea if it was still working after so long, or if Mesrra knew of it.

'We can pull in the energy from the suns and push it out. I do not know how we do it. My parents could destroy the ship because they had what they called "a machine". It increased their abilities.'

'So your parents could defend against another attack, if need be?' Amber said hopefully.

'I think I have said too much. Whether my parents could defend against an attack is irrelevant, isn't it?'

'We have a saying "never say never". Nothing is impossible. We thought the trade had stopped more than seventy years ago, then it started again. Do humans plan to attack your people again? No, because now we know what was happening, our leaders won't let them. But we don't know if there are others out there that will cause you harm.'

'I'm trying to understand. I am amazed at how big space is.'

'Space is very big, too big to ever be explored fully. The best we can hope for is to find out a little more every generation.'

Mesrra looked at her, as if trying to process what she had just been told.

'There are other people out there who are not human. And there are those of our kind who are evil and will act as they see fit. Those were the people who attacked your planet. Your telepathic abilities are different from ours. If you feel a threat, you must tell me. All the ship's telepaths know to let me and the bridge know if they feel danger. Do you understand?' Amber asked.

Conner had told Mesrra that the telepaths on the ship searched space around them. If she felt anything, she must tell someone immediately. Was the captain now asking her to actively search as the crew did?

'Of course,' Mesrra replied.

'That goes for anything else. You are now a member of this crew, so I want to know about any problems or concerns you have while you're on board.'

Chapter 17

CONNER sat with Mesrra in the hydroponics bay for her next language lesson. She had been spending her free time trying to learn Lismarian but was making minimal progress compared to Mesrra. In frustration she said, 'I started learning your language when I first met Brelsa but I can barely grasp the basics. How are you so much better at learning our language after only a few weeks?'

'Brelsa showed me.'

'Taught you,' Conner corrected automatically.

'No, she didn't teach me. She showed me her knowledge.'

'Telepaths can show each other memories? Is that what you mean?'

'We can share everything. It is how we learn, by sharing knowledge. What the parents know, the children know,' Mesrra explained.

'I think we may be talking about the same thing. Can you show me?'

'I do not know. I do not think it has been tried before with a human.'

'Please,' Conner pleaded.

'Fine,' Mesrra agreed. 'Relax your mind and open it up to me.'

Conner did as she was asked but could still feel nothing from Mesrra.

'I will try and show you our language in the way that Brelsa taught me yours. Are you ready?' When Conner nodded, Mesrra started.

Within seconds Conner threw up her mental shields to try and block her out.

Mesrra stopped. 'I'm sorry, are you alright?'

'Yes, it was just...' Conner did not have the words to explain it and her head was pounding, 'I'm sorry Mesrra, I need to go.' She stood up and stumbled out.

As the doors closed behind her, Conner paused and held her head in her shaking hands. After a few moments the pain eased and she went to the bridge. She needed to talk to the captain first, then painkillers and rest would be required. She was amazed at what she had discovered. There was more to the Lismarians than she'd expected.

As Conner walked onto the bridge, the captain turned to look at her and, without asking any questions, indicated the meeting room. As the doors slid closed Amber handed her pain relief. 'Are you alright to talk now, or do you want to wait?'

'I'm fine, thank you. How did you know?' Conner asked as she took the medication.

'I could feel your pain when it started. I was about to call a medic when it eased off. What happened?'

'It was my own fault. I thought Mesrra and I were talking about the same thing in terms of sharing information mentally and I asked her to show me to confirm it. I was proved very wrong.'

'What do you mean?'

'Mesrra kept saying that she had learnt so much of our language because Brelsa had shown her. I thought she was talking about sharing memories. It was more than that. They can – the best I can describe it as is "imprint" their knowledge,' she explained disjointedly, struggling to get her thoughts together.

'What did she imprint?'

'Some of her language. More than it has taken me a month to learn. It is so clear to me now.'

'You should have cleared this with the medical team and me first.'

'I know. I'm sorry. I didn't think she was referring to anything more than a simple mind share.'

'Be that as it may, report now to medical. I want to make sure you're alright, and this experiment of yours has not caused any damage, lasting or otherwise.'

❁

Conner listened to the lecture from the doctor. She was reminded what could happen to telepaths who abused their ability and the damage it could cause to their brains. The doctor ran several tests to make sure there was no damage and to try to understand what had caused the pain. Though it had been extreme at the start, it had quickly faded to a headache that went away with the painkillers. It did not return.

Conner was relieved when the results showed no brain damage. With that concern alleviated, the medical staff became very excited about what this could mean. She was told that a report would have to be made to the UTA, a thought that did not fill her with joy.

In the meantime, she was not to try opening her mind to Mesrra again. The doctor wanted to run further tests at twenty-four-hour intervals to make sure her brain function remained normal. If the results were positive, and unless the UTA or the captain said otherwise, any further experiments of this kind would be done under strict medical supervision. Conner was allowed to leave and, with relief, went back to her bunk to try and get some rest.

❁

When Conner returned to hydroponics, she was prepared to apologise and explain what had happened the previous day and why she had left abruptly. She was surprised by Mesrra getting there before her.

'I'm sorry I hurt you. Are you alright now?'

'Yes. It wasn't your fault. I asked you to try and did not understand fully what you meant. I should have asked more questions first. It's a very impressive way of learning.'

'Only a few of my people can read and write, so this is

what we do. It means that we learn quickly from each other – but we also lose knowledge if people die without sharing. Important information stays with just a few of us. It is not like here, where everything is accessible.'

Conner didn't like to explain how a lot of information was still withheld, such as why they had Mesrra on board their ship.

As if Mesrra had read her mind she asked, 'Who are the Urigans?'

'Where did you hear about them?' Conner tried to hide her surprise. Had Mesrra read her mind yesterday?

'From a few people.'

'People have been coming into the hydroponics talking about the Urigans?' Conner asked doubtfully.

'No. I know you consider it rude, but when people's minds are focused on me I cannot block them out. I heard people thinking about me and the Urigans and there was a lot of fear in their thoughts. I do not think the fear was aimed at me but it is connected to me in some way.'

'The fear isn't aimed at you,' Conner reassured her.

'Then why? Who are these people?'

'Ahhh...' Conner mumbled, trying to think of what to say.

After a few minutes of uncomfortable silence, Mesrra demanded, 'Why won't you tell me?'

'Because I ordered her not to,' another voice said. They turned around and saw the captain standing behind them. Neither of them had heard her enter. 'You may go, Conner,' Amber said.

Conner stood up and nodded goodbye to both the captain and Mesrra.

'Why is she not allowed to tell me about these Urigans?' Mesrra asked.

'Because I was ordered not to tell you. It's an order I disagree with, so I told Conner to let me know if you asked her about them.'

'That was the delay in her answering my question.'

'Yes. As soon as you asked about the Urigans, Conner

called me as ordered. The FWN was worried about you finding out about them.'

'Why?'

'They were worried about how you'd react to what they have done.'

'But I live with you now. Should I not know what everyone else knows?'

'Yes, you should,' Amber agreed. 'The Urigans are an aggressive race that is threatening us. They have attacked and destroyed a number of FWN ships near our space borders. They have attacked this ship before, which is why the crew are especially fearful.'

'I chose to travel with you and accept the risks. Ships have been destroyed in the orbit of my planet. My mother showed me what happened when the FWN first came to Lismar. My family know and accept the dangers and, under the terms of my leaving Lismar, I cannot disclose what I learn. Why are you worried about telling me about the Urigans?' Mesrra asked again, not convinced by Amber's reason.

'How much do you know about the attacks on your planet?' Amber suddenly changed the conversation.

'Just what I was told by my parents,' Mesrra admitted. 'Many years ago we were attacked and skinned. Hannoki saved us. Then the attackers come back and my parents fought them off with the help of your people. I do not know what this has to do with the Urigans.'

'During Hannoki's time, humans found out about the benefits from your people's wings. The skins were an additional benefit. How your people and that knowledge were originally discovered has never been found out. When the attacks started again two years ago, we struggled to find out what had happened before because so much information had been either hidden or lost. After your parents destroyed that ship in orbit, the debris was taken away and examined. The ship was not one of ours.'

'You had our skins but you think the Urigans were

attacking us? You have worked with the Urigans?'

'The people working with the Urigans were not good people. We believe the skins were a payment to get the Urigan ships through the outskirts of our space. Though the skins were being supplied to us, turned into clothing and our people were buying them, they didn't know they were from your people or from any living thing. Humans have not killed anything for their clothing for several hundred years. The knowledge of where the skins came from shocked our people.'

'But now it has stopped and the Urigans can't get to Lismar without going through your space.'

'Two years ago they could hide who they were. FWN ships sensed them but thought the ships were merchant vessels. Now some of their smaller ships are undetectable until they are very close. Since we stopped the Urigans attacking your planet, they've started to attack us instead. Though we had the skins, we never found any trace of your wings. At the time of Hannoki, we were using your wings as well and they were of much more value to us. We believe that this is what they still want.'

'How would they have found out about us?'

'When the original trade was discovered, the men behind it fled from FWN controlled space before they could be arrested. They were never found. We believe that they left our space and somehow encountered the Urigans. Maybe they shared their knowledge to save their own lives. Though why they waited so long, I don't know.'

'We thought that it was over, that my people were safe. Are they safe?' Mesrra asked bluntly.

'I don't know.' Amber repeated. 'We know that the Urigans are determined to get to your home. We have a sensor net around Lismar so we'll know when a ship approaches. And we're actively defending our space against any Urigan ships that try and enter.'

'You fear them. Do you think you cannot win against them?'

'They have better technology than us, and human telepaths can't sense them to locate them in space. I'm hoping that your telepathic talents may find something that mine can't. Our sensors have detected them at short range, but we've had limited success at longer range.'

'My parents think that our people are safe when they aren't. You have to let them know.'

'Why? If the Urigans get past us and attack, what will the Lismarians do about it? We don't want them to live in fear.'

'Why don't you replace the machine they had? Then they would have a chance of defending themselves. From what you have said, they destroyed a Urigan ship with it before.'

If they could work out how to replicate the machine – and Amber was sure that Cal could – would the FWN allow the Lismarians to use it if the humans failed to defend them against the Urigans? It was something she needed to investigate and possibly refer back to her father. She did not trust anyone else at the moment.

'I will ask if it's possible,' she promised. 'Is it only the First Protectors who can use the machine, or can other Protectors?'

'The machine couldn't be moved from the mountain range. In theory, any mated couple could use it but off the mountain peak we can't absorb as much energy. I suppose others could use it, but it would be less effective. Why do you ask?'

'I'm just curious,' Amber said, not willing to say anything until she knew if her superiors would entertain the idea of giving advanced technology to the Lismarians.

Chapter 18

MESRRA was angry and worried after learning about the Urigans. The FWN had withdrawn from Lismar without letting her parents know about the threat that still existed. She understood why Amber had not said anything before because she had been ordered not to; her own parents were good at giving orders and expecting them to be obeyed.

When Conner returned to the hydroponics bay, she was wary that she had not been honest with Mesrra. So it was with some tension that they sat down together later that day to continue learning in the non-mental way. Though Conner's test results had seemed to be alright, the captain had agreed with the doctor to await the response from the UTA before trying again.

Conner struggled to concentrate. At first she thought it was because they were going through the information Mesrra had placed in her mind and she was struggling to access it, but she started to realise something was bothering the Lismarian.

'We can do this later if you want,' Mesrra offered.

'No, now is good. I'm just trying to work through everything.'

'I didn't realise I had hurt you. I didn't mean to.'

'I know you didn't. As I said before, the fault was mine. Do you normally share so much in one go?'

'It depends on how strong the person is as to how much is shared. Brelsa and I do a lot more.'

'So you started out slow,' Conner said.

'I could go slower,' Mesrra offered.

They fell back quickly into their routine of Conner teaching Mesrra what she needed to know. The captain had given a brief as to how much Mesrra could be told about the Urigans, especially about scanning for them. Unfortunately, Conner couldn't say what the Urigans' minds felt like, as no one had been able to detect them mentally. Mesrra could not help; from the memories her parents had shared with her, she knew they had not tried to explore the Urigans' minds. They just knew they were a threat and acted on it.

The UTA had responded: although they were very keen to explore this sharing of information, they wanted to do it at one of their facilities, Conner was not to try again at the moment. She had to admit she was relieved; it had taken her mind a few days to process everything and she would not like to do it regularly.

Suddenly Mesrra sucked in her breath. She had felt something in space that she had not expected.

'Mesrra, are you alright?' Conner asked.

'I am fine,' she replied. As she looked into space, the viewing panels started to darken and there it was – a sun. She could only see its outline now the panels had turned opaque. Mesrra guessed they were cutting off a lot of the sun's radiation but they weren't blocking everything. For the first time since she had left Lismar, she could revel in the power of the sun.

She did not know enough to realise that ships rarely got this close to a sun's orbit and that Conner, on seeing the ship come so close, had thrown out her mind out to see if she could sense anything. But there was nothing outside, only the fear building inside the ship. Mesrra was so engrossed in what she was feeling that she did not pick up on the crew's fear as it was not aimed at her.

Suddenly Mesrra felt it: the hostility from space. She turned to tell Conner just as the red alert sounded.

'What...?' Mesrra started to ask.

'I need to go to the bridge. Stay here until you're told otherwise,' Conner ordered as she ran out of the hydroponics bay.

Mesrra sat there alone. The others who had been present had also left. Had Conner known what was happening before she left? Mesrra knew from her training that the red alert meant there was a severe threat to the ship. With the hostile feelings she was picking up, mixed with the fear she'd seen on Conner's face, she could guess what it was. They had encountered a Urigan ship.

She started to feel for minds around her. Reading a human mind was hard because they had natural barriers, but the overriding emotion coming from everyone was fear. They were under attack and no one was certain of the outcome.

The ship shook suddenly and Mesrra guessed that the fight had started. She felt she should be doing something, anything, to help. She was the daughter of the First Protectors whose sole purpose was to protect their people – but here she was, defenceless. She had not even sensed the threat in time. What use was she?

The ship shook again and again, groaning and hissing as if struggling with the movement the blasts created.

If they survived this, would they let her go home where she might be of use to her people, Mesrra wondered. She felt the crew's growing panic and knew that the fight was not going in their favour. She got to her feet and started pacing in frustration; she wanted to fight, she wanted to do something, but there was nothing she could think of. If the Urigans boarded them, possibly she could do something with the little she'd absorbed of the sun's power, but realistically Mesrra knew that the ship would be destroyed and she and the crew would be killed.

She stopped pacing as a message warned of an imminent hull breach in her location and called for immediate evacuation to different areas of the ship. As the announcement was made, she felt a massive surge of panic as she realised how many people were at risk.

'Mesrra?' Conner shouted.

Mesrra looked up and saw her friend running into the hydroponics bay. 'Here,' she replied.

'We need to leave now. Follow me and stay close.'

As they left hydroponics, the flashing colour and noise of the red alert was much louder. People were running past them, their fear and panic clear. Some staggered and fell. Mesrra stumbled; she was not used to feeling anything much from the humans, but now she was being bombarded with emotions and she found it very disorienting, Conner was having to drag her along. She had no idea where they were going.

'Hold on, we're nearly there,' Conner shouted.

Mesrra looked up and saw an airlock, a door that would be sealed at the last moment to isolate the damaged area of the ship. The ship shook again, making running difficult as the floor buckled slightly. A groaning and screeching noise could be heard and Mesrra wanted to cover her ears, but Conner wouldn't let her. The ship shook again and they staggered and lost their balance, as did several others. A crack appeared on the wall.

'Oh God!' Conner cursed. 'Quickly, Mesrra, we only have seconds.'

'We won't all make it,' Mesrra replied, looking at the others behind them. As she spoke, the hull started to disintegrate. Mesrra put her hand out and, with the energy she had absorbed from the sun they were orbiting, created a barrier over the breach.

'Run,' she ordered Conner.

'Mesrra!' Conner said, shocked as she realised what the Lismarian was trying to do and that while she was holding the breach she could not escape.

'Run!' Mesrra repeated. 'I can't hold this for long! You need to run.'

Conner could see the strain on Mesrra's face and did as she was told, screaming 'RUN' to those behind her. She got through the airlock and stood aside to let the others through. The rest of the crew ran in panic, aware that they had been given a last-minute reprieve. They were determined not to waste it.

'Mesrra,' Conner shouted, intending to tell her that they were safe and had made it through the airlock. Mesrra needed to drop her barrier and get to safety. But she was shocked as she looked at the Lismarian; her skin had turned grey and her body looked shrivelled.

Conner knew that Mesrra would not be joining them.

Mesrra dropped the shield and collapsed onto the floor. The second she did so, the hull breached and the airlock door slammed shut.

Conner screamed her friend's name, not quite believing that the hull had collapsed and her friend had been sucked into space.

'Section 8 from the bridge, report.'

The tannoy brought Conner back to her responsibilities and she hit the communicator. 'We lost Mesrra,' she informed them.

❀

'We lost Mesrra.' The words seemed to echo around the bridge. Amber should have felt sad at the loss, should have had questions about how that had happened when Conner and the others had made it through. Instead she just felt relief that Mesrra was going to be spared what was to come.

'Damage report?' Amber asked.

'Complete hull breach in section 8. The airlocks have engaged but shields are at a minimum. I doubt they'll take another direct hit. Do you want to sound the evacuation?'

'No, we're still too near the sun for the emergency pods to break the gravity field,' Amber pointed out.

When the Urigan ships had appeared there was not one this time but three huge ships, all in firing range. Amber knew that they did not stand a chance against them. She had moved the ship into the sun's orbit, hoping its radiation would mask their presence, but that meant the escape pods could no longer be used.

When the gamble had not paid off, and the Urigans had followed them and opened fire, the *Ottawa* had tried to move away from the sun but the Urigans had kept them pinned.

Another blast hit their shields, then another.

'The shields have collapsed, Captain! We can get them back if we divert power from the weapons but they won't hold for long. Do you want me to divert the power?'

'No, put everything into the weapons. We won't be taken by the Urigans.'

'Yes, Captain.'

Then Amber suddenly changed her order. 'Everything into the shields now,' she yelled. Her crew did as they were told without question.

'Yes, Captain,' the reply came. 'The Urigans are about to fire again.'

'Captain,' another voice interjected. 'We have a massive energy build-up out aft. The energy signature is Lismarian. How is that possible?'

'If we survive this, we can ask questions later,' Amber said.

The bridge crew sat there waiting, not knowing what was about to unfold.

Chapter 19

MESRRA was relieved when she saw all the crew escape through the airlock. Conner said something, but she was so exhausted she could not make it out. Her energy was totally depleted, and both she and the shield collapsed.

She felt herself being sucked out into space and was helpless to stop it. She closed her eyes and waited for death. She had been told about the effects of space on a human body and knew it would be painful and slow as her blood froze and there would be no air to breathe.

None of it came.

Not a single breath did she take, or need to take.

She felt powerful, so very powerful.

Mesrra opened her eyes and looked at the sun that seemed so close beneath her. The markings on her skin lit up in a way she had never seen before and were pulsing with the power they were absorbing.

She looked around her and saw the three Urigan ships that were powering up to destroy her friends. She could not allow that. Any questions or doubts she had would have to wait.

Out of habit, Mesrra went to pull in power from the sun. It almost overwhelmed her; there was so much power, she was not sure she could contain it. She was not sure what the result of her releasing it on the Urigan ship would be and if the blast would affect the *Ottawa* or not.

Mesrra called out to Conner and to Amber, *'Get your shields up,'* in an attempt to warn them before releasing her power on the enemy. She didn't know if they had heard her but she could not wait. The *Ottawa* would not last much longer and she expected that Amber would want to go down fighting.

The energy flew past the *Ottawa* and hit one of the Urigan ships. The first blast sent Mesrra hurtling towards the sun. In a panic she tried to stop herself with her wings, but they moved uselessly in the vacuum of space, so instead she released a small amount of energy towards the sun, hoping it would act as a counter to her momentum. She began to slow down.

Mesrra turned back and saw that the Urigan ship she had hit was losing orbit and falling towards the sun, a third of it missing. The other two still remained a threat to the *Ottawa*.

Smiling to herself, Mesrra let off a second then a third blast towards the Urigans, each time also releasing a counterblast to stop herself falling into the sun. Some of the blasts went wide; Mesrra's aim was poor in the vastness of space.

The Urigans now turned their attention to her but she was far too small and the few shots they released fell wide of the mark. Mesrra kept firing at them; she made her shots as wide as she could so as not to endanger the *Ottawa*, meaning her aim did not have to be great. It did not take her long to reduce the Urigans to debris. She felt satisfaction as the last ship crumbled.

⚛

'Something just took out the Urigans. The energy signature was Lismarian but how is that possible?' a bewildered officer asked. 'Mesrra is dead.'

'Are the sensors detecting any other ships?' Amber questioned.

'No, Captain.'

'I want a damage report as soon as possible.' Amber closed her eyes and concentrated. The report would take time to collate; in the meantime, she searched for Mesrra's mind and found it.

'*Mesrra*,' she called.

'*I'm here. Are you all alright?*'

Amber felt overriding relief when Mesrra replied, her mental voice strong. '*We are still alive, thanks to you. I heard you and felt what you intended just in time. Are you able to come back on board?*'

'*I don't think that would be a good idea. My markings are lit up in a way I have never heard about and I am fast recouping my energy. I am pulling in more power than I ever thought possible. I do not know if I would be a danger to you.*'

'*You can't stay out there. You won't be able to get back into FWN space. We can open the shuttle bay doors for you then the bay can be sealed if we think radiation is coming off you,*' Amber suggested.

'Captain,' an ensign said, before Mesrra had a chance to reply.

'Go ahead.' Amber kept the link with Mesrra's mind so she could also hear.

'Reports are still coming in. Apart from Mesrra, we didn't lose anyone – but there are multiple injuries. Sickbay will let us know shortly, but early indications are that none are life-threatening.'

'That's good to know. And the ship's systems?'

'A lot of our central systems are damaged. We have no engines and very little life support remaining.'

'How long do we have left?'

'It's hard to say – three to five days if everything is diverted to maintain it.'

Amber cursed the news. 'Can we send out a mayday?' she asked, hoping communications would be back up now that the Urigans were gone.

'No, communications are still down.'

If they could not move from the sun, their only chance of survival was for someone to come quickly and find them.

'Damn. Tell all the telepaths on the ship to meet me in the conference room in fifteen minutes,' Amber ordered.

'Mesrra, did you hear?'

'Yes. I will see if I am close enough to reach Brelsa and ask her to get help.'

'Thank you.'

✵

'Thank you all for coming,' Amber said as she joined those assembled in the conference room. She looked at the pale faces. 'I'm going to get straight to the point about why I pulled you away from your posts. The Urigans took out our communications, and we have no engines. We're too near the sun for the crew to evacuate using the emergency pods. We need to get a request for help to the FWN as a matter of urgency. There is no ship in my mental range so I'm proposing that we pool our abilities. Hopefully, we'll have the combined strength to get out a distress message. I know most, if not all, of you won't have done this since you finished training with the UTA. But we must try.'

Murmurs went round the room. The fact they had won at the last minute was still sinking in. Those who worked in engineering already had an idea of how bad the ship was without being told.

'I'm certainly going to try,' Conner said and looked around the room. Everyone was nodding in agreement.

'Thank you,' Amber said.

'I barely made it out of the UTA. How do we do this?' Ensign Jones asked.

'The strongest takes the strength from the rest – which I believe is you, Captain,' Conner said, smiling.

Amber raised an eyebrow at her over her use of 'believe'.

'I don't think I was told the protocol with so many. Do we start with the weakest and build up, or all merge together?' another asked.

Ensign Mann spoke up. 'There isn't a protocol for us. Telepaths in the FWN have done this before but with three or four minds, not the seventeen we have here. The UTA doesn't teach this at the level most of us leave at – this is advanced training. In theory, we need to get as much strength with as few minds as possible. I'm a level 6, Conner is a level 5. We need to start with the strongest first, and work our way down the scale.' He had not joined the *Ottawa*'s crew straight out of training. Unlike most telepaths, he'd worked in the UTA for many years before deciding to leave. He was not as strong as Amber but she had to admit he was much better trained, which was why she had fought to have him on board.

'What are the risks for us doing this if it's an advanced technique?' she asked.

'What does it matter? We're all going to die if we don't try,' someone else said.

'If we do it right, we might get a message out. Get it wrong and we won't,' Amber retorted.

'Most of the risk will sit with you, Captain. If you can't control the merger, you'll have a stroke. The rest of us will be released and should be fine,' Ensign Mann explained.

'I'm prepared to do this. Now is your last chance to leave if you're not, ' Amber said.

Everyone remained seated as she looked around the room.

'Alright, organise yourselves in order of your UTA levels so it's clear in what order you'll need to join the merger. Let us begin,' she said.

Several people changed places around the table. Amber was not surprised when not a single person asked for another at their level. Telepaths always seemed to know the abilities of others around them.

Once everyone had settled down, Amber put her hands out to those on either side of her. Closing her eyes, she opened up her mind and took in the minds of the next strongest. Once she had adjusted to them, she moved further down the chain of linked hands. As she continued it got harder, but she was determined to take as much as possible; the more minds she had, the stronger she would become. She slowly gained all the minds, her head swimming with the different consciousnesses. She knew she could not hold it for long, so she shouted out as loud as she could, 'Mayday, mayday from FWN *Ottawa*.'

Then she collapsed, releasing the merge. Someone jumped up and called for a medic as their captain started to have a fit and blood dripped from her nose.

※

Amber came to consciousness lying in the medical bay. Her mind felt foggy. She remembered the attack and that Mesrra was outside the ship; she tried to call her but her head exploded in pain.

'Captain, please don't try and use your telepathy,' said Conner, who was sitting by the bed.

'How long have I been unconscious? Is Mesrra alright?'

'You've been unconscious for two hours. Mesrra is fine but worried about you. She contacted me when she felt the merger collapse.'

'Do you know if anyone heard the call?'

'I'm sorry, I don't. You collapsed after getting the message out so if there was an acknowledgement, we wouldn't have heard it. Mesrra couldn't contact Brelsa either,' Conner said.

'Is there an update on the engines or life support?'

'Unfixable with what we have on board, but...' Conner said, stalling. 'Mesrra does have a plan of sorts.' She stopped talking as Doctor Lee showed up to run what limited tests were available with the lack of power.

'So what's the damage?' Amber asked.

'Your blood pressure is high,' the doctor said. 'But if you're asking if you have brain damage, I can't answer that until we're fully operational again. My advice is to be careful. Don't use your abilities again until I can confirm everything is alright.'

'I promise,' Amber said. As she swung her legs off the bed and stood up, her head exploded with pain again.

'Here.' the doctor injected something into her neck. 'It's

a powerful painkiller, that's all. Though my advice would normally be to rest, I know I'd be wasting my breath in these circumstances.'

Amber smiled at him gratefully before turning and leaving. Conner followed her to the bridge. Once there, after getting an update from the crew which added nothing to what Conner had already said, Amber led them into the meeting room. 'What's this plan that Mesrra has?' she asked as she eased herself into a chair.

'She wants to take in as much energy as she can from the sun and push us towards FWN space. She hopes to get us near enough for them to hear a mental call. The plan is full of problems, but we won't know if it's possible until we try.'

'That's an understatement. Does Mesrra know how long she'll last in space once we've moved further from the sun? What is she going to push against? She could easily punch another hole in our hull. And how fast and far will she have to push us? How will she know where to push us? She could move us further away. And another mental call? The next strongest telepath is considerably weaker than me. Those are the first few problems that come to mind.'

'We can route some of the remaining power and have the shields up where she'll be pushing us. The rest is unknown – but what other options are there?'

'You mean other than sitting here and hoping someone heard our message?' Amber asked.

'If our message was heard and ships are coming, they'll find us anyway – though if we stay here, it will possibly be too late. Mesrra is giving off a very distinctive energy signature that can be tracked.'

'If they are coming, we have no idea how many or from where. Ra is the nearest base and that may not be close enough.'

'Are you saying you'll go with the plan?' Conner asked.

'I don't think we have a choice. I'd prefer to fight for my survival than wait for death. But if she can barely move us, we stop. And if the hull can't take the force, we stop and re-assess.'

'Understood, Captain. I'll let Mesrra know and warn the crew.'

Chapter 20

MESRRA was floating in space, waiting to hear what was happening on the ship. She had been trying to call Brelsa but, since she'd not tried that since they had parted at Ra, she had no idea of the range they could achieve or if the extra power from the sun would increase her mental abilities. There was only silence.

She hadn't needed Conner to tell her that the attempts at telepathic communication had failed and the captain was sick; she had heard the mayday and the sudden silence from the captain. Conner had promised to keep her updated.

As Mesrra waited for news, she started to experiment in her new environment. Her wings were useless in space, not just because of the speed she was moving at as a result of the energy blast. She flapped them and nothing happened; they moved effortlessly and they had also taken on a luminescence she had never seen before. If she got out of this, she would ask why that was. The humans would be happy at being asked to look into it; they were desperate to know about her kind, but so far both she and Brelsa had refused to tell them much. For now, Mesrra folded the wings behind her back.

So how best to move around? Her blasts had pushed her far in the opposite direction. If she used a small amount of energy, how would she move? Her first attempt sent her hurtling away from the ship – so not that much, she thought. Slowly she reduced it so that she could alter her direction, and she worked out the position for her arms that gave her the best control. She didn't know how long she spent experimenting, but she loved the feeling as she started to move around the ship.

'Mesrra are you alright?' Conner called her.

'I'm fine. I am learning how to fly in space.'

'Be careful. There's no atmosphere in space, so there's no weight and nothing to stop your movements. It wouldn't take much for you to fall into the sun.'

'What do you mean by no weight? Is not the ship still very heavy?'

'It still has a great mass, but with no gravity there is no weight. I have to go. Just be careful, please,' Conner begged.

No weight. Mesrra looked at the ship. Would she be able to push it? Could she get it close enough to call for help? Out here a little energy seemed to go a long way.

'Conner!' Mesrra called.

'Yes, Mesrra.'

'If there is no weight, could I push the ship?'

'It would still take a lot of power to get it out of the sun's orbit. And even if we tried it, how would we stop you destroying us as you did with the Urigans?'

'Well, I wouldn't aim the blasts at the ship but behind me as I push it. I know you still have shields up to protect you.'

There was silence from Conner. Mesrra knew she had heard her, but someone was talking to her on the ship.

'I'm sorry, Mesrra, the captain is waking up. I'll think about what you've suggested and let you know.'

❖

'What do you make of Mesrra's suggestion?' Amber asked her senior crew.

'She's been practising propelling herself in space while she's waiting to find out what's happening here. She's getting very good at it – we've been tracking her power output to see how fast and far she goes. We believe she could move us but I don't know how it will affect her. I doubt she knows. It was such a massive amount of power that destroyed the Urigans that she should have ended up in the sun, but she must have corrected herself in time, which gave her this idea. If she can start propelling us in the right direction, it'll be worth it. Anything is better than sitting here waiting for death,' Conner said.

'We would need to divert extra power to the rear shields or she'll punch through the hull,' Lieutenant Commander Mike Hayworth, the head engineer, explained.

'Power supply is low. How could we facilitate it?' the captain asked.

'Mesrra will be doing the work. We shut down everything that is non-essential – sensors, navigation, lighting, even reduce the heating,' Hayworth explained. 'It won't be pleasant for us but it will only be for a short time. I should add that if we stay here, we would need to redirect a lot more power. The sun's gravity is pulling us in and we can't pull away. It won't be long until what protection there is on the ship will fail and the heat will kill us.'

'What's the risk to Mesrra?' Amber asked.

'Significant, the further she gets from the sun,' the Chief Medical Officer Doctor Lee said. 'But I can only guess. We know nothing about Lismarian biology.'

'We don't need to travel far. If Mesrra can get us out of the orbit, the crew can evacuate in the pods and wait to be rescued,' Doctor Lee pointed out. 'That way she wouldn't get too far from the sun.'

'We lost several pods when Section 8 was breached. There are not enough for the whole crew,' Amber said.

'She was prepared to die for us once and this is her idea. I think she's more aware of the risks she faces than we are,' Conner said.

'Be that as it may, it doesn't feel right to sacrifice her. But our options are limited so I'm of the opinion we let her try. Conner, you will monitor her mentally. If you think she's getting too weak, let me know. Hayworth, get me as much power as you can. If it's not enough to protect us then we'll stop. If all Mesrra can do is get us far enough out of orbit for some of the crew to escape, then so be it.

Any objections?' Amber was met with silence. 'Then let the crew know. Divert the power to create the rear shield. Conner, tell Mesrra to get ready and let her know that, whatever happens, we're grateful to her.'

⚛

Mesrra saw the slight distortion of the shield and hoped on Hannoki's name that her idea would not be a total disaster. She had absorbed as much of the sun's power as possible; she felt overloaded and desperate to expel it. She put her hands out and touched the shield, a solid invisible force.

Mesrra was surprised when Conner had come back to her an hour earlier to say that they were going to try her plan. She'd had to promise to let Conner know if the effort of pushing the ship out of orbit drained her of too much power. She had to make sure she had a lot conserved for when the ship left orbit.

'*Are you ready?*' Mesrra asked.

'*Yes, go for it.*'

Mesrra placed her right arm against the shield and her left arm behind her. She began slowly releasing her stored energy; she remembered what had happened to the Urigan ships and did not want to destroy the *Ottawa*. Conner gave her updates on how the shields were holding up.

At first nothing happened. Mesrra pulled more and more power from the sun to replace what she was expending. Then suddenly the ship was moving, slowly at first, but as she put more power behind her they picked up speed.

'*We are pulling out of orbit. You don't need to expend so much power now. Take in as much energy as you can — you're going to need it,*' Conner told her.

Chapter 21

'BRELSA, help us.' For a moment, Brelsa thought she'd imagined the quietly-spoken words because she was so desperate to hear from Mesrra. It came again: *'Brelsa, help us.'* Then there was nothing.

Brelsa tried to reach her mind out to ask Mesrra questions, to find out what had happened, but she did not have her friend's strength and couldn't contact her. She opened communication with the bridge. 'I have just heard Mesrra calling for help,' she informed them.

'Any information on the location of the ship and the status of the crew?'

'No, she just said "help us" and was gone. I tried to talk to her, but there was nothing. I think we must be heading in the right direction, though. If she has been calling out at random, this is the first time I have heard her.'

'Thank you, Brelsa. Let us know if you have any further contact.'

'Yes, Bridge.'

Brelsa had boarded the FWN *Cardiff* a few days earlier after several telepaths on the starbase had reported hearing a mayday call. One of the telepaths thought it was Captain Yoland, but the message had an echo effect indicating a mental merge. The base had sent out a call to the FWN *Ottawa* and received no reply. All attempts to the track the ship failed.

There had been a brief discussion about what to do. As the mayday calls implied that the *Ottawa* needed urgent assistance, the ships docked at Starbase Ra were deployed to the FWN *Ottawa*'s last known location near the Urigan border. With the Urigans habit of jamming transmissions and locators, if the *Ottawa* had encountered them the crew could not have called for help. But nobody knew if they had fought the Urigans and been destroyed, or had won and needed urgent help.

Brelsa was asked to join all the telepaths who had heard the call. If the human telepaths could not locate the *Ottawa* then maybe Brelsa could. And she had.

She was on one of three ships from the starbase; other ships were travelling in from other parts of space. She didn't know what the crews expected; they were hoping for the best and preparing for the worst.

Brelsa settled herself in hydroponics and concentrated on Mesrra, calling her name over and over. Time seemed to stand still until she suddenly got an answer,

'Brelsa, thank Hannoki.' Mesrra's voice was weak and Brelsa did not know how long the connection would last.

'What happened?'

'We were attacked by the Urigans. The **Ottawa's** *life support is about to fail. I didn't think we were close to the starbase.'*

'You are still a considerable way out. The humans heard the captain's mayday. I'm on one of the ships coming to you.'

'Thank Hannoki. I'm so tired.' The communication ended but Brelsa knew where they were now. She ran for the communicator.

'Bridge, we are close to them, they are here,' and she gave directions. 'Mesrra said the *Ottawa*'s life support was about to fail. I don't think there is much time.'

'Thank you, Brelsa.'

'Captain, Mesrra was very weak. I could not keep in contact with her.'

'I understand. We'll be with the *Ottawa* as quickly as possible.'

If Mesrra was struggling that much, what state was the rest of the crew in? Would they find and evacuate the *Ottawa* in time?

Captain Justin Smith spoke. 'Brelsa, please come to the bridge. I want to know immediately if you hear or sense anything.'

Brelsa looked around the hydroponics bay; the thought of leaving it was daunting but she knew she could manage away from the lamps for a while.

'Of course.' Taking a deep breath, she left.

❁

Brelsa was standing on the bridge when the FWN *Ottawa* finally appeared on scans. It did not respond to the requests for communication. Brelsa had felt Mesrra twice; she was weaker each time and begging for help. Now there was nothing.

'Captain, I don't understand it,' one of the bridge crew said. 'It took us so long to detect the *Ottawa* because it has no power. It's not moving under the thrust of its engines.'

'Could they have started the trip back before the engines failed?'

'Unlikely. They look like they were damaged when the hull was breached.'

'Maybe they got lucky and they had some thrust left. Let's concentrate on communicating with them so we can get shuttles on board.'

'Yes, Captain.'

'Anything from Mesrra?' the captain asked.

'Nothing, but I will keep trying,' Brelsa said. *'Mesrra, can you hear me.'* Silence. *'MESRRA,'* she shouted as loud as she could.

'Brelsa.' The reply was weak.

'We are here but we can't raise the ship. Are the humans still alive?'

'Yes, life support has failed but they are still alive. They have no communications. You will need to communicate with the ship's telepaths.'

'Why can't we communicate through you?'

'I am not on the ship.'

'I don't understand. If you are not on the ship, where are you?' The question was met with silence. 'Mesrra can you hear me? Where are you?' Brelsa repeated.

'Space.' Then nothing.

'Mesrra! Mesrra!' she shouted but got nothing back.

'Brelsa, what's happening?' the captain asked.

'The crew are alive but communications are down. Mesrra said to get your telepaths to communicate with them.'

'You and Mesrra can't facilitate communications?'

'She is very weak and she said she was not on the ship but in space. How is that possible? I cannot get her back.'

'Keep trying. Ensign Kadle, can you reach the telepaths on the *FWN Ottawa*? Let them know we're sending our shuttles to start evacuations. Let the other ships know as well.'

'Yes, sir,' Kadle said. *'Any telepath on the* **FWN Ottawa** *receiving from the* **FWN Cardiff.***'*

'This is Ensign Conner. It's good to hear you, **Cardiff***. Our life support has failed. We only have the oxygen left in the system, and we're about to start evacuating as many as we can in the remaining pods. Are you near enough to get any of us off?'*

'We're within shuttle range. We'll send them over to begin evacuation.'

'Thank you – but you won't get us all off.'

'I'm on one of three ships. Others will be here soon.'

'How did you find us?'

'We heard Captain Yoland's mayday so we came looking for you.'

'Thank God.'

'Do you know what happened to Mesrra? She told Brelsa she's in space?'

'She got blown out into space when the hull breached. We were in a sun's orbit at the time, and it had an unforeseen effect on her. She took on a massive amount of energy and destroyed the Urigan ships, then started to push us towards

home. We haven't been able to communicate with her for a while – we thought she had died.'

'Brelsa said she is very weak but she was alive a few minutes ago. I'll let the captain and Brelsa know what's happening. Get the crew ready – I'll let you know when the shuttles are en route.'

'They are all alive but everything on the ship has failed so they need to be evacuated quickly,' Ensign Kadle reported.

'Get the pilots to the shuttles and let the other ships know. We need to get them off the ship as quickly as possible,' Captain Smith said.

'Did they say what has happened to Mesrra?' Brelsa questioned.

Ensign Kadle recounted the conversation.

'What do they mean she is in space?' both Brelsa and the captain asked at the same time. When Mesrra had told her that, Brelsa thought she was delusional.

'That's what I was told. They haven't been in contact with her for some time. They thought she was dead.'

Brelsa could not grasp what she was being told. 'Can we find her? Bring her back on board? She is so weak.'

'We can't detect people unless they're in a spacesuit. I'm sorry, we have nothing to lock onto to find her,' Captain Smith explained.

'But she has spoken to me,' Brelsa said, then she shouted, *'MESRRA! MESRRA!'* She prayed to Hannoki that Mesrra would hear her.

'Please, Brelsa, I want to sleep.'

'No, Mesrra, don't sleep. Listen to me, please. If you have any energy left at all, release it now.'

'Can it wait until I have slept?'

'Listen to what you are saying! We barely sleep. We need to find you to save you. To do that, you need to release some energy. Please, Mesrra, let us save you.'

A small spark of energy appeared on the sensors.

'Captain, I think I have her. She's just off our aft and near enough for us to retrieve her without deploying a shuttle.'

'Then let's bring her in. Brelsa, can you go to the airlock to help Mesrra when she's brought on board.'

Brelsa went, not knowing what to expect. All ships had the same layout so she knew where to go. She had only been in this area before when she'd arrived on a ship and wanted to know where everything was. She had never seen it in operation before.

She watched as several of the crew put on suits and helmets, similar to the ones she'd seen them wear on Lismar, except they had a large rectangular box attached to the back that had tubes coming down through the arms and ending in some sort of hand control.

Once ready, they opened an airlock that revealed a small area. They went inside and the door sealed again, trapping them. A green light appeared; suddenly a door in the hull opened and they were pulled into space.

Brelsa watched as the humans oriented themselves and moved away from the ship. She couldn't understand how Mesrra was alive out there. She had lived among humans for long enough to know that they could not survive in space without one of those suits. Were the Lismarians so different?

Time seemed to drag as she waited for them to return. Lots of scenarios went through her head. Could they not find Mesrra? Was she dead and her body not retrievable? Then Brelsa saw them coming back to the hatch, Mesrra with them – but she was limp. Brelsa reached out to her mind but there was no response. Were they too late?

The crew entered the airlock and the latch sealed behind them. After a moment the second door released and Mesrra was carried onto the ship and laid on the floor next to Brelsa.

Brelsa was horrified. How could Mesrra be alive? Her body was very swollen, her skin stretched and distorted. She could not detect anything from her; Mesrra was not breathing – but then she wouldn't have breathed in space.

'Is she dead?' the person who had brought her in asked.

'I do not know. Can you help me get her to hydroponics?' Brelsa asked. 'If she is still alive, the solar lamps will help.'

'Do you want us to get a medic to join you there?'

'No, they do not know anything about how we work. They cannot help.'

Mesrra was carried to hydroponics and placed under the lamps.

'Is there anything we can do?' the crew member asked.

Brelsa knew they felt as helpless as she did. 'Not at the moment. Thank you for going out and getting her back.'

Chapter 22

BRELSA sat with Mesrra under the lamps. She was aware that the ship's shuttles were making repeated trips to the *Ottawa* and back, bringing as many crew members as they could each trip. She longed to know what had happened. She had asked the captain but there was nothing further that he could – or was willing to – disclose. At this time, it was a rescue operation.

Mesrra took a shallow breath; if Brelsa had not been watching her so closely, she would have missed it. Mesrra was still alive but Brelsa did not know how long she could hold on. The lamps were not enough to repair any damage to their bodies, let alone such serious injury. The only thing that could help her would be the sun. They needed to go to a planet.

She did not know what the captain would say to that, bearing in mind the number of extra people they'd taken on board, some of them injured. She would not know unless she asked.

The captain received the request. Brelsa was desperate for her friend and, if the accounts were to be believed, the crew of the *Ottawa* were only alive because of Mesrra. He contacted the sickbay. 'Do we have anyone that is critical?'

'No, sir, all injuries are minor.'

'Thank you.' The captain closed the communication then turned to the bridge crew. 'How far away is the nearest planet with a sun? Preferably a planet *near* a sun?'

'There's a sun two days away. There are only two planets in its solar system and both are inhabitable. We could land on the second planet for a short time, but environmental suits would be a must at all times.'

'Plot a course and open communications with the FWN so I can update them,' the captain ordered, before telling Brelsa what was happening. He'd been told of Mesrra's condition when she was brought on board; he did not know how she was still alive.

❀

Ensign Kadle came to carry Mesrra to a shuttle. They had arrived at a planet that had been described as a dust ball, with a surface temperature that made Lismar seem cold. The crew would have to stay in the shuttle in environmental suits all of the time.

Brelsa had been asked if the planet was suitable for them. She honestly didn't know so she said yes. If Mesrra could survive in space in the orbit of a sun, then she would survive here. It was this planet or the solar lamps, and Brelsa knew they were not working. With an occasional breath the only indication that Mesrra was still alive, Brelsa was willing to try anything.

The shuttle would take them down to the planet and stay with them, while the *Cardiff* took the crew of the *Ottawa* back to an FWN base. Brelsa prayed to Hannoki during the trip down; there were no lamps to help Mesrra on the shuttle and Brelsa hoped the limited time without them would not be disastrous.

The shuttle landed. Once Ensigns Kadle and Jones had put on their suits, the hatch was opened. Brelsa walked out and staggered under the energy of the sun.

'Are you alright?' Kadle asked.

'Yes. I didn't realise one sun could be more powerful than the two on Lismar.'

'We're much closer to this sun than Lismar is to either if its two suns. Are you going to be all right here?'

'Oh yes, this is the perfect place for us. If Mesrra has a chance of survival, it is here.'

Mesrra was carried out and placed on the ground near the shuttle. The crew flinched at the heat. How could

Brelsa walk on such a hot surface with bare feet?

'Thank you. Please go back into the shuttle. I will call you if anything changes.' Brelsa sat next to her friend and waited.

⚛

Brelsa had no idea how much time had passed. The heat remained constant and there was no sign of a sunset. One of the pilots came out occasionally to check on them but there was nothing Brelsa could tell them. There was no change in Mesrra, and Brelsa worried that her body might be too severely damaged. She cursed herself for refusing to let the doctors to run their tests. If she had, maybe they would be able to help now.

The only hope Brelsa had was the rare, shallow breath that told her Mesrra was still alive. Eventually she stood up to stretch and look around her. She dared not walk away when she had no idea of the hazards of the planet.

'Brelsa.' She thought she was dreaming when she heard her name being whispered. 'Brelsa, where am I?'

Brelsa turned and looked at Mesrra. The girl was still lying on the ground but her eyes were open and her breathing was normal. Her body was still swollen and her skin painfully distorted.

'I am here,' Brelsa said, grabbing Mesrra's hand. 'I do not know exactly where we are but the FWN *Cardiff* brought us here because of the sun. You need to concentrate on healing yourself.'

'What happened to my crew?'

'They are safe. We got to them in time.'

'Thank Hannoki,' Mesrra said, before closing her eyes.

Chapter 23

AMBER walked off the shuttle onto the FWN *Berlin*. The *Ottawa* was to be towed back for repairs. A doctor was in the docking bay, waiting to receive her and convince her to report to the medical bay.

'I will later. Right now, I need to make sure my crew are all accounted for.'

'You're the last to disembark, Captain. I understand that you could be suffering from brain damage. We need to run tests...'

'The cause of the brain damage was a few days ago. Other than a persistent headache, I'm fine and I've not attempted to use my telepathy since. Once I know the status of my crew, and once I've given my report, I'll come and see you,' she said firmly.

Without waiting for a response, Amber made her way to the bridge with Conner next to her. They walked in silence, With communication on the *Ottawa* limited through the telepaths, Amber was desperate to know what had happened over the last few hours and the status of her crew. Hearing that they were all safe was not good enough.

On the bridge, she smiled as she saw the *Berlin*'s captain, a friend from her training days. 'Captain Wallace.'

'Captain Yoland, it's good to see you. Care to join me in the conference room?'

'Thank you. This is Conner. I'd like her to join us. She has been coordinating all the telepathic communication.'

'If you're happy, then so am I.'

'Always the charmer,' Amber said, smiling again. John Wallace had always been a flirt.

They went into the adjoining room. As the door slid shut Amber asked, 'Is it true that all the crew are accounted for and they're all safe and well?'

'Your human crew, yes. The *Cardiff* found you just as your life support failed. The oxygen left in the system was just enough. They started evacuations immediately, as did the other ships, and you were removed in time. All reported injuries were minor. Our sensors showed that you suffered a hull breach but no one was lost, which is unusual.'

'That's because of Mesrra, a Lismarian, who held the breach long enough for the crew to get to safety. She was sucked into space. We know she survived because of the sun, but we had no communication with her for hours before the *Cardiff* found us. Do you know what's happened to her?'

'Brelsa made contact with Mesrra and she helped us locate you. My understanding is that Mesrra is very weak. She's being taken by the *Cardiff* to a planet in close orbit with a sun. No one knows if she'll be alright but we all hope so.'

'I feared she'd been left behind, that once we started moving at speed away from the sun she wouldn't be able to keep up.'

'She was floating in space. How long was she out there?'

'A surprisingly long time. I'm sorry, I've not yet made my report to the Admiralty. To say more now would not be appropriate,' Amber reminded him.

'Of course. I'll let you know any updates regarding Mesrra. Please make sure you go to the medical bay and get checked out.'

❈

Amber saw several of her crew in the medical bay. She was moving towards them to see how they were when she was approached by a doctor and taken away for tests. When she tried to protest, he insisted. 'None of your crew are seriously hurt. I'm currently more worried about you than them.'

She allowed herself to be led to a bed, where she lay down and let the doctors do their tests. Amber hated tests.

The medical results didn't take long to come through; they showed a small brain haemorrhage but nothing that couldn't be fixed. Amber was told that the bleeding would have worsened if she'd continued to use her telepathic abilities. That could have caused permanent brain damage but fortunately the bleed was small and should resolve itself. She would need to be monitored regularly.

Amber was commended on not continuing to use her telepathic ability and delegating to Conner. She bit her tongue at the comments, but she remained silent as the doctors ordered her not to use her ability until given the medical all clear.

'Am I fit to work?' she asked.

'With restrictions, yes.'

'I know – don't try to read someone's mind. That's easy – it's not something I'm in the habit of doing.'

The doctor grudgingly gave Amber the all clear and she immediately got off the bed. 'We would recommend that you rest,' he said.

'Don't worry, I'm more than happy to leave everything to Captain Wallace and his crew.'

Amber didn't leave the medical bay immediately; she spent time talking to her crew, then demanded information about those on other ships. It was not until she had spoken to them that she accepted they were alright.

Finding out about Mesrra's wellbeing was more difficult. Information about her was vague. Amber was reassured that as soon as an update came in she would be informed immediately, and she felt slightly better knowing that Brelsa was with Mesrra.

Once Amber was satisfied that she could do no more, she went to the room she'd been assigned desperate for some sleep.

❈

When they docked at the starbase, Amber connected with all her crew. Most of them had been medically cleared; those who hadn't would be soon. They asked her to join them for a drink. They were the only crew to have survived twice against the Urigans and they were keen to celebrate.

Declining, Amber returned to her room. There was a message from her father telling her not to disclose to anyone what had happened until they had spoken. That wasn't a problem, though she had to let him know that most of her crew and the captains of the *Cardiff* and *Berlin* were aware of some of the facts.

Her father said he would talk to the captains and asked her to advise her crew to remain quiet. She gritted her teeth; her crew knew better than to gossip about a mission.

Chapter 24

BRELSA pressed the communicator so she could talk to the two pilots who were waiting on the shuttle. She was met with silence when she told them that Mesrra had regained consciousness. She asked if they had heard her. They confirmed that they had and closed the communication.

Since landing, she'd had only occasional contact because the planet was far too hot for them. They had struggled even when wearing the environmental suits, so they had stayed in the shuttle.

Brelsa heard a noise and turned. The shuttle hatch open and both humans walked out in their suits. She stood up, surprised that they had come out to her. She waited as they approached. Mesrra pulled herself upright to watch them.

'I'm sorry – when you said she was better, we thought... We can't believe it. How?' Ensign Kadle stammered. When they'd taken the call, they had wondered if there had been a translation failure and Brelsa was telling them that Mesrra was dead. But here she was, sitting looking at them.

'The sun heals us,' Brelsa said, not understanding their confusion.

'Alright.' The ensigns still didn't not understand. 'It's good to see you looking so much better,' Louie Kadle said to Mesrra.

'Thank you.' Her skin was still swollen and her markings protruding, but not to the same extent as when they had carried her off the shuttle. They had not expected her to live for much longer; to see her recover so quickly amazed them.

'We'll let the FWN know the good news. Captain Yoland is keen for an update. How much longer do you need to stay here?'

'Two days at least; four would be better,' Brelsa said. 'It is hard to gauge for certain, as this has never happened to any of us before.'

'You think it might take two to four days?'

'Yes, that would be ideal.'

'I think it will take two days for me to get back to normal and another two for me to build up energy reserves and rest,' Mesrra explained, mistakenly thinking that staying so long would inconvenience the humans.

'Would there be any adverse effects if you had to stay longer?' Kadle asked.

'For us? No, we would be very happy to stay for a while longer. The conditions here are perfect for us,' Brelsa reassured the ensigns.

'We'll contact the FWN. I don't know how long it will be until a ship can come, but it's likely to be more than two days. When we know that one has been assigned, we'll let you know. Is there anything either of you need in the meantime?' The Lismarians had barely consumed any food or water since they had arrived.

'Thank you, we are fine. We still have water left,' Brelsa replied, pointing to the small container that had been left when they first arrived.

The ensigns nodded, reminded Brelsa and Mesrra to let them know when they needed anything and headed back to the shuttle. As the shuttle hatch closed, they released their helmets and looked at each other.

'I honestly thought the captain was mad dropping us off here. I thought there was no hope for her when I carried her off,' Kadle said.

'I know. It was hard to believe that she was still alive. I can't believe the change in just a few days,' Ensign Jones replied.

'I'll let the FWN know. But I've no idea how long it will be until we're collected.'

'Bet you it'll be longer than two days.'

'No way am I taking that bet.'

❁

'Two days? That's all Brelsa thinks it will take before Mesrra is ready to travel?' Justin Smith, the captain of the *Cardiff,* repeated when he got the shuttle crew's report. He had honestly believed the next communication would be that Mesrra had died.

'That's what she said, sir. Brelsa seemed to consider it a long time and was apologetic.'

'OK. I'm not sure what to say to that. We've just docked at the starbase. I'll let you know as soon as we have permission to leave. Brelsa will definitely have her two days. I will let you know how much longer as soon as I know!'

❁

Captain Smith finished his report and was about to submit it when he was ordered to report immediately for a meeting with Admiral Yoland in the starbase conference room. He assumed that the other captains who had assisted the *Ottawa* would be present and that the admiral wanted a personal briefing, so he was surprised when he saw only Amber sitting at the table.

'Amber! It's good to see you looking so well. How are you doing?'

'Very well, thanks to your timely arrival,' Amber smiled.

'Always a pleasure. Do you know if we're expecting anyone else?'

'No, I believe it's just the admiral and us.' As if on cue, Admiral Yoland called through to the conference room and appeared on the screen in front of them.

'Thank you both for coming at such short notice. Do you know how Mesrra is?'

'Still weak, but she'll make a full recovery,' Justin said.

'That's a relief. I'm sure you both have a lot you need to be doing right now but what I have to say can't wait. I want a formal report to show that Mesrra was pulled into space by a hull breach and died. She was found by the *Cardiff* floating in space near the *Ottawa,* having been caught up in the ship's shields.'

'Sir, how do I account for how we escaped the Urigans?' Amber asked.

'How do any of us know where the fight happened and when your engines failed? The *Ottawa*'s systems are badly damaged, the only formal account about what happened will be yours. I know I'm asking a lot, and I'll be asking the same from you as well, Captain Smith. When you return to pick up your crew and the Lismarians, I want you to report that Mesrra is dead.'

Justin tensed at the idea of making a false report to the FWN.

'I don't ask this lightly, but for now it can't be known what Mesrra was able to do,' Admiral Yoland continued. 'As you both know, the Urigans are pushing against us to get back to Lismar. At the moment they seem to be taking it slowly, testing us. If they find out what the Lismarians can do in space, I suspect that would change dramatically.'

'With respect, sir, if we submitted our reports correctly how would the Urigans find out about them?'

'I'm assuming the same way they found out about the Lismarians to begin with.' The message was clear: Admiral Yoland suspected there was a traitor in the FWN.

'I understand,' Justin said. Amber nodded her understanding as well. 'I received a message from the pilots. Mesrra will recover and be fit to be collected in two days. If we're pretending she's dead, what do we do with her?'

'Who else have you told?'

'No one. I was going to request permission to collect her once I'd submitted my report,' Justin said.

'I didn't expect her to recover so quickly,' Yoland said. 'I thought we'd have more time. Could they stay longer on the planet?'

'Mesrra and Brelsa could but my crew can't. The shuttle isn't equipped for a prolonged stay.'

'Could you keep her secure on your ship once you've collected her?'

'I don't know enough about the Lismarians to answer that,' Justin admitted.

'They're not very sociable. Mesrra's better than Brelsa, but she still didn't leave the hydroponics bay. She might not like it, but if you let her know the reasons I believe she'll keep to herself,' Amber said.

'I need Mesrra and her people on our side. Tell her whatever you need to so she understands that she can't pass information to anyone else. I want her willing to intervene again, if possible.'

'She is not a weapon to...' Amber started to say.

'Did I say she was?' her father snapped. 'I commend your defence of her, Amber, but think about it. If I wanted to use her indiscriminately, I wouldn't be going to these lengths to hide her. There may come a time when she's very necessary but I'd certainly never pressure her to repeat what she did.'

'I'm sorry.'

'The Lismarians' welfare is a priority for me, but I can't discount their potential. It needs to be explored quietly and tactfully. We must be led by them, by Mesrra.'

Amber knew what her father was saying: keep Mesrra's survival a secret and lie on official reports. She also knew what he was suggesting: convince Mesrra to fight with us. She even agreed – so why did it leave such a bitter taste in her mouth?

'What of my crew? I have two pilots on the planet with Mesrra. They know she's alive,' Justin said.

'Do you trust them to obey orders and keep the information to themselves?'

'Yes, sir. They're both very experienced. They were chosen for their discretion and their ability to deal with the unexpected because we didn't know what risks they'd face when they took Mesrra and Brelsa to an uncharted planet.'

'Take a skeleton crew when you return to collect them,' Admiral Yoland ordered. 'Tell the rest they can have leave. Amber, would you be in a position to leave on the *Cardiff*?'

'My absence will be noted. I still have a lot to do to arrange welfare for my crew. If we can wait a few days, then I'll be able to leave.'

'How about Conner? Unless I'm mistaken, she has a good rapport with the Lismarians.'

'She should be able to leave as soon as the *Cardiff* is ready.'

'Then talk to her and get her to report directly to Justin. Justin, I take it that's acceptable to you?'

'Yes, sir. I'll wait for Conner.'

⚛

Admiral Yoland felt reassured after talking to his daughter that she was alright. He had been told that she had suffered a minor brain haemorrhage caused by the multiple mind merge she had coordinated to get out the mayday.

The Admiralty was always informed when there was a concern over a captain being unable to fulfil their role. In this case, Amber had been unconscious for some time and the medical team was unable to discern the level of brain trauma. He'd been worried and frustrated, then relieved slightly by the reports from the *Berlin* and the starbase doctors. Telepathic injury was not their speciality, however.

He'd asked Amber how she was before the meeting and she had brushed him off, saying she was fine. But his daughter had not reassured him on a personal level. Taking a deep breath, he made a call.

The communicator buzzed and buzzed. Gareth was about to terminate it before it had the chance to go to message when it was answered.

'Gareth, this is unexpected. What can I help you with now?' Mary, his ex-wife, said.

'I'm worried about Amber.'

Mary had seen who was calling and been tempted to ignore it before realising that her ex-husband wouldn't contact her unless there was a problem. When he told her he was worried about Amber, her heart skipped a beat. 'What's happened? Is she alright?'

'She has a slight brain haemorrhage resulting from a massive over-extension of her telepathic abilities. She lost consciousness for a while and it was undiagnosed for a few days. She says she's fine. The FWN medics say she'll be okay if she's careful but FWN medics are not UTA medics.'

'She's sensible and she knows how to protect her mind. But if you can, send her medical file through to us and I'll make sure it's checked by the best.'

'Thank you, Mary.'

'She is my daughter too,' she reminded him.

❊

Conner was surprised and slightly annoyed when Captain Yoland asked to talk to her urgently. She had just been for a final medical check and had gone back to the room she had been allocated. She planned to sleep then try to source a change of clothes, as all her belongings were still on the *Ottawa*. With so many at the starbase and nobody able to live on the *Ottawa,* accommodation was tight. Conner considered herself lucky – some of the crew had had to slot into available sleeping bunks on the docked ships.

Conner tidied up as best she could and went to the captain's room. As she entered, she was surprised to see Chief Engineer Hayworth was also present.

'Thank you for coming so quickly, Conner.' Amber said. 'I have some good news for you. As you're aware, the crew of the *Cardiff* were able to get Mesrra and Brelsa onto a shuttle and to a planet.'

Conner nodded; she'd been relieved at first – until she realised how weak Mesrra was and that no one expected her to survive.

Amber continued. 'Mesrra will make a full recovery. They have asked for her to be collected from the planet.'

'I don't believe it,' Conner said, struggling to keep her tears at bay, remembering how for hours before they were rescued she had called Mesrra's name over and over again. 'Mesrra is going to live?'

'Yes. I want you to go on the *Cardiff* to collect her.'

'Yes, of course. Thank you, Captain.'

'Don't thank me just yet. I need you to convince Mesrra and Brelsa that they must keep quiet. As far as the FWN are aware, Mesrra was blown out of the airlock and died. She didn't push the ship to safety. Her body was retrieved after it was caught in the *Ottawa*'s shields. As was her wish and Brelsa's, her body was taken to a planet to be disposed of according to their customs. Captain Smith will talk to the skeleton crew who accompany you. The fewer people who know, the better.'

'Yes, Captain. Mesrra and Brelsa will ask why. What can I tell them?'

'That we want to keep Mesrra's capabilities a secret for now. We don't want the information leaked to the Urigans. I appreciate they won't like it, but it's for the best and only for a while.'

'Am I to bring them back here?'

'Yes. We're looking at where they can stay while we work all this out. I'll keep you and Captain Smith updated.'

Conner looked at the chief; she did not need to be a telepath to know that was why they were working together.

⚛

As soon as she left the room, Conner contacted Captain Smith. She had just enough time to pick up a change of clothes and some toiletries before boarding the *Cardiff*.

She was relieved to be shown a room to herself. There were so few people on board that there was plenty of space. She hated to think what the crew were experiencing in the tight living quarters on the starbase, but she couldn't wait to get a good sleep.

Conner had been told she wouldn't be needed until shortly before they arrived at the planet when the captain would want a briefing. Collapsing into bed and closing her eyes, she slept deeply for the first time since the *Ottawa* had been attacked.

❀

Conner stood on the bridge as they approached the planet's orbit. She had just come out of a briefing with Captain Smith. He wanted to know what she'd been told by her own captain, how she thought the Lismarians would take the news, and how the crew would manage them once they were on board. 'Do you think they'll cause us any problems?'

'No, sir. Both of them have always confined themselves to the hydroponics bay. If they can stay there for the trip back, everything will be fine.'

'That's not quite what I meant. One of them just blew up Urigan ships and pushed the *Ottawa* out of the orbit of a sun. I was told they wouldn't be a risk, but I understand you know them best.'

'They are powerful, but they only attack when they're under threat of death. Don't threaten to kill them and you'll be fine.'

Captain Smith looked at her with narrowed eyes, trying to make up his mind if she was being sarcastic or just pointing out a fact. She was saved by the communication that they had arrived at the planet. Smith dismissed her, contacted his pilots and told them to report to him as soon as they docked.

❀

'Mesrra, Mesrra, can you hear me?' Conner called.

Mesrra's happy shout sounded in her head. *'Conner, I am so glad to hear from you.'*

'The same here. I thought we'd lost you.'

'You nearly did. Brelsa was horrified when she saw me. I do not think I will ever hear the end of it.'

Conner laughed. 'I'm sure she'll give me a telling off as well for not taking better care of you. We're just entering shuttle range for you to board the Cardiff. I have what you might consider a strange request.' Conner recounted what had been explained to her about Mesrra pretending to be dead.

There was a temporary break in the mental connection when Conner assumed Mesrra was talking to Brelsa about the request. Finally Mesrra replied. 'If you think it is best. We will be led by you. But how can I leave here and return to a starbase and no one know about it?'

'There are hardly any crew on board. They'll be busy when you dock, so you should be able to get to hydroponics without being seen. I'll stay with you there and let the captain know if anyone approaches. He'll make sure they are called elsewhere. It shouldn't be a problem – the crew will have too much to do. Once we dock, they'll leave but you'll have to stay on board for a short while. Amber will talk to you there.'

Conner hoped the captain had a plan; they couldn't keep the crew off the ship for long.

'I understand. But what about the pilots here with us?'

'Their captain will deal with them.'

Conner stood anxiously waiting for the shuttle to dock. Though they had spoken and Mesrra sounded fine, she wouldn't believe it until she saw her. The only person waiting with her was the captain.

The shuttle landed and the hatch opened. A few moments later, Mesrra walked off. Conner went towards her excitedly, then paused for a second as she noticed differences. Mesrra looked well but her markings had widened and were more pronounced, and her skin had become even more translucent.

'How are you?' Conner asked.

'Very well. These,' she said, looking at the changed markings, 'seem to have happened because of being so close to the sun. On the planet they let me pull in more energy than I ever did before.'

'Will the markings revert?'

'I do not know. This has never happened before.'

'Do they hurt?'

'No.' Mesrra ran her hand down them. 'Brelsa thinks if they had not opened like this, I would not have survived.'

'I still cannot believe what you did,' Brelsa said, as she came up behind them. 'It is good to see you again, Conner.'

'Brelsa, thank you for all your help,' Conner said. 'Shall we make our way to hydroponics?'

'Yes. You can tell us everything that has happened. How is Amber? Has she recovered? Was anyone else hurt? We were told no one had died.'

They left the captain to talk to his pilots, not noticing how they all looked at them.

'I'm guessing girls and gossip are not just a human thing,' Captain Smith said.

Chapter 25

AMBER went to the *Cardiff* when she was told that the ship had returned. Conner had contacted her and let her know that Mesrra and Brelsa had agreed to the request, but they were worried about what would happen to them.

Amber could understand that – and the fact that she had nowhere yet to place them was not going to reassure them. Her father had said he would find somewhere they could safely stay; she just needed to give him some time.

Amber walked into the hydroponics bay. She was expecting the 'what happens now?' questions but the request that Mesrra made, even before Amber could ask how she was doing, stopped her in her tracks.

'You want to try and do what?' Amber asked, not sure for a moment that she had heard correctly.

'I want to go back into space again. I want to see what more I can do,' Mesrra repeated.

'I thought that was what you said. Mesrra, you nearly died only a few days ago. We have no way of knowing if you've fully recovered yet.'

'Look at me. I am fine.'

'You look different.' Amber pointed to the changes in her markings. 'How do we know what that will mean for you?'

'We don't. And please do not ask us to see your doctors,' Mesrra said. At the start of her recovery both she and Brelsa had thought it was a good idea but, as the sun healed Mesrra, they changed their minds.

'We think all the markings do is allow better absorption. Being near the sun opened up the markings to allow Mesrra to take in more energy,' Brelsa explained.

'Does that mean you're losing power quickly as well?' Amber asked, worried.

'No, we do not lose energy through markings. I am noticing a slight difference with the lamps. It is easier being on the ship than it was before.'

'How do you know that you can survive in space again? You may just have got lucky.'

'I will not know for sure until I try again, but if I am near enough to a sun I should be fine,' Mesrra said confidently.

'It may not be that easy,' Amber argued. 'If you're too near the sun, it could easily kill you. Too far and you won't take in the energy that you need.'

'But you know where the ship was when the hull breached.'

'Yes, but... '

'Then take us back there,' Brelsa said, as if it were that simple.

'We can't. The risk of the Urigans returning to discover what happened to their ships is too high.'

'Do you know how far I was from the sun?' Mesrra said.

Amber had that information; it would not be difficult to work out the equivalent distance with a different sun. 'I'll think about it and talk to my father,' she said. 'We will need his support if you want to try this.'

'Thank you, Amber,' Mesrra said.

'Now might be a good time to mention that I want to try as well,' Brelsa said. 'I know I am not as strong as Mesrra, but if I can fight in space as well it could give us a purpose for being here.'

'We would never ask either of you to risk your lives for us.'

'Why not? We have a common enemy. Why can't we learn if there are new ways to defend ourselves – very effectively, from what Mesrra has shown me.'

'That's true. I'll see what I can do but I can't make any promises. In the meantime, I came here to see how you're doing, Mesrra, and if there's anything you need. I hope to have you placed elsewhere soon,' Amber said, effectively changing the subject.

❋

Returning to her room, Amber put in a request for communication with her father. What he was going to think of the Lismarian request she was not sure, bearing in mind their heated exchange about using them as weapons a few days ago.

'I have to confess I'm glad they're asking to see what they are capable off, but I share your fears for their safety,' Gareth Yoland said. 'Could we get a doctor to monitor them, get some idea of their energy absorption rate compared to their life signs?'

'I doubt they would agree. Mesrra has already said she doesn't want to see a doctor, and Brelsa has always refused a medical examination. Added to which, how do we know what is normal for them? No doctor would know if there was a problem or not.'

'Understood. We could try allowing them out for a short period, one at a time, with some crew in a shuttle and space suits next to them to bring them in quickly if needed. Maybe choose a sun with a planet in close orbit.'

'It would certainly be the safest way to try it,' Amber agreed. 'But the *Ottawa* will be in for repairs for some time yet, and too many questions will be asked if we use the *Cardiff.*'

'Don't worry about it. I'll arrange a ship for you. I'll let you know when it's ready to go.'

❋

'Cal, how are you doing?' Admiral Yoland asked when he contacted him minutes after talking to Amber.

'With the increased Urigan attacks, very busy,' came the curt reply.

'How is Amber, Admiral?' Jane cut in 'I heard she was attacked by them again.'

'She suffered a minor brain injury but otherwise she is fine, thank you.'

'I'm sorry. It must be hard, not to be there with her.' Jane knew the Yolands well enough to read between the lines.

'Which brings me back to why I'm contacting you both. I need you to meet with Amber at Starbase Ra, where you will be very much needed.'

'Admiral, I'm sorry but I can't break off what I'm working on at the moment,' Cal protested.

'Please, Cal, I can't be there. I know how close you are to Amber. She really needs your support and I need you to find a way to be there for her and Brelsa.'

'Of course we'll go, Admiral,' Jane promised as Cal glared his frustration at her.

⚛

'What are you doing?' Cal asked a few hours later when he returned home. Jane had left their laboratory as soon as the call was over, ignoring him when he demanded to know why she had promised Admiral Yoland they would leave to be with Amber. He was sure that Amber didn't need their emotional support.

'Packing,' Jane said, as if that should mean something to him.

'You can't be serious about going to Starbase Ra? You know how much work I have here!'

'You heard the admiral. Amber needs us.'

'I can't leave now. And I didn't realise you were such good friends that you'd go running to her based on that call.'

A shoe flew at him and he caught it just in time. 'Amber and I have kept in touch. If I hadn't asked after her, you'd not have known who she was. That doesn't mean she isn't my friend.'

'I know who she is,' he defended himself. 'And I appreciate she's been through a lot, but why are we running off to hold her hand? I'm sure she has friends and family who can do that.'

'I love you, but sometimes you are so stupid. Gareth doesn't need us to hold her hand. Something happened where he thinks your skills will be beneficial and for some reason he can't say why. I guess it's something to do with the Lismarians since he mentioned Brelsa, so if I were you I'd pack bits to make some of those machines.'

Cal opened his mouth but Jane continued before he could speak. 'Don't tell me you haven't worked out how David built it or that you haven't improved on the design.'

'Stop!' Cal ordered. Jane stopped what she was doing and turned to look at him. 'This is ridiculous. How can you have read all of that into the conversation?'

'Think. The admiral called to ask how you are doing on a link he knows we share. He made out we were a lot closer to Amber than we are, that she needs us. She needs our skills – not us as people. Whatever's happened, the admiral is keeping it close to his chest and doesn't want to ask openly.'

'We don't know what happened with Amber.'

'After the admiral called, I got a copy of her formal report. Trust me, she needs help.'

'How? Was it sent to you?'

'No, and don't ask,' Jane replied. 'According to her report, Amber got into a firefight with a Urigan ship. They were losing and withdrawing but with a lucky shot they broke orbit and destroyed the ship. Their hull breached, they lost another Lismarian – Mesrra – and they lost their engines. The momentum carried them near enough to be rescued. I'm sure something else happened and I bet it has to do with Mesrra.'

'How many Lismarians are now in the FWN?'

'No idea – but definitely two.'

'Fine. It will take me a few days to get the parts together and leave my work in a place that I'm happy for others to continue. So please stop this frantic packing. And if you can find out anything else that would help us, that would be great.'

Chapter 26

'ARE you sure you both want to try this? It could have just been luck before,' Amber asked the Lismarians again as they stood by an airlock.

They had left the starbase a few days earlier on a small science ship that the admiral had appropriated for them. Only a handful of people were needed to crew it as they would only be gone for a few days. Amber had taken Conner and the two pilots, Kadle and Jones from the *Cardiff,* together with the telepaths who had helped to get the message out. If the FWN thought their training about being discreet was good, it was nothing compared to the education the UTA gave its people.

'It is not luck, it is how we are,' Mesrra said with total conviction

'Alright, but you need to know that this is the only sun that we have time to travel to and we can't get as close to it as we did before. This ship doesn't have the shielding the *Ottawa* had, and there are some other variables in play. This is a different classification of sun to the one you were exposed to.'

'Was that the same as our suns?' Mesrra asked.

'No, both of your suns were of different classifications,' Amber informed them.

'Then it is unlikely that your classifications will matter.'

'You're right, it is unlikely. We tried to take into account the differences between this sun and the other one, and where you were when you entered space. If the maths is correct, the radiation should be the same. But we had to guess what you needed, so our calculations may be wrong.'

'Is that why you want us to go one at a time?' Mesrra asked.

'I just want you to know the risks before you go back into space.'

'We will be fine.' Mesrra said with so much certainty that Amber wanted to scream at her about how dangerous it was. How could she not understand?

'I should go first,' Brelsa offered. 'What would I tell your parents if this goes badly?'

'No. I have a better chance of surviving. Look on the bright side – if we cannot make this work and I die today, considering how the battle is going with the Urigans you will not get the chance to go home and face my parents.'

'Mesrra!' Amber and Brelsa said.

'Am I wrong?'

'No,' Amber conceded.

'If this fails, the FWN has not lost anything. We have not contributed much to this fight. If we can make this work, we can be useful.'

'This conversation is pointless,' Amber said. 'If we're going to do this, I will let you out of the airlock. I'll have a shuttle on standby with the crew in spacesuits ready to pull you on board if necessary. We can't go out with you this close to the sun, even in suits. All communication will have to be via telepathy to Conner, who will be on the shuttle. I won't let Brelsa follow you until I know you are alright.'

'I understand. I want you to trust that I know what I'm doing. I do not plan to die today.'

'I believe you know what you're capable of, otherwise I'd not allow this.'

'You tell yourself that but it is clear you are unhappy. Now it is time for me to try again. I want you to experience what I do when I go out of that airlock. I want you to understand why I am so sure that this is a good idea.'

Amber had not told them about the brain haemorrhage after the mind merge; she had told them she was fine because she didn't want Mesrra to worry. She'd had another scan before leaving; her injury was healing well, with no signs of any further bleeding, but she had been told to avoid telepathic contact until she was cleared by the medical staff.

Was it worth the risk to connect with Mesrra to understand why she was confident that this would work? Conner had found it painful when she had opened her mind up to Mesrra for a mind share, but no damage had resulted. Everything Amber knew told her that it was a dangerous, terrifying endeavour, yet both Mesrra and Brelsa couldn't wait to throw themselves into space. What was she missing?

'Alright,' Amber agreed.

'Then I am ready.' Mesrra went into the airlock.

Amber locked it and released the seal. She and Brelsa watched as Mesrra was pulled into space.

Amber felt Mesrra's sudden euphoria and for a moment it took her breath away. Then there was something else, something building in her that she did not understand. She started pulling at her skin as if it felt too tight.

Brelsa grabbed her wrist. 'Mesrra is fine, she is just pulling in power.' The pressure eased slightly.

'I can't take this. I feel her joy, but I want to rip my skin off,' Amber said.

'Then cut the connection. She will keep pulling in energy – she is revelling in where she is. She may realise your distress too late.'

Amber took Brelsa's advice and withdrew, clutching her head as it started to pound. She had learnt enough. She had extended her telepathy too far, too quickly.

People were asking her if she was alright as she slumped into the chair. 'I'm fine,' Amber managed to say, and pull herself upright. 'Brelsa, how is Mesrra doing?'

'She is fine. I can feel her exhilaration. She told me about it, but I am only now starting to understand it.'

'Captain, there has been a massive energy surge just off our bow,' the bridge reported. 'It looks like Mesrra is experimenting with propelling herself in space using small energy blasts.'

Amber smiled as she pictured it in her mind. She tried to reach out again to Mesrra but the pain that ripped through her skull stopped her.

'She is all right,' Brelsa reassured her. 'But are you? Mesrra said she lost contact with your mind.'

'I'll be fine,' Amber reassured Brelsa.

'Which means you are not fine now,' Brelsa pointed out. Amber cursed at how well she had picked up their language. 'Mesrra is doing really well. Trust your telepaths. They will all tell you the same thing.'

'Will Mesrra agree to share with so many?'

'Of course, especially if it will get her what she wants.'

'Conner, can you link in with Mesrra and see if she's happy to share with the other telepaths? I want to be totally sure before I let Brelsa into space.'

It did not take long for all the telepaths to report to the bridge that Mesrra was fine and was having fun practising moving around. That was something the ship's sensors confirmed through the energy spikes.

Amber asked Conner to make contact for her.

'Mesrra, how are you doing out there?' Conner asked.

'Brilliantly. Brelsa can come out whenever she is ready,' came the reply.

Conner reported back. When Brelsa was asked if she was ready to go, she replied confidently, 'Yes.' Amber took a deep breath then agreed to Brelsa going into space. She knew that Mesrra would help Brelsa and the shuttle was there is if she could not.

Brelsa went into the airlock.

'Brelsa is about to join you,' Conner let Mesrra know. After getting an acknowledgement, she notified the crew on the shuttle and bridge before sending Brelsa into space.

Conner's mind was still open with her connection to Mesrra when Brelsa went into space; as a result, she felt a moment of panic when the Lismarian couldn't breathe.

'*Relax, Brelsa,*' Mesrra said. '*Take in the sun's energy. Accept it. Enjoy it.*'

And Brelsa did. Conner felt the moment the panic turned to joy and amazement. Relieved, she updated the captain and the shuttle was told to stand down. Conner remained in close mental contact with Brelsa and Mesrra as they worked out how to manoeuvre. She had to try really hard to keep her laughter from them.

'*You are failing,*' Mesrra told her.

'*Sorry,*' Conner said.

❈

'Captain Yoland, we may have a problem,' the bridge called a short while later.

'In what way? Are the Lismarians in danger?'

'I don't believe so, Captain. But if our sensors are correct, they won't be able to come back on board because they are emitting too much radiation.'

'How much radiation?'

'The amount keeps increasing, but the levels are already dangerously high for us. They can't safely come on board.'

'Damn it. Why wasn't this detected earlier?' Amber cursed as she remembered what Mesrra had said the first time she was in space.

'Mesrra wasn't pulling in that much energy and was expelling what she'd absorbed, but Brelsa pulled more in a lot quicker. The levels went from acceptable to dangerous in a moment.'

'I should have considered that.'

'There were no readings from last time, Captain. The *Ottawa*'s sensors were damaged. Accurate readings weren't possible, so we had no idea what radiation Mesrra was giving off last time.'

'I know, but this is not exactly the same. Is it both of them or just Brelsa?'

'I don't know, Captain. They're too close together for me to tell.'

'If we got a shuttle near to them, would that help in identifying if it is one or both of them?' Amber asked.

'Not noticeably. I'd suggest that they let off a few shots away from the ship and try to not replace what they expand. If the levels reduce sufficiently, then we pull them on board.'

'And if they don't? Mesrra was nearly dead the last time she was retrieved from space. I don't want to have to take that risk again.'

'There's no easy or quick way. We would have to build shielding to contain them in part of the ship.'

'I was afraid you were going to say that. Get the shuttle ready to go in case they release too much radiation,' Amber ordered. 'Conner, can you inform them of the problem and what we want them to do?'

'Yes, Captain,' Conner acknowledged. *'Mesrra, Brelsa, we have encountered a problem. You have now absorbed so much energy that you can't come back on board because the radiation you are releasing is dangerous to us. We need you to release some energy blasts to see if that will reduce the radiation.'*

'Of course,' Brelsa replied.

'We understand. Stand by,' Mesrra said, before letting two energy blasts into space.

'There is a reduction, Captain, but nowhere near enough. Scans show they are quickly increasing their radiation output.'

'Shuttle from the bridge, I'm going to have to ask Mesrra and Brelsa to expend as much energy as possible. As they do it, they must get as far away from the sun as they can so the amount of energy they absorb is at a safe level. I need you to be ready to follow them and pull them on board quickly, if need be.'

'Understood, Captain.'

'Mesrra, Brelsa,' Conner called. *'Sorry, you will have to release a lot more energy. Try and aim away from the sun so that after each blast you don't take in as much. The shuttle*

will follow you. If you don't reduce your energy, it will make us sick when you come back on board.'

'How sick would we make you?' **Brelsa asked.**

'The radiation you're giving off will destroy a lot of the ship's systems, and it's unlikely that we'd get back to the starbase without help. It will also give the crew radiation poisoning. We wouldn't live for long after direct contact with you.'

'Understood. We will give it a go.'

Amber knew that Brelsa and Mesrra had started to do as they'd been asked before she was told by her crew, who were monitoring the sensors. With each blast the Lismarians let out, the amount of radiation reduced. The power behind each blast also registered and Amber was amazed at the readings.

It was not long before Brelsa and Mesrra could be brought safely onto the shuttle. If they were willing, further experiments would be carried out to balance their energy input to power output. On this occasion, they had put everything into each blast, more than was needed to destroy a ship, but if they were not near a sun then they would soon be in trouble.

Amber knew that her father would be excited by the possibilities when she reported back to him. 'I want the results stored on an external drive for my eyes only and then deleted from the ship's records,' she ordered.

'Of course, Captain.'

'This experiment stays with those involved. I will share the information with Admiral Yoland, but under no circumstances is today part of public record. I won't put our Lismarian friends at risk.'

'Yes, Captain.' As far as anyone looking at the logs was concerned, the ship had paused temporarily at the sun before moving on.

'What is the status of our friends?'

'They're on board the shuttle. Radiation is now at acceptable limits. They're requesting permission to dock.'

'Permission granted.'

Chapter 27

AMBER met the shuttle as it docked, keen to see how Mesrra and Brelsa were after their experience in space, especially as Conner had expressed concerns over how weak they were. This ship had no hydroponics bay; the best they had were the portable lamps that had been taken from Brelsa's room on the base. If the Lismarians were too weak, they would go straight to a planet that had already been identified as suitable for them.

Amber was reassured when they walked off the shuttle. Giving them a visual inspection as she walked towards them, she could detect the signs of weakness that had worried Conner; they both dragged their feet and their shoulders were hunched. The signs of exhaustion were the same for the Lismarians as they were in humans, she realised. As she got closer, Amber saw Brelsa's markings had changed like Mesrra's had and were more pronounced.

'How are you both?' Amber asked.

'Drained but alright,' Brelsa answered. 'I have never felt anything so amazing in all my life.'

'Do you need to go down to the planet?' Amber asked them.

'Conner has already asked us. We think we are fine for the moment. We would have been happy to stay out and practise some more,' Mesrra said.

'I'm glad to hear that. I imagine that this time we picked up better sensor readings, which we'll need to look at. Maybe we can help you learn how to moderate your energy release better.'

'What do you mean by that?' Mesrra asked.

'At the moment you are guessing how much you release into space. When you fought the Urigans, your power ripped through those ships as if they were nothing. On that occasion, as here, you were near a sun so it wasn't a problem. If you had to fight further away, it would be beneficial to learn how much energy would cause the same result so you could ration what you had stored.'

'I understand. We will wait for you – but we would both like to go out again soon,' Mesrra informed her.

❁

Amber sat on the bridge going through the readings with Conner. 'What do you make of them?' she asked.

'Science is not my speciality; I can read them on a simple level. They fluctuate greatly. Brelsa was giving off the most powerful blasts.'

'Really?' the captain asked, surprised. 'I didn't expect her to be more powerful than Mesrra.'

'I don't think she is. I think Mesrra was being conservative in what she was releasing. She seemed to be more interested in coordination and movement in space. Brelsa was very excited after she realised she wasn't going to die, and she wanted to see how much she could expel.'

'She was having fun out there?' Amber clarified.

'Yes, Captain, they both were.'

'They've expressed a wish to go back into space. I'm happy to let them go again. I want to make sure that Mesrra was doing what we assume she was, and that Brelsa can rein it in and follow Mesrra's lead,' Amber said. 'But you're closer to them than anyone else. Do you have any objections to this?'

'No, Captain,' Conner replied.

❁

They went to the cabin that Mesrra and Brelsa were sharing. The Lismarians were huddled close to the lamp. Would letting them out into space again be such a good idea? This ship was clearly not able to meet their needs.

'Have you decided if we can go out again?' Mesrra asked. There was a look of hope on both their faces.

'Once more. This is what I want you both to try.' Amber took them through what she and Conner had assumed from the readings and how they wanted them to learn better control.

'Once more is not enough time to learn this,' Mesrra said.

'I know, but you shouldn't be left to suffer like this, and running you down to the planet each time would not be practical.'

'We don't mind.'

'I do, especially if there are other options. This was only ever meant to be a short trip. We'll work on getting another ship that will better fit your needs.' Amber would brook no argument. They could go out once more, then back to the starbase. She hope d her chief engineer could work out a better place for them to stay in the meantime.

As Amber walked out of the cabin, Mesrra followed her leaving Conner behind with Brelsa. 'I know you worry about our safety, but there is something else that is concerning you,' Mesrra said, getting straight to the point.

'I'm worried about how much you want this,' Amber replied.

'Why should we not want it? Surely it is a good thing?'

'That would depend on why. Being that close to a sun has changed you. We don't know how. Unless you and another Lismarian who has not been into space agree to tests, we'll never know what the impact is.'

'I have told you I am fine. If anything, I'm better than before. I can cope with the lamps more easily now.'

'I know, but there could be more than that. Your determination to keep going back out worries me. You're craving the euphoria you feel out there.'

'It feels wonderful, yes, but it is not the reason why I want to go out there.'

'Are you sure?'

'Yes. Why are you so worried about this?'

'Humans can suffer from addiction, where something makes them feel so great that they will do anything to keep feeling that way. That can be, at best, self-destructive to the individual and, at worst, dangerous to others.' Amber knew it was an inadequate and very simplistic explanation, but if the Lismarians did not have a problem with addiction trying to explain further would not be relevant.

'We crave the sun because we need it. It can make us feel really good but it is more like you are with food. Once we have enough, we stop the feeling of need for it. I am not standing here feeling I must go out into space. I want to go so much because, after the pain these Urigans have inflicted on my people, I finally have a way to make a difference. I do not want to sit on a ship or a starbase waiting for the outcome of a battle. I want to be out there taking part. Both my parents and Brelsa's are Protectors and that is what we want to do – protect others.'

There was a determination in Mesrra's voice that could not be ignored. Amber also felt Mesrra's confusion over the concept of addiction, which reassured her.

'Alright, we'll get the shuttle ready again. But my decision stands: once more, then we go back and look for a better ship.'

⚛

'What happened, Natalie?' she was asked over a secured communication call. It was a call she had been dreading.

'What do you mean? The *Ottawa* got lucky against you. It wouldn't have been the first time.'

'Last time it got the better of one scout, not three ships, one of which was a battleship. The *Ottawa* should be debris.'

'No. Captain Yoland reported that they encountered one Urigan ship, they got lucky and barely escaped alive.'

'Then she is lying. I want to know why and what happened to our ships.'

'Of course.'

'Be quick getting the answers.' The communication shut off. Admiral Webb sat and cursed.

When reports came in that the *Ottawa* had been found without life support and badly damaged but with all the crew alive, there had been great rejoicing. Amber Yoland was the first captain to have survived twice against the Urigans. Gareth Yoland had been evasive when Natalie Webb asked if he'd spoken to his daughter directly to see if Amber had given him any additional information.

Natalie tried to think of ways to get more from Gareth and couldn't. Having been married to a powerful telepath, he knew how to detect – and to a great extent block – a mind read. He had extra encryption on his computer. She had looked at his personal vulnerabilities but could find no scandal to use as leverage against him. But others were not as protected or as careful as him; surely some of the crew of the *Ottawa* knew what had happened?

Chapter 28

THEY had docked an hour earlier. Amber's chief engineer had met them and shown them to two rooms on the *Ottawa* in an area where the damage had been minimal. He had hooked up two solar lamps to a temporary power supply. Here the Lismarians could stay, safe from discovery from anyone else. It was not as nice as hydroponics, but it was just as effective.

'I'll get you back into space again as quickly as possible,' Amber had promised the Lismarians before going to her room to call her father.

'I have to admit you're back earlier than I expected. Did the experiment with the Lismarians not go well?' Gareth Yoland asked his daughter when she contacted him.

'Yes and no. They were both very happy out in space and keen to learn how best to help us. Which, if we can get the Urigans to fight us near a sun, would be great. The problem is that Mesrra and Brelsa took on too much energy and we had problems getting them to reduce what they'd absorbed so that they could return to the ship safely. The first time they coped on the ship for a while after returning, but they were weak. The second time they were out in space for longer and they seemed to have a harder time creating the balance. We had to take them down to the planet for an hour so they could take on enough energy to come back here.'

'That does cause problems. How much radiation were they giving off?'

Amber transferred the details.

'That's not a small problem,' Gareth said. 'We need to

work out a way to shield an area of a ship better. Cal might be able to assist with that.'

'I thought he was working on improving our ships' shields. Would the FWN release him for this?'

'As he keeps telling us, Cal is under contract and not employed by us. Readings from destroyed ships only get him so far. If we want effective shields, he needs the weapons themselves. Until we get those weapons, he has a team set up that can continue his work without him.'

'So if he wanted to come he could?' Amber asked. 'You couldn't stop him?'

'He's very wealthy and has powerful connections. Those were his terms of contract and we needed him too much to argue. His work ethic keeps him with us, but you have to admit it can also be useful.'

'Cal might be struggling to protect our ships without knowing more about the Urigan weapons, but the Lismarians are working with us. He should have all the information he needs to start working on shields.'

'If anyone can do it Cal can,' Gareth said. 'We just need to contact him and Jane diplomatically.'

'I can do that. I talk to Jane whenever I hit a starbase. It wouldn't be seen as unusual,' Amber informed her father.

'Sounds like a good idea.'

Gareth cut off the communication to his daughter. He was still worried that she was not as well as she seemed. Mary had reassured him that, if Amber was careful, the injury should heal on its own without leaving any lasting damage. Now he hoped that the call he had put into Cal and Jane a few days earlier meant that they were already delegating their work and preparing to leave.

⚛

Amber sat down and logged into the general communication unit where non-FWN messages were held. She played one from Jane and smiled as she listened to her friend asking how she was – Jane had heard what had happened. Amber knew Jane's means of 'hearing things' were not the same as everyone else's. She opened a link, expecting to leave a message, but was happily surprised when Jane answered.

'Amber, so good to hear from you. How are you doing?'

'Not great, if I'm honest. It's been a rough few weeks.'

'We heard. I'm so sorry. If there's anything Cal and I can do, let us know.'

'Is there any chance you can come here? I really need you both at the moment.'

'Of course. We'll be with you as soon as possible,' Jane promised.

Amber cut the communication, thinking that was way too easy. What did Jane know that made them willing to come at such short notice?

❊

'I told you she'd call for help. Aren't you glad that we're on our way?' Jane asked Cal after she had finished talking to Amber.

'What did you learn from that conversation that you're so happy about?'

'That she doesn't want me, she wants you! I knew something interesting was going on. Aren't you excited?'

'I'm sure I will be excited about the Yolands' problem when I've found out what it is. But until then, no, not really,' Cal admitted as he continued to work.

❊

A few days later, Amber stood at the docking bay waiting for Jane and Cal to disembark. They were arriving much quicker than expected. Amber didn't know for sure where they'd been based, but she assumed it was somewhere like Europa. She put the thought behind her; did it matter when they were here now?

Amber's face lit up when Jane walked briskly towards her. With everything that had happened, she hadn't realised how good it would be to see a familiar face – and one that was not FWN.

'It's good to see you. I didn't expect you to get here so soon,' Amber admitted.

'Like you, we have a lot of connections,' Jane replied, thinking of the call from Amber's father that had set them on this course days before Amber had called. 'You're looking well.'

Amber did not need to use telepathy to know what Jane was implying. Jane had gotten hold of her medical report somehow and had feared something worse.

'I'm fine, Jane. It was just a little brain haemorrhage.'

Jane shuddered. When Amber raised an eyebrow she admitted, 'The report didn't make pleasant reading.'

'Is that how you made it here so quickly? You left having read it?' Amber questioned. Jane and Cal had not come running after her first encounter with the Urigans and that time she had lost crew members.

'Amber!' Cal shouted as he entered the docking bay. Jane was relieved that the timely interruption meant she didn't have to reply.

'Cal, it's good to see you.' Amber was relieved that he'd come with Jane at such short notice. She had noticed Jane's pause before Cal had arrived; they were not here because of the call Amber had made and she suspected someone else's involvement. She was going to have a word with her father.

'Do you know if we have a place on the starbase or are we staying on our ship?' Jane asked, always the practical one.

'The base is full – all of the *Ottawa* crew are taking up the rooms, I'm afraid.'

'No problem,' Cal replied. Jane shook her head. Their ship had been built to their specifications and she doubted the starbase had many rooms as nice as their own quarters.

'Would you like to come on board to talk?' Jane invited Amber.

'Thank you, but I have a better place to tell you about

everything that's been happening.'

'Of course,' Jane said.

'Do you need me?' Cal asked, keen to get back to work and not interested in listening to Amber and Jane catching up.

'Yes. Sorry, Jane, I'm very grateful that you're here but it's Cal that I need most. I want to introduce you to two people. It will help you understand what I'm going to tell you.'

'Very cryptic,' Cal said.

'I told you so,' Jane whispered to him.

Yes, Amber thought, she was definitely going to talk to her father.

'Lead on,' she was told by Cal and Jane in unison. Amber led them to another dock, where the *Ottawa* was.

'What's this about, Amber?' Cal asked. 'I thought the *Ottawa*'s life support was badly damaged, as well as other systems.'

'It is, but the ship has some life support due to its link with the starbase. You will find the air thin. It's fine for short periods, which helps repairs where a suit might get in the way, but it's not sufficient for a crew to live on board as normal.'

'Still doesn't answer the question as to why we're here,' Cal pointed out. 'I really have too much work to do...' he started to complain.

'I need your help with the Lismarians, to build a shield for them.' Amber threw the statement at him now she knew they were safe from spying ears. She knew it would stop him in his tracks.

'Sorry, I don't understand. Why would you need a shield against the Lismarians? Don't attack their planet and you'll be fine.' He did not mention that, without their machine, he doubted the Lismarians would be a threat to a ship in orbit.

'Not to protect our ships from them,' Amber started to explain, then stopped. 'This will start to make sense in a few minutes, but you must promise that what I'm going to tell you – what I'm going show you – will go no further.'

Cal and Jane promised, clearly curious. It was not long before they walked into a room on the *Ottawa;* sitting in front of them were Mesrra and Brelsa.

'The Lismarians, as in two, not the race in general. I thought Mesrra had died,' Jane said, guessing who she was by her markings, which were the same as her parents'. 'I'm sorry, I didn't mean...' Jane was mortified that she'd been overheard and understood, especially when Mesrra turned around and smiled at her.

'It's fine. Mesrra is well aware everyone thinks she's dead. That's why she's hiding on the *Ottawa,*' Amber said when she saw the exchange of looks.

Mesrra smiled again. Jane thought the situation amused her.

'We have gone to great lengths to make sure that is what people think,' Amber continued. 'And I guarantee that any account of the battle you've heard is wrong.' She sat on the floor next to the Lismarians and, after a brief hesitation, Jane and Cal joined them. There was not much room and Jane and Cal were slightly uncomfortable with the seating arrangements, but their curiosity was now well and truly spiked.

Quickly Amber completed the introductions. She felt Cal and Jane's shock as they tried to comprehend that Mesrra, by human standards a young adult, was the daughter of the First Protectors they had met when she was only a few years old. Jane had read the reports, but seeing her was another matter.

Suppressing her desire to ask what she assumed would be irrelevant questions about the Lismarians, Jane continued with the matter at hand. 'The official account is that you encountered a solo Urigan ship during the fight, the hull was breached and Mesrra died.' Mesrra smiled back, unconcerned. 'Amber, you destroyed the Urigan ship before it destroyed you, then you started back here before your engines failed. All very tragic and heroic, but I'm also starting to think it's a work of fiction.'

Amber didn't doubt for a moment that Jane had not been given the report through official channels; if there were other versions, Jane would have found them. 'That was my official report to the FWN,' she said. 'The reality, as you can imagine, was somewhat different. We weren't attacked by one ship but by three. We detected them when it was too late – they'd already jammed our communications and were heading towards us. We couldn't outrun them so I decided to try and hide in the sun's orbit, in the hope that the radiation would make us undetectable to their sensors.'

Amber paused, then continued. 'Unfortunately, that didn't work and the Urigans locked their weapons on us. Our shields lasted for about fifteen minutes before the hull gave way. Thanks to Mesrra, no one was lost. She was able to hold the breach until everyone got through the airlock, then she was pulled into space.

'We thought that we'd lost her, but being that close to a sun had an unprecedented effect on her. I guess the best way to describe it is that the sun supercharged her and she destroyed the Urigan ships that were about to kill us. Once the Urigans had been destroyed, we were stranded. We were caught in the sun's gravity with no engines. Mesrra pushed us – she gave us the momentum we needed to get away from the sun and towards help.'

'Amazing!' Cal said. 'I've seen the energy readings from the battle at Lismar, when Lovoa and Solvan destroyed a ship in orbit. Do you know how these differ?'.

'No. The scans at the time were limited due to the damage we'd sustained, but we know that the readings were significant.'

'I'd love to know more. But why do you need me? I can think of other departments that would be in a better position to work out how to use Mesrra's ability.'

'Amber does not trust her people,' Mesrra said bluntly. 'She fears that if whoever is working with the Urigans finds out what we can do, they will try and harness it for themselves. Or, more likely, destroy Lismar from orbit as we could be a threat.'

Cal knew this better than most. Jane had been trying to track Diaz and Gallo and keeping close attention on all their family members to identify any connections. She had found one who was significant – and that Amber's father was aware of – so Cal could understand their caution. Admiral Webb was well-placed to gain all this information if Amber went through the FWN.

'I can understand the need for secrecy but I only work on defensive technology. Did you want me to look at the *Ottawa*'s shields? Do you think they were sabotaged and gave way too soon?'

'No. After the battle we went back into space on a science ship to let Mesrra and Brelsa experiment in space. The power that they produced was more than anything our weapons can generate. I can give you that data. The only problem was that Mesrra and Brelsa couldn't come on board until they'd depleted the energy they'd absorbed,' Amber explained.

'Why not?'

'They were giving off high levels of radiation that would have been harmful to the ship's crew if we'd brought them on board too soon. I want to know if it's possible to shield an area of the ship so we can bring Mesrra and Brelsa on board safely and transport them to another area of space when they've absorbed as much energy as possible.'

'You're wondering if we could use them as weapons against the Urigans, aren't you?'

'I am,' Amber replied. Cal and Jane looked shocked at her reply.

'What do you think about being used in that way?' Cal asked Mesrra and Brelsa.

'Who do you think came up with the idea?' Mesrra replied. 'Amber was not happy to start with.'

'Strangely, I'm not surprised,' Cal admitted. 'I understand

why you've not gone through official channels, but is your father fully aware?' He suspected the admiral knew because he had contacted them days before Amber had asked for their help.

'My father is fully aware and asked me to liaise with you. I'd be more than happy to get him to confirm that.'

'That won't be necessary at the moment. If I need confirmation, I'll contact him directly. I don't know if I can help until I've seen the data, and that might not be enough in itself.' Looking at Mesrra and Brelsa, he continued. 'To start with, I'd need to know how much you could both hold at capacity and how long you could retain the energy once you're away from a sun.'

'Of course. Does this mean we get to go back into space?' Mesrra asked.

'Yes Mesrra, we'll be going into space,' Cal replied. The Lismarians' smiles relieved his concerns about how they felt at the prospect of going out into a cold, dark vacuum.

Chapter 29

'WHAT are you looking at?' Jane asked. Cal jumped when she spoke; he'd been so engrossed in his work, he had not heard her enter the room.

After several calls that had not been picked up, Jane had gone looking for him to try and convince him to take a break. Though they had secured a room on the base, she found him in his office on their vessel. Cal had bought their ship when he started working for the FWN and it became evident that he would need to travel. He wanted the independence to go to damaged ships without waiting on the FWN; also, Jane insisted on her computer systems always travelling with her. Some of them were not portable so had had to be installed. She did not trust the FWN network and wanted her own more advanced build in place.

'Amber sent me through the data,' Cal said, as if that explained it all. Jane had been with him long enough to fill in the rest.

'Can you build the shielding they need?'

'I don't know. I believe I can build something that could contain the radiation Mesrra and Brelsa give off in their little experiment. But the energy they released so they were safe to come on board was less than that given off by Lovoa and Solvan when they destroyed the ship in orbit in Lismar.'

'Meaning?'

'Brelsa and Mesrra were nowhere near capacity. Until I know how much they can absorb, I don't know if it will be possible to build the shielding.'

'You don't sound optimistic. Surely the shields that surround a ship are strong enough to protect against the radiation they could give off?'

'Yes, easily.'

'Then can't they be replicated inside the ship?'

'No. The shields reflect the radiation out into the vastness of space. In the small confines of a ship, the radiation has to be released otherwise it will continue to build. I don't know how that will affect the Lismarians.'

'You want me to talk to Amber and see if we can arrange another experiment with them?' Jane asked.

'Yes, please.'

As Jane turned to leave, another issue occurred to her. 'How are you going to explain being absent to the FWN? Surely they'll be after you for a report on possible improvements to their ships' shields?'

'Easy. We've come here so you can offer moral support to Amber, and I've come to inspect the FWN *Ottawa*. I've requested the official report and I'll be looking at the damage. If the shields failed so quickly against one scout, there are serious concerns about their effectiveness. However, against three ships, and combatting the radiation from the sun, I honestly wouldn't have expected them to have held for so long.'

'That's going to cause serious questions if Amber sticks to the official account of one ship and not three. I don't see how the investigation will hold against this.'

'They were in the sun's orbit. The debris would have been pulled into the sun's gravity field, so an accurate accounting of the wreckage wouldn't have been possible. I doubt anything retrievable remained.'

'I was thinking more about the standard of the shields. Won't that cause questions at the Admiralty?'

'Yes, unless Amber and I can find a way to justify it. However I don't expect those types of questions to be asked for another few weeks – and a lot can change by then.'

'Do you think you can hold the enquiry into the *Ottawa* at

bay long enough to help Amber out?'

'I've spoken to Admiral Yoland and he has it all in hand,' Cal said. 'What worries me is that we can hide what happened from our people, but what if the Urigan ships reported back before they were destroyed?'

'Oh God! They would have known what was in the area at the time.'

'And if there's a leak in the FWN, that we are hiding something.'

⚛

They were all sitting on the floor on the *Ottawa*. Amber had been trying to find another ship to take Mesrra and Brelsa back into space. The *Ottawa* was still not an option and the science ship was due to leave with its own crew. Amber had said she would contact her father about getting another ship for them.

'What about ours?' Cal asked. 'It's small but its technology is better than anything the FWN could give you at such short notice.'

'Thank you for the offer but it's too small for a shuttle bay. If the Lismarians get into trouble in space, we'd need to help them get back on board. Help would be slower in coming, as we'd have to go out in space suits to pull them back, and that would put my crew at risk,' Amber pointed out.

'We are willing to try it,' Mesrra said.

'Not a chance in hell,' Amber said. 'I have no problem in arranging further experiments, but we have to do it as safely as possible. I won't risk losing you because we cut corners.'

'Your father can't keep appropriating ships without questions being asked,' Cal challenged. 'We have one that can be used without raising those questions. The FWN has no authority over my ship.'

'I appreciate that, and it'd be perfect if we could fit a shuttle on it. I'm sure you have technology that will be of great value – but I won't risk losing Mesrra and Brelsa.'

'If we are near a sun, we are not at risk,' Brelsa pointed out. 'And we could stay out there for a considerable time. It is you that are at a disadvantage if you get too close at the wrong time. We could use it as an opportunity to learn better control. Until we can safely manage our absorption and expulsion, don't come to collect us.'

'If we fight for you, there won't be a shuttle hovering close by. You will come and collect us as and when you can,' Mesrra added. 'Now is not a good time to be safe, because a fight is not safe.'

'You're right,' Amber conceded. 'A fight is not safe and it will be a lot worse than not having a shuttle because you'll probably be on your own for some time.'

'So we go out on Cal's ship?' Mesrra asked.

'Yes,' Amber conceded. She had to remember that she was trying to get them ready for a potential war. Pushing them to their limits would be a good idea. She had to forget that they were only a few years old. They were not children, they were adults and they knew what they could do better than she did.

❄

Just before leaving the starbase, Amber checked her status to see if she needed permission. She was still shown as on medical leave as a result of the brain haemorrhage. She was annoyed because she was okay, other than the limits on her telepathic abilities. The headaches had gone entirely. As far as she was concerned, she was just like any non-telepath. On the other hand, she was not deployable.

She needed to make a follow-up appointment with the doctor. He would probably tell her she was fine, but no one would be looking for her until then. As long as she informed her manager, who happened to be her next of kin, about any travel then her commitments were fulfilled. It was with a sense of amusement that she contacted her father to tell him where she was going – as if he did not already know.

The next day Amber travelled with Mesrra, Brelsa, Conner, Cal, Jane and Ensigns Jones and Kadle. They had all agreed to go back to the sun they had been to previously.

Now, a few days later, Amber sat behind Cal and Jane eagerly waiting for the readings as Mesrra and Brelsa prepared to be pulled into space. Conner was down there with them, making sure that they were alright.

On being given the go-ahead, and having made sure everyone was ready, Conner released the airlock and watched the Lismarians being pulled into space. The first time Conner had watched this she'd thought she had lost her friend. Knowing that Mesrra was fine still felt wrong and left her worried. She had a space suit ready to be put on if there was any indication of a problem.

Amber knew that Cal had seen the results, both the limited ones from the battle with the Urigans and the more detailed ones from their last trial. She wondered what he would make of them now.

Conner called and confirmed that Mesrra and Brelsa were now in space. Amber saw Cal's excitement and knew he was already monitoring and tracking them.

Through Conner, Cal passed communications to them one at a time. He wanted to know the most power they could pull in, the maximum they could expel in a blast of energy, and how depleted they could become before they had to pull in power. They reported back that, being this close to the sun, they were always replenishing their energy supply so it was hard to calculate.

Mesrra and Brelsa were happy to comply with everything that was asked of them. Amber sat and watched. As time went on, they started to gain an idea of what the Lismarians pulled in and how controlled their blasts were. Brelsa and Mesrra's control was incredible; Amber could not believe how quickly they taught themselves what was needed.

Amber heard Cal calling a halt and realised that they had been at it for hours, Conner was asked to relay the message to Mesrra and Brelsa, asking them to expel as much energy as they could. Conner and Louie Kadle put on their spacesuits in case they needed to go out and pull the Lismarians back on board.

On receiving the instructions, Brelsa and Mesrra did as they were asked. Compared to the last time, they were much more controlled. After only a few hours they could balance their absorption nearly perfectly, leaving the watchers amazed.

Chapter 30

AMBER had just been down to see Mesrra and Brelsa. They were starting to feel frustrated; they wanted either to return to the starbase, where the solar lamps met their needs better, or to be allowed back into space.

Amber was waiting to see if Cal needed any further information before heading back to the starbase; they might not have another chance to get data. She knew Cal and Jane were working all hours but the waiting seemed to take forever.

The Lismarians said they understood but expressed a desire to go back into space, even if there was no need for readings. As before, they had enjoyed themselves, using their power to propel themselves. They had seen Cal's instructions as a challenge. They had improved very quickly, to the point that when it was time to come back on board they could gauge what power they should be holding so they did not over-expend it and become weakened.

Amber was about to find Cal when she was informed that her father had requested a private communication. She headed to her room and opened the secure transmission. Expecting him to be checking on her and how the Lismarians were doing, her heart sank when he broke the news to her.

'You're out of time, Amber. Intelligence suggests that the Urigans are massing their fleet.'

'How long do we have?'

'I don't know, but we're calling in all ships. We're working on the assumption that it won't be long.'

'We'll head back in. I need to check how far the repairs

have progressed on the *Ottawa*...' She doubted the ship would be ready to fight in time.

'I'm thinking of a better use for the *Ottawa,*' her father interrupted.

She listened to his plan.

❀

'So can you do it?' Amber asked Cal, once she'd tracked him down. He had been hidden away in his office for the last few days; with the new developments, she was determined to get some answers quickly.

'It depends on how much time I have. I can definitely build some insulation into a large area like a shuttle bay, which would mean the Lismarians wouldn't have to expend as much energy before returning on board. But to get the shielding in place so they can be at full power will take more time than I suspect we have.'

'The insulation would be a good start. How many Lismarians would we be able to house there?'

'You have more Lismarians working with the FWN that I don't know about?'

'No, but I don't want to rule out any possibilities.'

'You're thinking about going to Lismar and recruiting more? They wouldn't have a clue what to do, and there's no time to train them,' Cal said indignantly.

'I'm more than thinking about it,' Amber stated. 'Why not? They don't need training, they learn by mind shares. Mesrra and Brelsa can pass on what they know. This will become their fight if we fail. I think we have a better chance of winning by working together.'

'We do,' Cal admitted. 'The power in their blasts is greater than anything our weapons can produce – or what we've seen the Urigans produce. If they aimed at us, our shields wouldn't come close to protecting our ships, and from what I have seen the case would be the same for the Urigans. Going back to your original question about whether I can do it, I don't know at the moment. It would depend on how many more Lismarians we're talking about and how much energy each one is storing.'

'So the answer is no?'

'It will likely take too much time.' Cal saw the disappointment on Amber's face. 'I'm sorry. I can guess why you want this and maybe, in time, I can create the shielding you need.'

'Thank you, Cal. Anything you can do would be a benefit.'

'I'll do what I can, Amber. Luckily, with your ship in for repairs and me being here to assess the damage and how your shields held up, I should be able to make the upgrades without any questions being raised. But they're unlikely to be at the level you want, so please don't get your hopes up.'

❀

'You seem unhappy. I thought you were pleased with what we could do,' Mesrra commented when Amber came to find her a short while later.

'I thought there would be more time, that Cal could create what we need, but it's likely that the Urigans will attack us soon. Cal hopes to build shielding on *Ottawa*'s shuttle bay so you and Brelsa can be on board with more stored power, but it will be limited.'

'We are ready to fight with you. Why would that not be enough?'

'I was thinking about going back to Lismar and asking your parents if anyone wanted to join us in the fight. But it's pointless if we can't transport you ready to fight.'

'There would be people willing to go. We don't want to risk the Urigans ever coming back,' Mesrra said.

'That's what I had hoped.'

'If there were a risk of them attacking our planet again, I expect my parents would want another machine,' Mesrra said hopefully.

'I have no idea what can be done about getting them another machine. It was old technology. Cal will know if it can be replicated – I can ask him. For now, if your people are ready to fight or not is irrelevant if we can't transport you to the battle.'

'Then why mention it?' Mesrra asked.

Amber was not sure. She'd hoped that by some miracle she would have an answer, but she had just caused worry and disappointment.

'When we were brought on the ship from Lismar, how did you manage? There was no mention of this shielding,' Mesrra asked suddenly as Amber was about to leave.

'It wasn't needed. You don't pull in enough when you're on Lismar for it to be a problem.'

'You were also happy with the balance we created before we were brought back on board last time.'

'That you and Brelsa managed such a level of control in such a short space of time is amazing,' Amber admitted.

'Then why is it a problem now?' Mesrra questioned.

'We won't know where this battle will be. If it's not near a sun, there would be no point in any of this.'

'Then bring the battle to a sun,' Mesrra said as if it were obvious. 'We are best the nearer we can get to the sun. That is why the First Protectors are on the highest peak on Lismar. We fight near a sun.'

Amber was about to explain why no one had ever wanted to fight near a sun. Then she stopped. No one had ever had the Lismarians fighting with them before. Would her father accept the risk?

Chapter 31

RETURNING to the starbase, Amber went to the *Ottawa* to meet her chief engineer, Mike Hayworth. He had been overseeing the repairs and she was keen to see how far they had progressed.

She had spoken to her father on the trip back. He'd been interested in what she proposed but agreed that they should keep it to only a few people. 'I understand your thinking, Amber, but unless you can guarantee the Lismarians' help, we'd be putting ourselves at a greater disadvantage by starting this fight near a sun.'

'Do we have any real hope against the Urigans, regardless of where the fight happens?' she asked.

'If we had Mesrra and Brelsa, then yes. But if you go to Lismar with them and don't get back in time, the fleet will be doomed.'

'Without the Lismarians, we will be doomed anyway. Mesrra and Brelsa may be able to tip the scales in our favour, but our ships would have to hold back or risk going down under friendly fire. Though the Lismarians' aim has improved, I'd not want any FWN ship near them.'

'I'll see what I can do, but without being able to tell the others your plan, I don't know how successful I'll be.'

'There's nothing you can do about Admiral Webb?'

'Jane can find nothing to indicate she is giving intelligence to the Urigans. The only thing against her is who she is related to.'

'If I could get in the same room with her, I could tell you if she's guilty or not!'

'Amber!' her father rebuked her.

'Don't tell me you haven't thought about it?' she questioned.

Of course he had. He also knew that Natalie worked pretty much in isolation and always had the same telepathic aide with her when she went out. An illegal mind read was not going to happen. Gareth Yoland could not even accuse her of abnormal behaviour as, with the growing power of the UTA and the acceptance of telepaths, such behaviour was becoming more common.

'I can argue that being near a sun is a good place to amass the fleet. The radiation will help to hide us. After that, we'll be driven by what the Urigans do,' he said.

'Thank you.' Amber hoped that the rest of the plan would fall in place.

When she walked into engineering on the *Ottawa*, it was a hive of activity. What reassured her most was the number of systems that were operational. 'You've been busy. What's the status?' she asked Mike. He was standing at the back, keeping a close eye on everything.

'We have life support in the main areas but where the hull breached is still inaccessible. It will take time to repair the damage in that area of the ship.'

Amber was not surprised, but that meant that Brelsa and Mesrra could not use the hydroponics bay. They would have to use the lamps that were on Cal's ship, which would not be ideal.

'What about the engines and shields?'

'The shields are sufficient for travel but not for defence – they won't withstand anything being fired at us. The engines are working. They were in better condition than we originally thought and repairs are going faster than expected. But they won't get you anywhere far or fast, Captain. The *Ottawa* won't be ready to meet the Urigans.'

'I didn't think she would be. Do you have a few minutes to walk with me?'

'Of course.' They went to an area where they would not be overheard. Amber explained what she wanted and why, and what Cal wanted to build in the shuttle bay.

'Can the *Ottawa* do it?' she asked Mike. 'Will the ship take the extra power draw from Cal's shields and make it to Lismar and back?'

'I'd need to talk to Cal, but it sounds like the shields will be a minimal power drain. If Cal wanted to protect against a lot of fully powered Lismarians, that would be a different matter. The engines should get us to Lismar and back if you don't push them too hard. I'd not want to try going any further until they've been tested.'

'Thank you. I'll make sure Cal comes and talks to you. For now, this is just between us.'

❈

With growing frustration, Amber waited for Cal and Mike to complete the work on the *Ottawa*. They had reassured her that they and the crew were working around the clock to get the repairs done.

'They're going as fast as they can,' Jane reminded her.

'I know. I just feel I should be doing something and not sitting around.'

'It won't be long until you're wishing for some rest.'

'I doubt it. I've always had something to do before but now I don't have the engineering knowledge or the computer skills to help.'

'Then why don't you go and talk to Mesrra? If you plan to recruit her people, why don't you learn more about them? From what I can see, Brelsa – and Mesrra after her – adapted to us but we've learnt very little about them.'

'Conner and I have been learning their language and we work telepathically with them.'

'Because it served a purpose. What do we know about their culture? What do they like? Dislike? We have killed them, probably led the Urigans to them, and we are about to ask a lot from them. But we've never bothered to understand them as people.'

❈

A few days later Mesrra looked around the large, sterile shuttle bay. There was nothing to break up the cold atmosphere. She was surprised at the lamps that had been installed; she had expected Amber and Cal to move the ones from his ship to here. They were more powerful than lamps in hydroponics and the bay was big enough to take them, unlike the small rooms on Cal's ship.

Amber explained all this when she caught Mesrra looking at them. 'I know it's not the hydroponics bay, but you don't have to spend the whole trip here. One of the sleeping rooms has a lamp installed as well, so you can go there. Cal put some extra shielding in place in case it's needed if your people agree to join us.'

'I'm sure we can make ourselves comfortable. Thank you,' Mesrra said politely. 'When do we leave?'

'Very soon,' Amber promised.

The ship was ready but Cal had delayed their departure while he waited for some essential equipment. His lack of explanation about what it was irritated Amber, but gut instinct told her not to leave without him, even after the shields had been installed.

Mesrra and Brelsa waited on Cal's ship for the last few days while the lamps and shielding were put into place. They were getting frustrated; their attitude had changed since they had discovered the freedom of space and the genuine threat against their people.

❋

When she received the information from Cal and Jane that they were ready to leave, Amber called her father. She wanted to know if there was any indication of how long they had before the Urigans attacked.

'I can't give you an exact time, I'm afraid,' Gareth Yoland told her. 'But we don't think it will be long, I'll keep you updated with information as soon as I get it. Now life support is stable, I'm giving you orders to pull the *Ottawa* out of dock to make room for other ships coming in for resupply. I can't give you any further orders without revealing where you will be going,' he warned.

'I'll be seen as going AWOL.'

'Yes. I'm sorry, Amber. With what's happening with the Urigans, I'll argue it's a waste of resources going after you.'

'Thanks for letting me know,' she said. She was not surprised but it still worried her; she knew that others would think she was scared, that she'd taken the *Ottawa* and run instead of joining another crew. If her plan was successful she would be exonerated; if she failed – well, that was not something she wanted to think about.

'You might want to ask my mother for help,' Amber told her father before he could sign off.

'What do you mean?'

'We always lose communication when the Urigans attack. How can a battle be fought if our ships can't communicate with each other?'

'We were hoping to get as many FWN telepaths onto our ships as possible and use them to communicate and pass on orders.'

'I doubt that would work. Most of the FWN telepaths are not of high level because the strongest telepaths tend to stay in the UTA. What you're asking them to do – to manage multiple telepathic communications – takes a lot of strength and skill.'

'You're telling me it's not a solid plan?' her father asked.

'Using telepaths for communications is – but you need *UTA* telepaths.'

'The UTA would never agree to that. The risk would be too high.'

'How do you know? Talk to Mother. Make her understand what will happen if the FWN fails to defeat the Urigans. It wouldn't take long for the UTA to fall to them if they advance into our space.'

'I'll talk to her,' Gareth promised.

'Thank you. Hopefully I'll be in touch soon with news.'

'Good luck.'

Amber recalled the minimum crew she thought would be necessary. She started with telepaths and those who were sympathetic to Mesrra, before pulling in those with skills she knew were required.

All those who boarded were told only that they were pulling the ship out so others could move in for resupply. Once they were on their way, when the ship's communications were closed down, she would brief them on the plan.

Chapter 32

'WHAT has happened? Is Amber alright?' Mary said as her ex-husband was shown into her office. He had called her an hour earlier asking to meet urgently and she had been worrying ever since.

'Amber is fine,' Gareth reassured her. It had not occurred to him that Mary might be alarmed by his request, though with recent events he should have considered it. The last time they had spoken was when Mary had allayed his concerns about Amber's health after she'd had one of the UTA doctors review Amber's scans.

'In fact, it's on her advice that I'm here,' Gareth continued.

Mary sagged briefly in relief before pulling back her shoulders, all business again, and inviting Gareth to sit opposite her.

'I'm sorry, Mary. I didn't think how you might see my visit here.'

'It's fine,' she replied, but he knew it wasn't and she was right. He'd told her that their daughter had been hurt and asked for her help without giving her any details, then shown up at her office with no notice.

Before he could say anything, she continued. 'Even with the number of telepaths entering the FWN over the years, I still feel we're left very much in the dark about what is happening. How did Amber get hurt?'

'I must thank you again for not disclosing that I came to you for a second opinion.'

'How many times do I have to remind you? Amber is my daughter too,' she snapped. 'I know I acted inexcusably in trying to stop her joining the FWN, but I'm paying for that now. She wants nothing to do with me.'

'I know she trusts you. As I said, I'm here on her advice. Can you activate that extra security you have?'

'I did it before you came in. Two visits in two years, Gareth. And whatever happened with Amber, though neither of you has explained it, I know she must have been desperate to inflict that damage on herself. If you're not here to break bad news about our daughter, I hope you're here to tell me what is going on.'

'Your father told you everything he knew about the Lismarians?'

'I told you everything that was pertinent, and I shared the more personal memories with Amber. I don't know anything else. If you're here to see if I withheld anything, I didn't.'

'No, I mentioned it only because the Lismarians are central to what's happening now.' He briefed her about the potential Urigan attack.

'Why has this not been broadcast everywhere?'

'The FWN thought we had more time to prepare. They didn't want to cause panic among the worlds.'

'People have the right to know, Gareth.'

'I agree, but the panic will pull resources away from the Urigans into peacekeeping on the planets, resources we don't have. There are no inhabited worlds near the Urigan border so if we fail, we don't even know which worlds will be affected first.'

'Why did Amber think I could help? I can't see how we can help manage several world populations if you fail. She should know better.'

'She suggested the UTA telepaths help coordinate the attack against the Urigans. The FWN have telepaths but we don't have many powerful ones.'

'Why do you need us for that? What's wrong with your own communication system?'

Gareth pulled out a data chip and handed it to Mary. 'This is everything you need to know. Most important is that the

Urigans can block our communication system when they get close. I'm not authorised to tell you, but I disagree with the decision. To get your help and support, I feel that you should know everything.'

'You're kidding me! Why didn't you come to us sooner?'

'The incidents were isolated and an active communication wouldn't have changed the outcome of the battle.'

'Even with Amber?'

'There were other factors in play with her. They're documented on the chip.'

'Will you get into trouble for showing me this?'

'Only if they find out.'

'Then why? Why not go through correct channels?' Mary asked.

'I have a suspicion that at least one admiral is corrupt and is feeding intelligence to the Urigans. I don't know if she's working alone or with others. Amber and I have a plan, which we're keeping to ourselves, but it means it's unlikely that Amber will arrive in time to start coordinating the fleet. Once we get close to the Urigans, we'll lose communications. We'd hoped that the FWN telepaths could pass important messages between ships, but Amber thinks they won't be up to the task.'

'She's right. You need strong, highly trained telepaths on each ship to facilitate complex communication in a battle.'

'Do you have them?'

'Yes. How dangerous will this be for them?' When Gareth didn't answer immediately, Mary nodded. 'I see. I can't make you any promises. I'll read through this information and let you know. If the UTA agrees to help, the telepaths will be volunteers.'

'Thank you – but please be quick in making a decision. We're calling in our ships in preparation.'

'I'll let you know as soon as possible.' Gareth got up and turned to leave, but Mary stalled him. 'You implied that Amber was off doing something else, that she might not be back for the start. Did you send her away deliberately?'

'If you're asking if I sent her away to keep her safe, no. The plan is hers, with my support, but it's nothing the FWN has tried before. If it works, it will place her on the front line, Mary, but it will also be our best chance.'

'Do you plan to tell me what she's doing?'

'Not at the moment, no.'

❁

Amber was lying on her bunk, recalling the memories her mother had shared about her grandfather. Most prominent was his work building the machine and how it had been used – a machine that was broken, according to her cousin. She knew Cal had looked at it on Lismar when Amber had first taken Brelsa back. She wondered what his thoughts were about repairing it.

They were now going to Lismar to ask the strongest to leave their planet and their people. If the Urigans got around them, then the Lismarians would have no way to protect themselves. If the Lismarians accompanied them, they could help win the battle and the Urigans would no longer be a threat. But what if it was not enough and they failed? The Lismarians would be left with no way to protect themselves from genocide.

Getting up, Amber went to seek out Cal.

❁

'Are you alright?' Jane asked as she opened the door to Amber.

'A while ago my mother shared some memories with me which are now raising questions. I was wondering if you and Cal had a few minutes. I don't know if it's anything you can help with.'

'Come in,' Jane said.

'How can we help you?' Cal asked, looking around. Amber saw that he was trying to build something, or two somethings to be more accurate.

'I'm sorry to disturb you. I've been thinking about the

Lismarians. My cousin Alex told me that the Lismarians had a machine they used to defend themselves. They used it to save him from another ship, but it was damaged in the battle a few years ago. It's what I believe you were so interested in the first time we met, and it's still on Lismar. What I want to know is, can it be repaired?' Amber asked.

'No. Some of the parts overheated and fused together, and those parts are not made any more,' Cal replied. 'But I could build a new machine.'

'I take it what you'd need would not be routinely found on a ship.' Cal shook his head. Amber's face fell. 'We can't risk stopping off anywhere to pick up the relevant parts.'

'I never said we needed to.'

'What do you mean?'

'I knew the FWN was against giving the Lismarians another machine so I didn't tell you, but that is why we delayed leaving for a few days. I was waiting for parts to build new machines for them. This time they'll have one for the northern and southern hemispheres, giving them better defensive capability than they had before.'

Amber smiled in relief. 'The machines will be ready when we land?'

'They will be built and, in theory, they will work. But the parts that were used in the original created by your grandfather are obsolete, so I can't replicate his machine exactly. I hope my machines will be an improvement but they'll need testing when we land to make sure the replacement parts work.'

'Why didn't you tell me you were doing this?'

'I didn't know if you'd approve. If I'd asked, you could have refused.'

'You do realise that nothing we're doing at the moment is approved by the FWN,' Amber pointed out.

Chapter 33

AMBER had chosen her crew for the *Ottawa* carefully. Once they were underway, she called them together and explained exactly what had happened during the battle with the Urigans. Most of them were shocked; if they had not been on the bridge, they had only heard the official communication. The number of Urigan ships – and what Mesrra had done – was news to most of them.

'Why are you telling us this now?' someone asked.

'Because it's important that you understand what we're hoping to achieve and why. We're not just making way for other ships to dock, we're heading to Lismar in the hope of getting other Lismarians to join us.' This was met by a lot of murmuring.

'This isn't an authorised mission. I take full responsibility. My log already states that no one here knew about my decision. If we fail, blame will lay with me,' Amber reassured them.

'What makes you think the Lismarians will join us? You said Mesrra nearly died, so it's not exactly safe for them. And why would they want to help us after what we've done to them?'

'Mesrra has practised in space and has taught Brelsa. They are confident that they can share their knowledge effectively with their people. Mesrra is also confident that her people will join us. If we fail against the Urigans, it will be the Lismarians who suffer next.'

'How can they survive so long in the vacuum of space?'

'That's something I'm sure every doctor would love to know,' Amber retorted. 'I'm not sorry this was kept from you but it was essential for the integrity and safety of this mission. You've all been chosen for telepathic, engineering and piloting skills. For the engineers, you know the state of this ship – get us to Lismar and back. That's all I ask of you.' They nodded, accepting the challenge.

Amber went on. 'If the Lismarians come with us, all communication will be telepathic once we engage with the Urigans and other FWN ships.' She nodded at the telepaths. 'You will be needed to pass on orders.'

'How will they understand us?'

'Mesrra and Brelsa have learnt our language. Pilots, though we only have shuttles in Bay 2, you will be responsible for helping the Lismarians get back on board if they can't do so themselves.'

'Why are there no shuttles in Bay 1?' a pilot asked.

'That's where Mesrra, Brelsa and any other Lismarians who come with us will stay,' Amber replied. 'I recommend that the telepaths and pilots to go down there and talk to them. Get to know their minds and what they can do. It may help when the time comes. Any further questions?'

⚛

Ensign Jay Winsor went down to the shuttle bay. He had been on the *Ottawa* and had run past Mesrra as she'd held the hull breach; he had heard Conner screaming her name when she was sucked into space. He had not known that she'd survived; he thought she'd died when she was pulled into space. He thought the *Ottawa* had just got lucky in fighting off the Urigans. After all, the *Ottawa* had done it before.

Jay had never spoken to Mesrra before and had only seen her that one time. Now he was going to the shuttle bay to say thank you.

⚛

As he walked in, he saw Mesrra and another Lismarian sitting on the floor. There was no furniture and the temperature was surprisingly hot. Then he saw several solar lamps.

Mesrra and Brelsa turned and looked at him. For a moment Jay thought about leaving but Mesrra stood up and smiled. 'Hello,' she said simply.

'Hello,' he replied, suddenly embarrassed. 'I didn't mean to disturb you. I just wanted to say thank you.'

'For what?'

'For saving me – us. I was one of the people you allowed to get behind the airlock before the hull breached. We've been told what you did.'

'It is what we do,' Mesrra said simply.

'I...' Jay was not sure what to say next.

'He is being polite, Mesrra.' Brelsa spoke up. 'Except for a few, like my father, it assumed that the Protectors will protect and they get the benefits for doing so. Here, if someone helps you, you say thank you.'

'I did not mean to be rude,' Mesrra apologised. 'Please come and sit with us.'

Not knowing what else to do, Jay joined them. He sat cross-legged on the floor, something he'd not done since he was a child. 'I have not met many people here. What do you do on the ship?' Mesrra asked.

'The captain asked me because I'm a good shuttle pilot.'

'You pull us back on board if we are too weak?' Mesrra clarified.

'Yes. The captain told us what happened before. Can you tell me more about it?' he asked.

What started as a conversation opener developed into one about tactical flying.

❈

Cal went into the shuttle bay to test how the extra shielding he had added was performing against the more powerful solar lamps. As the doors opened, he was surprised to see Conner and a cluster of crew members in their shirt sleeves sitting on the floor with the Lismarians. It looked like they'd been there a while, judging by the drinks and food next to them.

On seeing him, they all jumped to their feet. 'As you were,' Cal said, and watched as they returned to their conversation. Their voices were quieter, as if they didn't want him to hear. He listened as best he could as he examined the shields and was surprised at what they were discussing.

After he left, he went to see Amber. 'Is everything alright, Cal? Is there a problem with the extra shielding?' she asked, worried by his expression.

'No, it's operating better than I expected. Did you know that your crew are discussing flying tactics with Mesrra and Brelsa?'

'Yes. Ensign Winsor came to me a few days ago and asked if it was alright. I should have thought of it myself. If it helps them face a Urigan fleet, the Lismarians should have as much knowledge as possible. I'm glad that it's not just Conner talking to them.'

'There were several of the crew there. It looked like they'd been there a while.'

'I understand Brelsa and Mesrra are becoming quite popular.'

Chapter 34

THE tension on the ship increased the nearer they got to Lismar. Most of the crew had taken the time to go to the shuttle bay, and with the visits came more hope. The telepaths spent as much time as possible with Mesrra and Brelsa to learn, and become comfortable with, the differences in the way their minds worked.

Conner fed back regular updates to the captain, saying it was a shame that they would not be able to put into practice what everyone was learning.

'It would be useful but, with not knowing how long we have until the Urigans attack, we may not arrive on Lismar in time if we wait. If my father can give me a more accurate projection for the attack, then I'll reconsider.'

'Thank you, Captain,' Conner said.

'How are Brelsa and Mesrra doing?'

'Alright. The shuttle bay is stark but that doesn't seem to bother them. The increase in the solar lamps has made them more comfortable, and they seem thrilled to be talking to the other officers. I think this is the first time they've had so much interaction with humans.'

'That's good to know. Can you tell them we should arrive at Lismar shortly? Ask Mesrra to tell me when her planet is within her mental range.'

'Of course.'

❈

A few hours later, Mesrra called down to Lismar requesting permission to send a shuttle to the peak. Talking to so many humans during the journey had helped to keep her excitement at bay.

When she finally felt the minds on Lismar, she worried about how her parents would receive her. Conner and Amber had come to the shuttle bay to help her answer any questions from her family – and to give her support if she met any resistance from them.

'Mesrra, I did not think I would hear from you again. Are you alright?' Lovoa asked, her mental voice tinged with both worry and excitement at the return of her daughter.

'I am fine, and so is Brelsa. She is with me. But I need to talk to you about what is happening to the humans.'

'Of course. Come down to the plateau whenever you are ready.' Her mother could not hide her joy at seeing her daughter again.

'We can go down whenever we are ready,' Mesrra told the captain.

'Good. Conner will fly you and Brelsa down. If your parents are open to the idea, I will come down later,' Amber said, surprised at how brief the communication had been. Had Mesrra's parents asked her anything? It was not an encouraging sign.

'Why not come down now?' Mesrra asked.

'It's your first time back and a lot has happened. I know you can share information, so it won't take long to make your parents aware of what is happening. If they are happy to talk, I will come down.'

Mesrra understood. Amber wanted to give her a little time to reconnect with her parents before pushing her request for Lismarian help.

⚛

'Mother! Father!' Lovoa and Solvan heard their daughter calling them.

After the humans' last visit, Lovoa had not expected them to return unless something was wrong and they were under threat. She turned and looked at Solvan, experiencing joy, worry and fear.

'Mesrra, I did not think I would hear from you again. Are you alright ?' Lovoa asked. When Mesrra and Brelsa confirmed they were both alright, she just wanted her daughter back on Hannoki's Peak.

Lovoa kept the conversation short; the longer they talked, the longer it would take for Mesrra to come down to Lismar. And she needed to get better control of her emotions, which were in danger overtaking her.

Solvan wrapped his arms around his mate. 'I can't believe she is back,' he said.

'Neither can I. And though I am so happy to see her again, I worry about what has brought them here.'

'I do not think we will have to wait long. Should we call Kelvic?' Solvan asked. Their son was working with Issac on better ways to manage crops.

'No. I think it is better if we hear what Mesrra has to say first. If the reason is just for us, he will not take being excluded well. I sometimes think he spends so much time on the collectives because being here reminds him too much of Mesrra.'

'He will not forgive us if he finds out she was here and you kept it from him.'

'He is not as strong as us. How would he know?' Lovoa challenged him.

Solvan did not like keeping the news from Kelvic that his sister was returning, but he understood his mate's reasoning and conceded.

❊

Conner flew Mesrra and Brelsa down a short while later. As soon as she landed, Mesrra was on her feet waiting for the hatch to open. Brelsa hung back, waiting.

'Aren't you going to join her?' Conner asked as Mesrra left the shuttle.

'In a moment. I am giving her some time. She has missed her family a lot.'

'So have you.'

'They are my people, not my family. I have not seen my brother since I left.'

'I'm sorry, it must be tough for you.'

'I liked my brother before he mated, but I was never close to my parents,' Brelsa explained.

Conner was tempted to ask more about how Brelsa's brother had changed but worried it would be impolite.

❋

As Mesrra left the shuttle, the hatch closed behind her and she saw her parents waiting for her. She was so happy to see them again; she hadn't thought it would be possible when she had left Lismar all those months ago, when she had divorced herself from them. She could see and sense that her mother was happy to see her – but would Lovoa forgive her for abandoning them?

'Mesrra,' Lovoa called, and they ran towards each other and embraced. Solvan gave them a minute before joining them.

'Is Brelsa not with you? Is she alright?' Lovoa asked a few moments later, pulling away.

'She is fine. She is on the shuttle with Conner. She is giving us a few minutes together before joining us. When Brelsa arrives, Conner will go back to the ship and wait until we contact them.'

'I am sure she is keen to leave the shuttle,' Solvan said.

'Brelsa, thank you. You can join us,' Lovoa called out.

The shuttle hatch opened again and Brelsa walked out. Unlike the last two times, she did not stumble with the sudden increase in sunlight, which made Solvan look at her more closely.

'Your markings have changed,' he said as she joined them. Then he looked more closely at his daughter. 'So have yours. Not the pattern, but the shape of them.'

'Solvan,' Lovoa reprimanded him. 'Brelsa, it is good to see you again.'

'Thank you, Lovoa. But Solvan is right, we have changed.'

Lovoa took Mesrra's arm, running her hand over skin that used to be smooth. Now the markings were more pronounced and broader. 'What happened to you both.'

'That is part of why we are here,' Mesrra said. 'We have a lot to tell you and not much time.'

❈

'Are you going to say anything?' Mesrra asked her parents. To save time, she and Brelsa had both shared their knowledge with the First Protectors.

'You got sucked into space?' Lovoa stated, still shocked. 'We can absorb energy in space? We can survive in the orbit of a sun?'

'I appreciate this is a lot to take in...' Mesrra started to say.

'I think that is an understatement,' Solvan said. 'The captain, Amber, thinks that we could leave here and fight with the humans against these Urigans?'

'Yes. They believe that the Urigans will soon attack in force. They fear that they won't win and then the Urigans will come back here and start killing again.'

'The captain said that she would come down and talk with us?' Solvan asked, Mesrra nodded. 'Then invite her down.'

'We should call Kelvic back from Isslac's collective,' Lovoa added, revising her earlier thoughts.

❈

Amber landed on Lismar with Conner and Cal. They had tried to convince Jane to come as well but she was not impressed by the suggestion; she hated environmental suits and wouldn't be able to answer any questions about shielding technology or the Urigan threat. That was all Amber and Cal.

'I've enough to do here, Cal,' Jane protested. 'It's bad enough that I don't have all my computers here, which makes trying to find out how the Urigans are being communicated with a lot harder.'

'I know, but we needed your skills to make sure the *Ottawa*'s systems were secure and gave false readings once we disobeyed orders.'

'I'm not complaining about coming here. Whoever is leaking information is being very clever about it. If they try to access the *Ottawa*'s systems, that might be the clue I need. What I'm saying is let me stay here where I'll be most effective.' So Cal and Amber had left without her.

As they walked off the shuttle, all of the Lismarians were waiting for them, including a male Amber had not seen before. His markings were different to Mesrra's and her parents, but from the protective stance he had taken towards Mesrra he was obviously close to them. Taking a deep breath, Amber was glad of the environmental suit that hid her face. She and Cal went forward to join them.

'It has been a long time, Amber. Thank you for coming down.' As Lovoa spoke, she led them all off the plateau and inside her home. Once they were seated and had received a proper welcome, the male was introduced as Kelvic, Mesrra's brother.

His different markings confused Amber. She thought that all families had the same patterning; she must ask Mesrra about it later.

Lovoa spoke. 'I was very shocked by what Mesrra and Brelsa showed us. I admit I struggle to understand it. I have no concept of space beyond what little I have seen. I gather that surviving in space is unusual.'

'Until now it's been unheard of, unless we're wearing special equipment,' Amber said.

'But Mesrra and Brelsa were fine. In fact, they said that what they could do far exceeded what the machine allows us to do here.'

'Only when they were near a sun. We didn't try – and I'd not recommend – them entering space away from a sun, knowing how important it is to you.'

'I gather that is why Mesrra weakened the first time you

moved away from the sun's orbit,' Lovoa said.

'Yes – and she was expending all the energy she had absorbed as well,' Amber explained.

'How significant to you was what Mesrra did in destroying those three ships?' Solvan asked.

'We've not been able to match what Mesrra did. We have destroyed one or two Urigan ships, but it has always been at a cost. Before that battle my ship, the FWN *Ottawa,* was one of the best. We were seconds away from losing the battle and everyone dying but Mesrra saved us. There hasn't been an FWN victory on that scale before. I know what I'm asking is extreme, asking you to leave your planet and venture into the unknown, to risk your lives against an enemy that is stronger than the FWN, in an environment that is totally alien to you.' Amber paused, then continued. 'But I truly believe that without you we'll lose. And then the Urigans will head straight here and start skinning your people again.'

'If this is so important, why keep it a secret from your own kind? Why hide my daughter?' Lovoa asked.

Amber had not expected that question, though she should have; what Mesrra knew, her mother now knew.

'I'm afraid that there is someone in the FWN who is working with the Urigans. If we didn't tell anyone our plans, no one could reveal them. I came here against orders, so my leaders will punish me for that, but I honestly believe that without you all will be lost.'

'If that is the case, won't these Urigans be ready for us when we arrive?' Solvan asked. 'This person will have told them if they suspect what Mesrra did.'

'Very few people know what Mesrra did. My official report was false and states that Mesrra died when the hull breached. As no one had ever survived in space before, that was obviously not questioned. The Urigans will not be expecting you. They won't know what you can do.'

'Where will the fight take place? Will it be near a sun?'

'I don't know yet but my father, who is the only admiral

who knows what's happened, is trying to make sure that it will be. But I can't make you any promises.'

'It is a lot that you ask,' Lovoa stated.

'I know.' When no one said anything for a minute that dragged into two, Amber suspected that they were talking amongst themselves. For the first time, she knew what it must feel like not to be a telepath. Other than her mother, she had never had anyone capable of blocking her out of their minds.

'If we leave here, our people will be vulnerable if the Urigans get past you,' Lovoa pointed out suddenly. 'Is it possible that you can fix our machine so we have some chance to protect ourselves?'

'Cal?' Amber asked, turning to him. Until now, he'd been sitting quietly in the corner. He had examined the Lismarian machine that Amber's grandfather had built and had a good idea how it worked. The machine had been left behind, hidden. The decision had been made to leave it so that no one else in the FWN would know how the Lismarians could destroy a ship in orbit.

'Your machine cannot be repaired. The last time it was used, parts overheated and fused. Those parts can't be replaced as they are too old,' Cal explained as simply as he could.

'So if you fail to hold the Urigans back, they will return here,' Solvan pointed out. 'We are already vulnerable. If our strongest go with you, there will be no hope for our people.'

'If we go with them, there is a better chance of the Urigans being defeated. Then we would not need Protectors. We would not need a machine,' Kelvic pointed out.

'You didn't let me finish,' Cal broke in. 'I can't fix your machine but I can replace it. I know how David built it. The parts are not made any more but I've worked out how to replicate them with current technology.'

'You would not replace it before because you did not want your people to know about it. Why now?' Lovoa questioned.

'We never told the FWN about the machine. We didn't want to cause further complications by them knowing you'd had our technology for so long. But now, it might lead them to believe that you could blow a ship out of orbit on your own. And if someone is leaking this information to the Urigans, hopefully that will serve as a deterrent,' Amber explained. 'Also, two years ago the FWN were paying too much attention to you for us to bring you another machine. If they'd run high-level scans then they might have detected it. Now the Urigans are coming. If they get past us, it will be your only chance to defend yourselves.'

'How long will it take to build?' Lovoa asked.

'I've already started working on it during the trip here. It's nearly done,' Cal admitted. He had delayed the *Ottawa*'s departure for a few days, waiting for the parts to be delivered to the starbase.

'We will have an answer for you soon,' Lovoa promised, effectively dismissing them back to the *Ottawa*. Mesrra said she would call them when her parents had made up their minds.

Chapter 35

ALL the Lismarians watched as the shuttle left their plateau. They did not return inside but stayed outside for the benefit of Mesrra and Brelsa, though they did not seem to be struggling as Brelsa had done the last time she had returned.

'We have all heard Mesrra and Brelsa's view on this, that we need to help the humans to save ourselves,' Lovoa said. 'If they can give us a machine, I am willing to consider this request. But I will not leave our people unprotected.'

'Mother...' Mesrra started.

'I know your thoughts on this, but in helping them you nearly died. If this battle takes place away from a sun, we will be useless and we will be killed alongside the humans – and the Urigans will still come here.'

'Even with the machine, I doubt we could hold them off for long. We have only used it against a single ship in orbit. They will send many ships,' Mesrra pointed out.

'An early and effective attack may be enough to make them think twice. I will not leave my people with no chance,' Solvan said adamantly.

'Kelvic, what are your thoughts? You have spent a lot of time with the other Protectors – will they fight if we ask them to?' Lovoa asked, stopping what was likely to become a heated argument between father and daughter.

'I believe they will,' Kelvic said. 'There is a lot of guilt and disgust over what happened when the traders – or should I call them Urigans now? – came. As you know, a lot of the Protectors did not believe that they had returned. Even after Gilcan's collective fell and all were killed, there were still some who denied the truth.'

Solvan paled; he had been to Gilcan's collective after the attack. The memories of his helplessness after the killings started and the horror he had witnessed still haunted him, Lovoa reached over and took his hand.

'When the threat proved to be real, a lot of Protectors started to get their collectives in order,' Kelvic went on. 'There is still a deep fear that the Urigans will return. If there is a chance of ending the threat forever, you will have volunteers.'

'Can you give us the names of the mated couples you think would be most open to the idea?' Solvan asked.

'Why just mated couples?' Kelvic asked. 'I thought you said Mesrra had already been in a successful battle with them, and Brelsa had been practising with her.'

'You're right,' Solvan replied. 'The machine, and managing the power from it, needed a mated couple but that is not necessary for this. But I have to confess it would be interesting to see the difference. Being mated creates a stability in how we manage the sun's energy. Would a mated couple be more effective?'

'We will take those willing to go, mated or not. Only testing in space will prove if being mated is better or not,' Mesrra said.

'It was just an observation,' Kelvic pointed out. He left his family and moved to the far side of the plateau so they could continue to talk. He decided it would be best to start by contacting those closest to him who would be most likely to join the fight. With this thought, he contacted his mate, Derla, who was still on Isslac's collective.

'Is everything alright? What was so urgent that you had to return at once?' she asked. When he'd received the call from his mother asking him to return immediately, he had been filled with dread that something was very wrong – a feeling that had been borne out.

'Mesrra and Brelsa have returned.'

'Surely your mother could have told you that instead of

making you worry so much. Are they staying long?' Derla asked.

'No. The news they have brought with them is not good. They are looking for our help in a battle.' Kelvic told her everything he knew. Once he had finished, he was met with silence as she took it all in. It was very similar to his own initial response.

'Do you want to go with them?' she asked.

'I want to do what is best for our people.'

'I will come with you if you leave,' Derla said. *'You know that, don't you? You won't go alone.'*

'I do. Can you talk to Isslac and Gilcan? Let them know what is happening, but tell them to keep it to themselves for now. I want to know what they think. It will give me an idea of how other Protectors will take the news.'

'Of course. Are you staying there?' Derla asked.

'I don't know. I want to talk to those most likely to join us, but I will wait until my parents have decided what they want to do. Gilcan's and Isslac's opinions may be important in the final decision.'

⚛

Derla pondered on what Kelvic had told her. Her family had been lucky; they had not been attacked the last time the traders had come. But her parents had not believed the First Protectors until the last moment. They had since repaired their battlements and had given a place within the collective to the few independent farmers on the borders. Those who had refused were told that they would be welcome if the traders returned and they changed their minds.

Kelvic worked closely with Derla's parents, and their collective was now one of the best run after Isslac's. Derla would have to let them know what was happening; she could imagine her parents wanting to go. It would make way for her sister and her mate to take over from them.

'Derla, are Kelvic and the First Protectors alright?' Isslac asked her. She turned and saw him standing next to her.

'We need to talk, and with Gilcan and Cardoc as well,' Derla said.

Gilcan, and those of his family willing to work with Isslac, had been allowed to stay since they had no collective and nowhere else to go.

❀

They all sat together as Derla explained what was being asked of them and why. It took time for them to understand concepts such as space.

It was Isslac who spoke first. 'My sister is here? She is back?'

'Yes, she is on Hannoki's Peak with Mesrra and the First Protectors.'

'Have you spoken to her? Is she well?'

'No, I only spoke with Kelvic. But I believe she is fine.'

'And she's been in space?' Isslac asked. 'I know she said she was leaving but I never really thought about where she was going.' When Derla nodded in confirmation, he got up and started to walk away.

'Where are you going?' Gilcan asked.

'To see my sister.'

Isslac went to the battlements and ran for the edge. At the last moment, he jumped and spread his wings. What Derla had told him was incredible but, on hearing that Brelsa was back even for a short time, he could not think of anything else.

He had missed her. When she'd returned that first time, he had just mated Erle and he had not been at his best. He had mated in order to gain control of the collective from his father. Erle had some personality traits that, together with the demands of his new position, had taken their toll on his temper. He had not been pleasant to be around. Isslac wondered if Erle had helped drive Brelsa away.

As Isslac arrived at the peak, he saw that Brelsa was waiting for him. He did not know if she had felt him or been told that he was coming, and he did not care. He stood there for a moment gazing at her. She did not look any older than when he'd last seen her.

'Brelsa.' He was suddenly lost for words.

'Hello, Isslac. How are you?' she asked, and he walked forward and folded her into a tight embrace.

❀

After Isslac left and people had run out of questions, Derla let them decide what they wanted to do. When asked where she was going, she said, 'To see what Kelvic and the First Protectors want to do next.'

'Well, I don't know about anyone else but I plan to go with them,' Gilcan said, breaking the silence.

'You can't go, Father,' Cardoc said. 'You are too old and your ability to absorb energy is starting to fail.'

'I'm fully aware of that, but I'm still capable of absorbing and expelling energy. And if what we are told about being near a sun is true, I will be able to help in this fight,' Gilcan declared.

'You have done enough for our people.'

'After abandoning my collective to the traders, I will never do enough to make up for it.'

'Mother won't agree to it,' Cardoc pointed out.

'I don't care. I will go and she can stay or come and fight with me.' Though Gilcan's mate, Pesline, still lived with them in Isslac's collective, he hardly ever saw or spoke to her; she kept to the room and balcony that had been assigned to her.

'Stay here. I will go,' Cardoc said, surprising Gilcan. 'I should never have helped Mother stop you from going to the battlements. I should have made her go with you. I should never have supported Ovato in his attack against his workers. You have nothing to repent for; you would have done the right thing if you had not been stopped. I should never have listened to Mother.'

'Be that as it may,' Gilcan said, 'I cannot forget the pain

of all those deaths. I should have been able to stop them. If I had listened to Solvan and his father when they first warned us, instead of waiting until it was too late, maybe they would have had a chance. Their deaths still haunt me. I have nothing left to lose, but you do. You have a mate and two children.'

'Who are both grown. They do not need me. And my eldest is due to mate soon – she will be a good Protector,' Cardoc reminded him.

'What will your mate think of your decision?'

'I support him.' Turning, they saw Helie walk in; she must have flown over from her parents' collective as soon as Derla told them what had happened with Mesrra.

Gilcan was more than a little jealous; Cardoc and Helie had a closeness of mind he had never had with Pesline.

'It will be good to have company,' Gilcan said.

'If you insist on coming, at least tell Mother what you plan to do,' Cardoc insisted. 'She has a right to know – it is not fair on her otherwise.'

❋

Amber arrived back at the plateau with Cal and the machine. As always, most of the Lismarians were waiting for them. Brelsa was there, and Amber wondered if she had talked to the other Protectors. Unlike previous times when Brelsa had returned to Lismar, when she had only been allowed to communicate with the First Protectors, this time Amber needed her to talk to as many people as possible. What the FWN would say about that, Amber had no idea. It was another thing that she could be prosecuted for later.

Amber helped Cal and Conner carry the machine off the shuttle and place it in the centre of the plateau.

'It's a lot smaller,' Solvan said, looking at it.

'Yes. It should work in the same way as the previous one, but it needs testing to make sure,' Cal said. 'I only saw your other machine when it was broken, so I had to make certain assumptions based on what I knew about the parts that were used.'

'Will it still need a mated couple?' Lovoa asked.

'The original machine didn't work if you weren't mated?'

'We never tried. Legend has it that Hannoki died on this peak when he tried to use the machine by himself. After that, only mated couples used it,' Solvan explained.

'If it's always been mated couples then I'd keep to that,' Cal said. 'I've tried to copy David's design as much as possible. But I'd be very interested in the contrast between a single person and a mated couple using it.' It had not occurred to him that it made a difference. 'Do you want to try it now?'

Nodding, Lovoa and Solvan went to the machine. Though it was smaller, when they got closer they saw that it was similar and they did not need to be told what to do.

'Can you start with a small amount of power first?' Cal asked. Lovoa and Solvan placed some energy into the machine and sent it out.

Amber left Cal working with them and went to Mesrra, who was watching. 'How are you doing?' she asked.

'It is strange being back. Though I love my family, I'm frustrated and want to be back there,' she said, looking up.

'You don't regret leaving Lismar?'

'I have missed my family, but no. I have been of more use to you than I ever could be here, and I need to be of use.'

'What of Brelsa? She is not here?'

'No. Her brother found out that she'd returned and she has gone with him. She has a family she has never seen and wants to try and get others to come with us.'

'You don't want to do the same?'

'I'm helping my parents here. We must make sure that the right people stay to keep the peace. We worry what the people will think if too many Protectors leave.'

'How much of a problem would that cause?' Though Amber had started to learn about Lismarian society, she didn't know enough.

'We have collectives – a group of farmers and other skilled workers. Each collective is largely self-sufficient and is run by a Protector. The Protector is responsible for running the collective day to day, for example bringing in the harvest so it can be distributed fairly among the people. When there is trouble, like the traders' attack, the Protectors receive power from the First Protectors and either divert it to where it is needed, for example, destroying the traders if possible, or use it to shield the people. The Protectors' authority was failing and there was unrest before I was born, then the traders returned. There is still a lot of fear among our people.'

'So my coming here and asking for help could undermine your society?' Amber asked worriedly.

'No, it is just a question of making sure the Protectors who go are replaced and their replacements don't try and get control of the collective, causing a power struggle.'

'I'm sorry, I didn't think of the impact on your people.'

'I knew, though. Most Lismarians are not as strong as Brelsa and me. Those that are, are in positions of authority. It is a matter of meeting our people's needs and yours. But I think we will have enough volunteers,' Mesrra reassured her.

A sudden shout of excitement from Cal diverted their attention. 'I think it's going well with the machine,' Amber said.

❁

Once Cal was happy that his new machine was working, he and Amber left Lismar. The First Protectors would let them know when they had Lismarians who were ready to leave with them. Cal was buzzing with excitement; his rebuilt machine was working better than expected

'I anticipated making changes to the original design because nothing had been recorded about how they feed the power into the machine. But your grandfather's design was so elegant that my replica works well. If we're given permission to do more work with the Lismarians, I'll be interested to learn about how they pull in the sun's energy and manipulate it. And the difference between a mated couple and a single Lismarian. All Lovoa and Solvan could say was that a mated couple's power was more stable, but they couldn't go into detail. Do you think mated couples could be more effective than Mesrra?'

Amber gave half-hearted responses, paying little attention to what Cal was saying. Other than that the machine was working and the First Protectors were happy, she wasn't concerned about the minor details that excited Cal. He didn't seem to notice that Amber was not sharing his enthusiasm.

After her talk with Mesrra, Amber was worried about how many Lismarians would volunteer. She knew that the planet's population was sparse compared to their own worlds, and only about one per cent of them had Mesrra and Brelsa's strength. Had the trip here been worth it? Mesrra seemed hopeful; all Amber could do now was to wait.

⚛

'Captain, there are massive energy spikes from the planet,' the bridge ensign informed Amber soon after she returned to the ship.

'Are any aimed at us?' she asked worriedly.

'No, Captain. Nothing is breaking the hemisphere.'

'Do we know what's causing them?'

'No, Captain.'

Amber asked Conner to call down to the planet.

'Mesrra,'

'I'm here. Is there a problem?'

'We're picking up several energy spikes. Though nothing is directed at us, we're concerned. Do you know what's happening?'

'It's nothing to worry about. Several strong couples are mating.'

'That's not what I expected as a reply. Why is it relevant?' Conner asked, somewhat confused.

'To hold a collective, you must be mated. And as I said before, being mated allows better control and balance if you need to manipulate the power from the machine. The people leaving with us are getting ready in case they are attacked again. It has never been known for so many to take to the skies at the same time. It is a beautiful sight.'

'I will take your word for it, but I still don't understand the energy spike,' Conner replied. She wondered what the captain would think of the explanation.

'When we mate we – I don't know the best way to explain it – we merge ourselves? It takes energy to do that. The stronger you are, the more energy it takes.'

Conner couldn't understand what Mesrra was saying; she realised she'd just have to accept it. 'Does this mean you'll be ready to leave soon?'

'We will be ready tomorrow morning,' Mesrra promised.

Amber sighed with relief when Conner relayed the conversation; it was sooner than she'd hoped.

⚛

When Mesrra finished talking to Amber, she turned her attention back to what was happening below. Standing on the plateau with her brother and parents, she watched the play of light. There were several couples in the sky tonight; rightly or wrongly, the sight brought a feeling of hope for what was about to come.

Many of the Protectors had decided to accompany the *Ottawa*, leaving their collectives to be managed by their strongest child. Those who had not already mated were doing so now. If this went badly, the next generation would be ready for the Urigans.

⚛

The next morning Amber and Conner returned to the Lismar. They'd been told that, through mind shares with

Mesrra and Brelsa, all the Lismarians who were willing to leave would have assembled, that they knew the risks and what they were expected to do. They would be given the chance to withdraw. Though Amber appreciated the amount of detail the Lismarians could pass quickly between themselves, she wanted to make sure that they understood the conditions they would be living in and the risks they faced.

As Amber and Conner walked off the shuttle, Mesrra and her family greeted them. It was almost dark; the suns were low, creating the impression of a sunrise and sunset to the north and south poles.

'They should start to arrive soon,' Mesrra said with a confidence that Amber did not feel.

⚛

The first to arrive were Gilcan and Cardoc, with his mate, Helie. Amber didn't know them but, judging by their markings, there were powerful.

Lovoa and Solvan greeted them as old friends. 'Is Pesline not here?' Solvan asked.

'She chose not to participate,' Gilcan replied.

'Are you alright with that decision?'

'She took away my opportunity to save our collective. I do not care what she thinks. I asked her to come and she declined. I will not let her stop me doing the best for our people again.'

Pesline had never accepted that she'd done anything wrong. When Gilcan had told her what he was planning, she had been furious. She had pleaded with him not to go, saying that it was not only his life that he was risking but hers as well. Gilcan did not care; he'd made it clear that it was her actions that compelled him to go, so she deserved any negative repercussions from his departure. Pesline had protested that if he died in the fight, it would kill her too. Gilcan had replied that would be a bonus before walking away from her. He had felt her screaming her frustration and anger in his head for a long time afterwards.

Gilcan and Cardoc were not the only Protectors congregating on Hannoki's Peak. Judging by the numbers of young couples that had suddenly decided to mate, Mesrra and Brelsa had expected several volunteers – but they were still surprised by how many arrived. It was a mixed group. There were mated couples who had been Protectors when the traders last attacked and who regretted their lack of action; now they had offspring who could take over the collectives they were determined to make amends. The rest were young and unmated, those who had no hope of a collective of their own and wanted to make their mark in another way.

Mesrra was shocked to learn that so many felt as she had, and wanted to try and make a difference. Though she rejoiced that they had a chance to find their way, as she and Brelsa had done, what future awaited them when – and if – they were lucky enough to return home?

'Thank you all for coming,' Lovoa said. 'If you leave here with the humans you must know what you agree to, the danger you will face and what the humans need of us. Once you leave here, it will be too late to change your mind.'

'After hearing what our human friends have to tell you about what is expected, I will ask all those here to agree to a mind share to see what I have been through, to see what may happen. We need everyone to be prepared,' Mesrra said.

As one, they listened to Conner's briefing. Afterwards, Mesrra took over. She was selective about the memories she chose to share, so she did not reveal the temptation of the humans' technology. What she did show was how hard it was on a ship, being sucked into space, and fighting and destroying the Urigans. She let the Lismarians feel her panic and fear; she showed them the damaged *Ottawa* with the enemy getting ready to fire again. She wanted them to know the worst of what was to come. When she had finished, she expected most would leave and return to their families and collectives.

Hardly any did. Her brother and Brelsa had recruited well.

※

Conner watched the Lismarians as Mesrra explained the risks; none of them seemed fazed by anything she said. She was relieved; when Mesrra reinforced the message, she was convinced that they truly understood what might happen. Though none of the Lismarians had such extensive markings as Mesrra, most were similar to Brelsa's.

There were so many volunteers that it would take several shuttle trips, or the captain would have to send other shuttles down to collect them. Conner wondered if the shuttle bay could accommodate them all. Cal would have to keep a close eye on the shields in the shuttle bay.

The numbers gave her hope. Maybe they could win this.

Chapter 36

ADMIRAL Gareth Yoland looked at the reports in front of him. He was disappointed. The simulations with the FWN telepaths, who were trying to coordinate and manage the mental conversation flow that would be needed in battle, had not gone well. It was exactly as Amber had predicted: most FWN telepaths were not strong enough, and none were adequately trained.

He suppressed the urge to call Mary to see if she had anything for him. She would call him when she had a definitive answer; he hated to think about what political wranglings she would have to do to fulfil his request.

Nothing further had been learned about the Urigans' location or how many there were. Gareth hated this uncertainty.

The report that Jane had sent him before she left with Cal to go to Lismar was the same as always. Gallo and Diaz's families were not acting suspiciously and there were no notable spikes in their financial activities. The only thing of note she'd uncovered was a large payment to Stuart Webb, Natalie's brother, but Jane had not identified anything that showed Natalie was involved. Jane seemed convinced that Natalie was the leak and had some other way to communicate with either Gallo and Diaz or the Urigans.

With no evidence, Gareth could take no action against Natalie; even if he was tempted to break the law, he had no idea what the repercussions would be. It could make the Urigans strike earlier.

A buzz from his com unit pulled his mind back to the

present. It was Mary contacting him; she wanted to see him at the UTA.

Mary was waiting for him when he arrived at the UTA offices. 'Thank you for coming, Gareth,' she greeted him.

'You said you had an answer for me.' No matter how hard he tried to hide the worry in his voice, he thought that Mary was aware of it.

'I do. Please follow me.' She smiled reassuringly.

Gareth expected her to lead him to her office where they'd spoken in the past, so he was surprised they went to a large conference room which was full of people. He stopped and looked around.

'This is your answer. Everyone here has volunteered to join you. They are all ranked between Levels 7 and 11, and all excel at managing complex mental communication. A few are also teachers and can help train your more powerful telepaths in case there are not enough of us.'

Gareth was overwhelmed; he had hoped for a few volunteers but he had not for a moment thought that Mary would get so many. 'Thank you all for volunteering. For those who don't know me, I'm Admiral Gareth Yoland. Am I right in assuming that Principal Wilhelm has explained everything she knows?' Everyone in the room nodded in acknowledgement. 'If you have any questions then please ask them.'

The room was silent.

'I made sure everyone knew what was needed and the risks involved. All we need to know is when and where we must be,' Mary told him.

'A lot of ships are coming into Europa; others are heading to several other starbases,' Gareth said. 'I need your details and a way to communicate with you. I will need to look at deployments but I should be able to tell you in the next forty-eight hours.'

'Thank you, everyone. Please wait until you hear from

the admiral or one of his staff.' As one, they got up and walked out of the room leaving Mary and Gareth alone.

'Thank you, Mary,' Gareth said. 'I didn't expect so many. What did you tell them?'

'Everything I could. We're privy to a lot of information that we're not allowed to discuss, so when I started looking for volunteers a surprising number signed up. They knew that the Urigans are looking to attack. And they understand the repercussions if we lose. One or two of them even knew that FWN communications went down when your ships were near them. There's a lot of frustration because we couldn't help and many are desperate to do so. We can't afford to lose against the Urigans. All of my people know the risks, that they might not come back, but it gives them a chance to play a part and not be relegated to the sidelines.'

'They all seemed very calm for a group that might not live much longer.'

Mary smiled. 'We're good at controlling our emotions and excellent at keeping a straight face. Remaining neutral is necessary in all our negotiations.'

'You mentioned a Level 11; I thought you were the only functional person at that level.'

'I am. Did you think I'd send my telepaths to their likely death and not be prepared to join them? Besides, you need the best to coordinate the communication, and Amber would not forgive me if I didn't give it to you.'

⚛

As Mary promised, forty-eight hours later all the UTA telepaths had their orders about when to go to Europa's FWN port and which ships they would be assigned to. All were boarding ships at Europa; some would stay on those ships, others would be taken to ships docked at various starbases or ships that would rendezvous nearer to the proposed battle location.

Admiral Yoland met Mary as she boarded the FWN *Sydney*. 'Welcome on board, Principal Wilhelm.'

'Thank you, Admiral Yoland,' she said, returning his formal greeting. She introduced the telepaths who had boarded with her and who were transferring to other ships. They were welcomed and passed to one of the officers to show them to their quarters.

'Can you give me a few moments of your time before going to your quarters?' Gareth Yoland asked.

'Of course.' Mary followed Gareth out of the shuttle bay and down several corridors to a small meeting room just off the bridge. She put a device down on the table and activated it.

'What's that?' Gareth asked.

'Amber didn't tell you about it?' When he shook his head, Mary continued. 'It's a portable shield and replicates the security in my office. I assumed you wanted this conversation to be private.'

'You're right. What I'm going to say is just for you. I need your support when the time comes and for you not to think I've lost my mind.'

'If whatever you've planned will put my telepaths at risk then I can't promise you anything.'

'The only thing that will put your telepaths at risk is if they can't get the crews of the ships they are on to obey my order,' Gareth said. 'Which is why I'm having this conversation with you now. You'll hear that the ships plan to rendezvous near the orbit of a sun, supposedly to hide in the radiation from the Urigans while the fleet congregates. I'm hoping that the Urigans will see this as a good place to corner us and start the fight.'

'It is an awful place for the fleet to be attacked! What are you thinking?' Mary said furiously.

'That Amber will arrive on time.'

'You'd better explain more clearly than that. And where has my daughter gone?' she demanded.

'This stays between us. No one else can know. Promise me, and I'll tell you everything.'

It was clear to Mary that whatever Gareth was planning

worried him more than anything she'd seen before. 'Of course, I'll promise. I want to know what my daughter is up to and what I've involved my telepaths in.'

Gareth bit his tongue; Mary had not been interested in Amber for years.

'I've always cared about her,' she retorted. 'No, I didn't read your mind – your face said it all. I was wrong, very wrong, in the way I behaved towards her. I know that. Just because I've respected her wish to have nothing to do with me doesn't mean I don't care.'

'She cares for you, you know. When she spoke about your meeting, where you shared the information about your father, she was happy about that connection. She's missed your closeness.'

'If that's the case, she shields her emotions very well,' Mary retorted.

'She's learned from the best. That aside, you know from our fathers' memories what the Lismarians can do when they take in enough sun.'

'Yes. Hannoki killed some of the traders, and destroyed a few shuttles with the machine that my father built. I don't understand how that equates now.'

'What your father witnessed was only a start of what they can do. I don't know if you're aware of everything that's happened to Amber recently.'

'Of course I am. You had me get a UTA doctor to check her results and told me she'd suffered a brain injury.'

'Tell me what you know,' Gareth pressed.

'This is ridiculous!' Mary replied angrily. 'She encountered a Urigan ship and destroyed it. She and her the telepaths made a mind merge to get a message out for help. It was reported that the Lismarian on board was killed.'

'That was the official report. Amber and I kept the truth between those who were there and myself. The report she submitted was false.'

'That's a court-martial offence! What were you both

thinking?'

'That we don't trust the truth to be leaked to the Urigans, so we hid what happened and what we plan to do,' Gareth explained. 'Amber wasn't attacked by one Urigan ship, she was attacked by *three*. When she detected them, they were too close. She took the *Ottawa* into a sun's orbit to get away from them, hoping to hide behind the radiation. She thought that the Urigans would pass them by, but it didn't work. The Urigans knew where they were and attacked. The *Ottawa*'s hull breached and Mesrra, the Lismarian, was pulled into space. Surprisingly, being in space and that close to a sun did not kill her. It made her very powerful and she destroyed the Urigan ships.'

'If you think there's a leak in the FWN, I can understand you not wanting that to come out,' Mary conceded. 'Mesrra has gone back to Lismar, hasn't she? She's going to try and convince the Lismarians to leave their planet and help us?'

'Yes, but they'll only be effective near a sun, hence the strange location for the ships to gather. When the *Ottawa* gets here, all the ships will need to drop their weapons and put full power to the shields. There will be resistance to this but...'

'But you don't expect the FWN fleet to win against the Urigans, you just want the fleet to hold out long enough for Amber – and hopefully the Lismarians – to arrive. And when they get there, you don't want the Lismarians getting caught in the crossfire.'

'We don't have a hope on our own, regardless of where we fight them,' Gareth admitted. 'The Urigans have better shields and weapons than we do. We've not even been able to take one of their ships to examine it. On the rare occasions we've won a fight against them, they've had some sort of auto-destruct. And they've tried to take us with them.'

'If the Lismarians don't come, if Amber is late, this could go so wrong.'

'The Urigans are pushing for this fight – we can't avoid

it. They'll win if Amber doesn't come through, regardless of where we make our stand.'

'So we need to make it in the best place possible in case she does get the Lismarians' help.'

'Exactly.'

'I just hope you know what you are doing.'

Chapter 37

THE shuttle bay was crowded and uncomfortable. Cal and Amber had not expected so many Lismarians would be willing to leave their planet to go out into the unknown.

When they had first boarded, the Lismarians came off the shuttle nervously and did not know what to make of this alien space they were now in. The First Protectors, who'd been the first to arrive with Mesrra, were quick to reassure them. It was a testament to Mesrra and Brelsa that they had done their job well in showing their people what to expect once they were on board.

Amber worried that one or two of them might panic when they realised that they could not pull in power as they could on their planet. How would that panic manifest itself?

Having remained on the bridge until the *Ottawa* left Lismar's orbit, it was some time before Amber went down to the shuttle bay to see how her new passengers were faring. She'd told Mesrra to let her know immediately if there were any concerns, but she had heard nothing. As she walked in, she saw the Lismarians sitting on the floor holding hands; there was not a sound from them. They all looked calm. Not wanting to disturb them, she quietly left.

Later she questioned Mesrra about it. 'Brelsa and I were sharing our experiences, reassuring them that what we had said was true, that they would get used to it, and answering questions.'

'I didn't think you needed to hold hands for that.'

'With contact comes greater reinforcement and comfort. Also, with so many minds with so many fears, contact makes it easier to filter the minds of those who all want to talk at once.'

Amber found herself wishing her mother was here; she would love to talk to Mesrra and compare the differences in telepathy.

Though the solar lamps were stronger than those in the hydroponics of the previous ships Mesrra and Brelsa had been on, they were not sufficient for the number of Lismarians. As the days passed, panic set in. Many Lismarians were fearful; if it was like this now, what would it be like in space? Though they had Mesrra's memories, the thought of going into the unknown grew more intimidating.

Mesrra and Brelsa reshared their memories and tried to reassure them, but that got harder as the Lismarians got weaker. If they were on the ship much longer, Mesrra feared she could not stop her people giving in to their fears.

Her parents added their authority and support. 'Is there anything that can be done?' Lovoa asked her daughter, worry in her face.

'I do not know. I did not expect it to be this hard for everyone.'

'Neither did I. Many are stronger than Brelsa, but they are not coping as well as she did.'

'She was on her own so she had to manage. I think the Protectors are feeding each other's fears and doubts. We are also heading to a war, which was never the case for Brelsa or me. The risk now is greater than any of us have ever faced.'

❈

'How much longer will be on this ship?' Mesrra asked Conner after her conversation with her mother.

'We are still several days away. How are your people doing?'

'Not well. They are weakening quickly, and fear is growing over what is expected of them. They doubt that they will

survive. Do we have time to stop near a sun to let them know what it feels like, and give them a chance to experience being in space? They know the theory but they are anxious.' **Mesrra paused.** *'I do not know how long Brelsa and I can help. We are asking them to throw themselves into space and fight for us when they are feeling weaker than they have ever done.'*

'I understand. Let me see what the captain says and if there is a sun nearby. I'll keep you updated.'

'What did Conner say?' Brelsa asked Mesrra.

'She will check and get back to me.'

⚛

Amber cursed when Conner informed her of the request. She could not imagine what it was like for the Lismarians, with no knowledge of space travel or other races except for the traders who had killed so many of them. But she could well believe how scared they were.

Taking a risk, she opened communication with her father.

'Amber, do you have an update?' he asked, ignoring any niceties.

'We're heading back to FWN space but the Lismarians are not doing so well. I wondered if you had an update on the Urigans' arrival?'

'The fleet is converging around sun P215. We haven't picked up any intelligence on the Urigan fleet yet but that means little, as you know. How far out are you?' Amber told him. 'You could divert to sun P574. You'd only lose a few hours.'

'I know. But knowing how quickly a fight with a Urigan ship could be over, is it worth the risk?'

'How effective will the Lismarians be if you don't?'

Amber knew the answer to that. 'Thank you. You'll keep me updated if anything changes?'

'Of course,' her father promised.

⚛

Mesrra lined up her people by the shuttle bay hatch, after telling them that she had got them a small amount of time in space, and reminded them what to expect. When the hatch opened, they would see into space for the first time. If anyone didn't want to try, they would have to leave the shuttle bay. A shuttle had a sensor on it that allowed it to pass through the force field but this would not be possible for the Lismarians, so the force field would be lowered and the Lismarians would be pulled into space.

Mesrra felt their terror as the bay hatch opened up and they saw space and a huge sun. 'There is nothing to fear,' she tried to reassure them, though she knew most – if not all – were petrified at what they were looking at.

The first few were about to refuse and wanted to leave the shuttle bay; Mesrra knew that if one went, others would follow. *'Release the shield,'* she ordered quickly, not giving anyone a chance to pull back. 'Get ready,' she shouted, as the shuttle bay was opened up to the vacuum of space and they were all lifted off their feet.

Mesrra gently pushed herself out and into space, followed closely by Brelsa. Once they were out and directly exposed to the sun, they opened up their minds to let the others know that they were fine.

Fear started to be replaced by curiosity. Mesrra watched as most of the Lismarians tried to use their wings, even though they'd been told they were useless, and were frustrated that they didn't work. Mesrra sent the image of how to move using a small amount of their power.

Slowly, one by one, the Lismarians moved from the shuttle bay into the expanse of space. As they got used to it, Mesrra felt their fear and uncertainty being replaced by joy.

⚛

'How are they doing?' Amber asked.

'Very well. They are learning quickly. I was worried that some would refuse to go into space, but they're all out there,' Conner replied.

'We'll have to get them back on board soon. It worries me that the FWN don't know what's happening with the Urigans, and I fear a surprise attack. Can you ask Mesrra to tell them to start releasing their energy? The shuttle pilots are ready to pull them in.'

'I think we should be alright getting back on board. We have not gone far from the ship,' Mesrra said. Her telepathic connection with Conner had been getting stronger, but to have her hear the conversation with Amber?

'I want the pilots to get some experience. Better now, when you don't need them to than when you're reliant on them for survival,' Conner pointed out.

Mesrra spread the word and slowly power was released. When the levels were safely reduced, a shuttle arrived with crew members in space suits to pull the Lismarians on board. After everyone had been successfully retrieved, the *Ottawa* continued to the rendezvous point at the FWN.

Chapter 38

GARETH turned off the communication unit; it had been a relief when Amber contacted him for an update, though he had nothing useful to tell her about how far away the Urigans were. He knew she was worried. At best the enemy was still a few days away but, if the Lismarians were not in a position to fight, then it would not make a difference if she made it back in time or not. At least he knew that she had several Lismarians with her; all he could do now was hope.

The next day he was leaving Europa with his ex-wife to join the fleet, together with the UTA telepaths. Over the last week, ships had been arriving to collect the UTA telepaths; tomorrow the last would leave with them.

⚛

'You're very quiet. Are you worried about tomorrow?' Mary asked.

When Gareth had invited her to join him for dinner, he'd been surprised that she'd agreed. 'Do you have your thing with you?' he asked.

Without asking questions, Mary placed the portal shield on the table and activated it. Gareth continued, 'Amber called me just before I joined you. She's on her way back and wanted to know if there was an update about when the Urigans would arrive. I had nothing to tell her.'

'Do you think she'll arrive in time?'

'I hope so. Knowing that she's on her way is a relief. I feel reassured about my decision about the location of the rendezvous point for our fleet.'

'The others would understand, if you told them what you and Amber have planned.'

'I know, but I don't want it getting back to the Urigans.'

'Ahh, the leak,' Mary remembered. 'Do you have any idea who it is?'

'I do, but I can't find any evidence.'

'Do you want my help?'

'What could you do?' Gareth asked. 'I only suspect her because of her family connections. It was believed that her brother was involved in something dishonest – he committed suicide after the Lismarian trade was discovered. She said he did it out of guilt at not realising what was happening, but I'm not so sure. She's used this to get involved in the investigation, saying she wants answers for closure. But there's no evidence that she's done anything wrong.'

'Is there anyone else who you think might be involved?'

'No. I asked Jane to look at all the admirals and staff but she found nothing.'

'Did you get a telepath to try and read her?' Mary asked.

'Of course not. That would be illegal – you, of all people, should know that.'

'There are certain exemptions where we're allowed to violate a person's mind. National security is one of them.'

'I know that, but I thought the accusations had to be beyond reasonable doubt, which we don't have.'

'They should be, unless there is a direct and immediate threat. Then it's a balance of probabilities. With the Urigan fleet descending on us, I'll happily argue that in court afterwards if need be.'

'That's vague. What does it mean?' Gareth queried.

'Is it more likely that she is working with the Urigans than not?' Mary said simply.

'I still think it's not enough. If she's innocent, she'll haul you and the UTA through the courts.'

'If we survive the fight she can try. I can shield the UTA well enough. If she's not the leak, and if Amber doesn't get here in time, will there be a UTA or a court for her to drag us through?'

'If we do this, how do you plan to get close enough to her? Do you want me to tell her what is happening, or just make an introduction and let you do what you do? Though I should warn you that she has telepaths with her all the time and she's been trained to block out attempted mind reads.'

'So have you – and I can still read your mind anytime I want to.' At his surprised look, Mary continued. 'What you can do is good at holding out telepaths with limited training, like most of those who enter the FWN, but you could never block out highly trained or high-level telepaths.'

'You never told me that before.'

'It wasn't in my interest to do so,' Mary retorted. 'Don't be mad. If it were common knowledge, there's be no way your suspected leaker would let me anywhere near her. Who is she by the way?'

⚛

'Gareth, this is unexpected. What can I do for you?' Admiral Webb said when she answered his call.

'I thought I'd better let you know that I've formulated a better plan for communication during the battle with the Urigans. I want to discuss it with you.'

'Brilliant news! I can't wait to hear it,' Natalie said.

'I was hoping to meet in person.'

'Why? This is a secure link and we both leave Europa tomorrow. I'm sure you're as busy as I am.'

'I want the person coordinating the plan to be there to answer questions, and they're not here at the moment. Also, Admiral Holl is still here and I want her to have the chance to ask questions as well.' Gareth had no idea if Karen Holl was available or not; he cursed himself for using her name and bringing her into it.

'Why can't we all conference call later?' Natalie asked.

'We could,' he conceded. 'But this is the last night we'll

be here together. With what's coming after today, do you really want to spend it alone?'

Mary raised her eyebrows as he squirmed at his lack of finesse.

'I'll meet you at 1800 hours in my office,' Natalie said.

'Thank you, I'll see you there.' The communication link was terminated.

'"Do you really want to spend it alone?"' Mary quoted.

'After years of being diplomatic, I panicked,' Gareth admitted.

'Just as well you didn't tell her that your coordinator is your ex-wife.'

'What do you mean by that?'

'I think she hopes you'll stay afterwards.'

'No!' Gareth denied, shocked.

'Yes! And I think you better call this Karen Holl as well.'

'You think she'll want to stay as well?' he asked sarcastically.

'No, but Natalie might check that she's been consulted, and you don't want her to cancel if she thinks you are lying,' Mary pointed out. 'But you're still handsome, so you never know.'

Chapter 39

A few hours later, Gareth was being led into Natalie's office. Mary would join them a few minutes later. Before arriving, they had discussed the best way to proceed.

'Get there a few minutes early and flirt with her,' Mary advised.

'No way.'

'Your somewhat clumsy comment about not wanting to be on your own got you this meeting. If Natalie is emotionally invested in you, I'll pick up on it easily – and it may distract her when you start talking about the Urigans.'

'What happens if she recognises you as my ex-wife?'

'We've been divorced for years, and it's well known that we're not on the best of terms, so I doubt she will see it as a plot against her. Spin it that you came begging to me out of desperation. If she's jealous, it will just make her easier to read.'

'I'm learning so much about your techniques that it's unnerving,' Gareth exclaimed. 'Could she use that shield thing against us?' He was worried it could undermine what they were trying to do.

'Those are the intellectual property of the UTA. The FWN had no part in their development so she shouldn't have access to them. If she's got one, I will know quickly because she won't come close to us and I won't be able to read her. I can activate my own shield. The two won't be able to operate together, and that in itself would cause uncomfortable questions,' Mary reassured him.

At 1755 hours, he went into Natalie Webb's office. He saw the two telepathic staff officers she employed and made sure that he protected his mind against them.

Mary had reassured him that he could block them out. 'I'm the best teacher, and I checked the UTA records for who was on her staff,' she had said. But after her comments that there were telepaths who could read his mind no matter what, he was no longer quite so sure. For the first time in years, he felt a certain nervousness.

'It's good to see you again, Natalie,' Gareth said. 'I've spoken to Karen – she's unable to join us.'

Natalie didn't seem surprised and it confirmed his suspicion that the two women had spoken. 'I'm sure she'll get the briefing, together with the rest of the FWN. I'm intrigued by what you have planned. I know the tests with the FWN telepaths haven't been successful.'

'I know. If we survive this, we really must work with the UTA to see if we can continue our telepaths' training.'

'I don't think that's necessary. Regardless how good a person is, I doubt they could cope with these high-level communications.' As she spoke, one of her aides interrupted them saying that Principal Wilhelm had arrived. 'What..?'

'She's the person coordinating the plan. I did tell you that I wanted her here to go through the details with us.'

'I know, but I didn't expect it to be your ex-wife. Like I said, I don't think telepaths are the way forward in this.'

'I thought that maybe our officers weren't good enough. I didn't take the decision lightly. You must have heard that my relationship with Mary hasn't been good for a very long time. But my personal feelings for her are irrelevant in light of what's happening. Surely you agree?'

'Of course. Please show her in.' Natalie's tone was frosty.

They stood in silence for the few minutes it took for Mary to join them. To Gareth's surprise, Mary was right: Natalie was very unhappy at his ex-wife showing up.

'Principal Wilhelm, thank you for your time this evening,' Gareth said as Mary walked in. 'May I introduce you to Admiral Webb?'

'It is a pleasure to meet you,' Mary said. 'Admiral Yoland hoped that I could brief the remaining admirals.' She looked around her as if expecting to see other people.

'It will be just us,' Gareth informed her.

'We're all being very formal,' Natalie said.

'This is business, is it not?' Mary questioned and shot Gareth a look of disdain.

'Of course. Admiral Yoland had just started to explain the plan,' Natalie said.

⚛

When she arrived, Mary was relieved that the staff officers were who she'd expected to see. She had read their files and they posed no threat to her: both of them were sycophants with delusions of grandeur. Neither of them were suitable for the positions they thought they deserved. She felt them start worrying when they saw her – and so they should.

Mary felt nothing, but the office was shielded so that was not a surprise. She was left to wait for a few minutes; that wasn't something she was used to, but she guessed that Admiral Webb was not happy about her presence. Would she dare refuse Mary entry?

Mary was not left wondering for long before being shown into the office. As she walked in, Mary knew two things immediately: Natalie was not pleased to see her, and she was determined to block out any mind read. Mary was tempted to smile but kept her best 'principal demeanour' in place instead.

'This is business, is it not?' she retorted after Natalie's dig about the formalities.

'Of course, Admiral Yoland had just started to explain the plan,' Natalie said.

'Then maybe he can continue. He knows better than me what he's doing with my telepaths. If you have any questions afterwards, I'll be happy to answer them.'

'Of course. Please sit.'

As Gareth talked, Mary worked her way carefully around the mental blocks that Natalie had put in place. Whoever had trained her had not been as good as Mary. Gareth had been told to keep talking about the Urigan threat and oncoming battle as it would push thoughts associated with them to the surface.

It was not as difficult as Mary had anticipated. Natalie was terrified of the Urigans, of being found out, and for her family. Gareth was right: she was the leak.

'I know you've been giving the Urigans information and I know why,' Mary said suddenly, interrupting Gareth.

'What? How dare you?' Natalie snapped back.

'The Urigans killed your nephew. Your brother helped them because they threatened to kill the rest of his family. The trade was discovered so they killed him and made it look like suicide. But they told you what they did, didn't they? Then they threatened your family.'

'How...?' Natalie asked as the colour drained from her face.

'Easily.'

'The Urigans are going to kill my children.'

'They're going to kill everyone,' Gareth pointed out. 'Once they destroy us, no one will be safe, including your children.'

'What happened with Amber? What happened in that battle?' Natalie asked suddenly changing the topic of conversation.

'Why is that important?'

'Because until that point the Urigans were only interested in trying to get around you. After the battle with your daughter, everything changed. They saw us as a threat for the first time. That's why they are attacking now, because they're worried that if they delay we'll become more powerful than them. They want to stop us while they can.'

'Bloody hell! When they decided to come straight at us, why didn't you speak out then? Give us a chance against them?' Gareth demanded.

'Everything seemed pointless,' Natalie replied. 'I don't know what Amber did, but they said she destroyed three of their ships. Her report said one. But how could she have done that? The Urigans must have been wrong. I told them they had to be wrong, but they wouldn't listen to me,' she pleaded.

'God, Natalie, what have you done?' Gareth asked. She did not reply, just sat there crying. He turned to Mary, a question on his face. Was Natalie faking it? Mary shook her head.

'Where are your children now?' Gareth asked.

'With my husband. I haven't told him anything. He doesn't know.'

'How do you communicate with the Urigans, and how often?' Gareth asked.

Slightly taken aback by the sudden change of tack, Natalie replied, 'They gave me a device so nothing is on the FWN network.' So that was why Jane had found nothing linking her and not suspected her. 'At the start, it was a report once a month, but recently it's been more regularly.'

'What did you tell them about our daughter?' Mary wanted to know.

'Nothing! I didn't know anything other the official report. That's why I told them they had it wrong but they didn't believe me.'

'Do you know when they will engage with our fleet?'

'They'll kill my children,' Natalie pleaded.

'I'll do my best to keep them safe, but how many people will die if you don't help us now? How many people will lose their mothers, fathers, sons and daughters because of you?'

'They don't tell me their tactics.'

'You must know more than we do. Ask them to see if they give you anything. If we even knew when and where they'll attack it would help us.'

'I'll give you what I can,' Natalie promised.

Chapter 40

WITH the revelation from Natalie, Gareth was now faced with the problem of who to tell. Natalie did not know if the Urigans had any other people giving them information – and if they could get to her, they could compromise others. The three of them decided not to inform the other admirals and Natalie would excuse herself from the upcoming conflict.

'How do you propose I do that?' she demanded.

'I'm sure you could suddenly become very sick.'

'It will end my career. Whatever I decide to be sick with will prove false if they test me. I'll be seen as a coward.'

'Once this is over, do you honestly think you'll still have a job in the FWN, let alone a career?' Gareth asked brutally.

They thought about moving Natalie's family but felt it would raise questions. If the Urigans had others giving them information, it could indicate that Natalie had been compromised. Instead, security was increased around her home.

'Won't anyone think that's suspicious?' Mary asked.

'Once the media have wind of the coming clash with the Urigans, there'll be a lot of panic. The increase in security shouldn't raise any red flags.'

'That could also be the excuse when your "sickness" is looked in to – you wanted to be with your family,' Mary pointed out to Natalie.

'I'll be seen as a coward by everyone in the FWN,' she protested.

'Would you prefer to be seen as a traitor?' Gareth asked. She shook her head.

Unless she had any further updates, the Urigans were not expecting Natalie to contact them again. She admitted that she'd not told them about her meeting with Gareth as she'd not had enough information to give a complete report. She had been waiting to see what plans they discussed.

After Natalie had given the information she had about the Urigan movements and the details she had passed to them, she left Europa for home with a few trusted people from both the FWN and UTA. Gareth hoped that no one else had been threatened or corrupted.

Once Natalie had been dealt with, Gareth reached out to Amber and left a message letting her know the expected arrival time of the Urigan fleet as Natalie understood it. From where he estimated Amber was after their last communication, he didn't know if she would arrive in time.

✺

Gareth, Mary and the remaining telepaths left that morning to join the rest of the fleet.

'Why so depressed?' Mary asked him.

'It's possible that Amber won't arrive in time and the Urigan fleet will arrive sooner than we hoped.'

'Those were variables that we were already aware of. The difference is that now you know for sure and you can do something about them. Your position is no worse than it was before.'

'You're right. I just didn't expect it to be so bad.'

'I know, but we're in this together. Though I don't fully understand what Amber is doing, you have faith in her and so do I. There's still a chance she'll make it.'

Though Gareth had told Mary everything, she still struggled to appreciate how a few Lismarians with no technology could be as effective as he hoped they would be.

✺

The FWN *Sydney* joined the converging fleet around the

sun's orbit. The news that Natalie Webb was ill had been met with cynicism by the other admirals and a belief that she had no faith in Admiral Yoland's tactical decisions. Discussions about moving the fleet started to filter through the Admiralty – but to where? Everyone had different ideas, and in the meantime the Urigans were approaching. Other than retreating further into FWN space, or moving away and allowing the Urigans a clear path, they were limited in where to stand their ground.

The UTA telepaths on the *Sydney* were taken to other ships. Once everyone was in place, they started practising passing messages, getting used to their locations, strengths and skills.

'How are your telepaths doing?' Gareth asked when he caught up with Mary a short time later.

'Good. But worried, like your officers.' He imagined that was a massive understatement. Mary went on, 'Are you going to tell the other admirals what you've planned?'

'No. Just in case Natalie wasn't the only leak, I'd prefer to keep my plan as close as possible,' he said. Natalie had not known of anyone else but that didn't mean that there weren't others. 'I'm glad you're here.'

'Just like the good old days,' Mary agreed.

❃

'I hate this waiting around,' Ensign Ward said from his place on the bridge of the FWN *Sydney*.

'The sooner we move, the sooner the Urigans get to kill us,' his colleague pointed out.

'At the moment, I think I'd prefer that to this waiting.' As Ward spoke, the terminals started to indicate something big coming towards them.

'I think you just got your wish. Captain, we're picking up multiple ships approaching the sun's orbit.'

'How many?'

'Unknown at this time. They're too close together for me to get any details, especially with the radiation from the sun.'

'Keep trying,' the captain said. 'Admiral Yoland, receiving from the bridge.'

'Go ahead,' Gareth said.

'Sir, can you please come to the bridge? We're picking up non-FWN ships approaching our location.'

'I'm on my way.'

The yellow alert sounded through the ship.

⚛

'Damn!' Gareth said as he closed the communication.

'I thought you wanted them to find us here,' Mary pointed out.

'I did, just not so soon. I hope that Amber didn't delay too long, or this could all be over before she arrives.' Gareth had let her know what the situation was when Natalie had confessed to him and Mary.

He typed in a secure communication code to call Amber, to see how far out she was and tell her that the battle was imminent, but the code failed to connect. The Urigans had already taken down their communications. Frustrated, he stood up, 'Join me on the bridge?'

'Of course,' Mary said. Together they made their way there. On his request, Mary had contacted the telepaths on the other ships to let them know the situation.

'Report, Captain.'

As the captain relayed the little that he knew, Gareth's heart sank. His gamble looked like it was going to fail. Communications were down and he was grateful for the telepaths. He just hoped they would offer some advantage.

⚛

As the yellow alert sounded across the fleet, fear rippled through the crews. They were not going to meet the Urigans; the Urigans had come to them. The thought going through everyone's mind was that they had limited manoeuvrability, and no emergency pods could be deployed this close to the sun's gravity and radiation.

As Gareth listened to the crews voicing their fears, he did not tell them that this was where he'd hoped the fight would take place, albeit a little later. He wondered if the Urigans had somehow found out about Natalie and pushed for a quicker confrontation.

All the ships were communicating through the telepaths. The absence of the *Ottawa* was noted – the only ship that had twice gone against the Urigans and survived. Gossip was rife, speculating that Amber had run scared and left half her crew behind, which had been incorporated into other ships. Those who knew her could not believe it. Another rumour was that the *Ottawa* was severely damaged and not fit to join the fight. The dissenters could understand that, but then where was Captain Yoland? Why was she missing? No one could give a definite answer, other than that she must have a good reason. She was not a coward. But others said that a person could only take so much before they broke.

The consensus was: would it make a difference now? No one had been in this position before.

⚛

'Admiral, we've analysed the results of the scans. We don't believe that there are many Urigan ships at the moment and we outnumber them comfortably.'

'Have they done anything yet?' Gareth asked.

'No, sir. They seem to be waiting, probably for further ships to arrive.'

'Can we leave the sun's orbit without engaging them?' Gareth asked.

'No, they're holding orbit above us.'

'Principal Wilhelm, can you detect anything from the Urigans?' Gareth asked.

'Very little. Their minds are closed off. But with so many of them, I'm getting the feeling that they are waiting.'

'If they're waiting for more ships, we'll have no chance

against them when they arrive. From this report, we vastly outnumber the ones that are here. We'll have a good chance of winning and finding a stronger tactical position. We can't afford to wait for the Urigans to make their move. Get your crews ready and await further orders. Principal, can you please send the details to the other ships?'

'You don't want to wait until Amber arrives?' Mary asked him after the captain left to pass the order to the crew.

'I wish I could, but I don't know how far away she is. And unless she's in your range, there is no way to find out.'

'She's not. I've already tried calling her.'

'Tactically, we're in a bad place. We can't afford to be attacked here. Our best chance is to take the fight to the Urigans.'

⚛

Mary gave the word to the other ships to prepare to break the sun's orbit and attack the Urigan ships. She could feel the turmoil of emotions, not just on the *Sydney* but on the surrounding ships as well. It had been a long time since she'd had to deal with such mental volume.

She felt the change when the yellow alert escalated to red as the order to break orbit was given. The Urigans started firing as soon as the FWN fleet moved towards them, but they'd expected that and had coordinated their return attack.

As she received the details of damage on the individual ships, and as the shields started to fail, Mary relayed them to Gareth. He ordered those ships back so the ones behind them could take the lead and offer some defence. Eventually the Urigan shields started to collapse under the continued bombardment of fire from so many FWN ships.

'We're not looking to take any of their ships. I want them destroyed, not disabled,' Gareth ordered.

Mary acknowledged the order and relayed it. There was a feeling of satisfaction as the Urigans' shields failed and exploded. Relieved, the FWN ships were able to pull further out of the sun's orbit.

'Sir, communications are back online.'

'Good, I want damage reports from everyone,' Gareth ordered.

Chapter 41

MARY stood on the bridge with her ex-husband. Her heart sank as the communications went down again almost immediately. Shortly afterwards, more Urigan ships arrived on their sensors; they had not been far away, just masking their presence until they were close enough so it was too late to do anything about them. This time it was not a few ships; with the size of mass moving towards them, Mary suspected it was the main fleet.

Gareth placed his hand on her shoulder and she felt the message he was trying to communicate. Stay strong. She understood and shut her emotions down tight. She could not allow her fear to take control because it would be evident in any telepathic message she sent and could cause panic. Then there would be no hope.

'Tell them to stand by for new orders,' Gareth told Mary. He turned to the captain for an update on the number and location of the enemy ships before deciding how to move what was left of his fleet.

'Wait.' Mary cut into the conversation.

'What is it?'

'It's Amber. The *Ottawa* is here.'

'Thank God.'

'Does she know the current situation?'

'Yes, and they are ready.'

'Then let's hope we can rise from the ashes.' Mary could feel Gareth battling between fear and hope. This would be a gamble that could save or destroy them.

Gareth looked at the size the Urigan fleet. There were now more ships than he had ever thought possible. The

Urigans wanted to make sure this would be the only significant battle. The FWN could not win by conventional means – but what would happen when the Lismarians joined in? He was about to find out. This strategy was based on an isolated incident. Amber had said she'd been successful but now he had doubts.

Before he could second-guess himself he told Mary, 'Give the order.'

'To all FWN ships, power down your weapons and full power to shields. On the order of Admiral Yoland. Repeat power down all weapons and full power to shields.'

Mary got the expected wave of concern and fear as the order went out but, as one, the fleet did as it was ordered.

❈

'Captain, the FWN *Ottawa* has just arrived.'

'Better late than never. But I'm surprised Captain Yoland is bringing such a badly damaged ship into this fight. Can you reach her?' Captain Alex Wilhelm asked. He'd never believed that his cousin would abandon them but, when he saw the size of the Urigan fleet, he knew she was coming to join them in death.

'Ah, Captain,' the UTA telepath said nervously. Then he suddenly added. 'From Admiral Yoland, all ships to power down our weapons and full power to our shields.'

'Please confirm that order,' Alex said. Surely the order was suicide?

'There are multiple requests for confirmation. The order stands, sir.'

Alex bet there were. 'What is it?' he asked as he saw confusion on his telepath's face.

'I'd started to reach out to the *Ottawa* before the order came in. Everyone apart from the *Ottawa* is scared about what's about to happen.'

'How are the crew of the *Ottawa* feeling?'

'Excited. Hopeful.'

'Let's hope they – and the admiral – have a plan.' What

was his cousin planning?

The *Ottawa* moved closer to the sun, a dangerous trajectory that could see them trapped in the sun's orbit. Some of the Urigan ships started to move to intercept her. What was Amber thinking? Then the monitors lit up.

'What's happened?' Alex asked.

'I'm not sure, but it looks as if the *Ottawa* has exploded.'

'How? Did the Urigans fire on them?'

'No, it's a Lismarian energy signature.'

'How? Why?' Alex asked, but no one had an answer.

Amber was not surprised when she received the message from her father about Natalie Webb. She knew Jane would be pleased with the news, though she wondered how her father had found Natalie out if Jane hadn't discovered anything substantial. Amber's heart sank, however, when Gareth disclosed that the Urigan fleet was not that far away. He was about to leave on the *Sydney* with her mother to meet the fleet.

Amber knew that the sooner the *Ottawa* got there the better. How would the Urigans react when they discovered that Admiral Webb had been compromised?

She called a meeting with the senior engineers 'Can we get more power out of the engines?'

'Captain, we're struggling to keep them maintained as it is.'

'What if we reduce the living and operational space to an absolute minimum and strip everything that's not needed. Would that help?'

'The extra power would make a difference if the engines can take it, but it means running the ship on absolute basics. It'll be very uncomfortable.'

'It's only for a few days, the crew will cope. We have to make it back before the Urigans attack.'

'Yes, Captain. We'll do everything possible.' And they had. The next few days had been highly unpleasant for everyone.

As the *Ottawa* neared the place where the fleet was meeting, Amber tried to open communication with her father but there was nothing. Her heart sank; were they too late? She tried calling out mentally for the first time since her brain haemorrhage but all she got back was blinding pain. Her injury had not healed enough.

She checked their location; they were not far from where the fleet was converging. She called the telepaths together.

'I know I've asked a lot of you recently and I'm afraid I'm going to ask more. We are close to where the FWN was congregating. The Urigans are due to arrive at any time and the fleet's communications are down. I fear that the battle has started. I've tried – and failed – to use my telepathic abilities. I know that the UTA are working with the FWN to facilitate communication. I need you to reach out to find the ship my father is on. Tell him where we are.'

Amber sat there as they merged their minds. For what seemed like ages nothing seemed to happen and she felt like clawing the table in frustration.

She received an update from the bridge about weapons' fire and a lot of both FWN and Urigan ships ahead. She was about to go to the bridge when Conner spoke.

'Captain, we're picking up a lot of minds. The fleet was attacked but they punched through the Urigan line. But most of the enemy fleet is now approaching. We can't isolate who it is you need to communicate with. None of the minds are familiar and there's too much mental noise.'

'I'm going to try and come in at the bottom of the feed.'

'Captain, is that wise?' Conner asked.

'I won't be taking the mental strain – that still falls to Ensign Mann. But I may be able to direct the focus.'

It was the first time she had not been at the centre of a mind merge and the feeling was strange. Instead of leading, her mind was being led and she had to relinquish control to Conner.

It didn't take her long to hear a very familiar mind giving

orders. For some reason, she was surprised that her parents were working together.

As one mind, the telepaths reached out to her mother.

❊

Amber was relieved when her mother responded to the merge. Mary confirmed that she would make sure that her father was aware and the order would go out to the rest of the fleet. They were to await confirmation that it had been given.

In the meantime, Amber had Conner released from the merge. 'We won't need a merge this close to the fleet. Ensign Mann can maintain contact. I need you to go down to the shuttle bay. Make sure Mesrra and her people are ready to go. Let them know about the current situation. Keep us updated.'

'Yes, Captain,' Conner confirmed and left the room.

Everyone else sat there in anticipation. Communication from the bridge was that they would be within the sun's orbit in the next five minutes.

If the fleet had not been told what was happening, Amber imagined that the captains would think the order was insane. She hoped their training to follow a lawful order would stand so the Lismarians didn't get fired on by the FWN ships.

'Order has been received, you are good to go.' Amber released the breath she hadn't realised she was holding as the message came from her mother. She broke from the mind merge, ordering the others to tell her if there were any updates.

Instead of calling Conner, she ran to the shuttle bay. As the doors opened, she could see that the Lismarians were ready to go.

'It's time. Any questions?' she asked. When no one said anything, she continued, 'Conner and I have to leave the shuttle bay. But thank you and good luck.'

As they left, Amber gave the order to release the hatch.

She ordered the *Ottawa* to fly close to the sun then along the Urigan line, hoping to spread the Lismarians as far as possible.

❀

Mesrra stood with her family and friends after Amber and Conner left. Though they'd had a chance to practise flying in space it had been brief, and only Mesrra had been in a fight. Her shared memories had given the others an idea of what that was like, but now the fight was in front of them. Their feelings were mixed: finally they had a chance to take revenge on the people who had been skinning them alive but there was also a fear of the unknown. Would they come back from this?

They watched as the shuttle bay doors opened onto space with the huge hot sun in front of them. The FWN should have still been in orbit but it was clear that something had happened that had pulled them further away than Amber and her father had planned.

When Mesrra had spoken with Conner, she'd decided it would be best to release near the sun so they could take in as much power as possible before engaging the Urigans. Mesrra thought the fleet was still near enough to the sun for them to keep up their energy levels but she didn't want to chance it.

'*You can go when you're ready,*' Conner told Mesrra.

'*Understood,*' Mesrra said, before turning to her parents. 'They are ready for us to go and fight.'

'In this you are the leader. You are the First Protector. We will follow you,' Lovoa said.

Mesrra smiled before turning to her people. 'We go now to fight. If we fail today, the humans will also lose. Our people will be lost. I cannot guarantee we will all return, but we must win today if our people are to survive. You all volunteered to come here. Now is the time for us to be the Protectors we were born to be.'

'*Release the shuttle bay's shield,*' Mesrra ordered Conner.

As before, the area became a vacuum. Mesrra immediately pushed herself into space and waited for the others to join her. As they pulled in as much power as they could, she felt the euphoria taking over from the fear.

Once they were ready, Mesrra made sure the Lismarians knew which were the enemy's ships. They broke into three groups, her parents leading one, Brelsa, Isslac and Erle leading another, and Mesrra taking the ships that were the furthest away from them.

The Lismarians started their attack.

⚛

'Sir, the *Ottawa* hasn't been destroyed. They're still there,' the telepath informed Captain Wilhelm.

'Are you sure?'

'Yes, sir. I can still sense the crew. They're fine – if anything, their feelings have intensified with anticipation.'

'Ensign, what exactly are the scans showing?'

'There is a massive power surge. The *Ottawa* should be gone, but the energy is blocking accurate readings. I don't know, sir,' the ensign admitted. 'I've never seen anything like it.'

'Keep me updated on any change,' the captain said. If this was part of the admiral's plan, he wished he knew what it was. He had experienced first-hand the power the Lismarians could wield but that was with the help of a man-made machine. He had no idea what was happening here.

'Sir, the massive energy signature is moving away from the *Ottawa* and heading towards the Urigan fleet. It seems to be breaking up slightly.'

'Any indication as to what it is?'

'No, sir, just that it has a Lismarian energy signature.'

'But they have no technology. How is that possible?' one of the crew asked.

'I don't think it's technology, I think it's the Lismarians,' the telepath said.

'Explain.'

'I couldn't sense them before – they must have been shielded. But that moving energy is a cluster of a lot of very determined minds.'

'How is that possible?' the captain asked.

Chapter 42

MESRRA led her people towards the Urigan ships. It was different this time, knowing she would have to fight further away from the sun, that she was possibly leading her people to their death. She could still feel the heat from the sun and common sense told her they would be alright. They were still closer to the sun than she was on Lismar – but on Lismar they had atmosphere and air. Here they had to keep pulling on their power to survive the vacuum of space and to manoeuvre themselves.

They would have to make every move and shot count, and hope that the FWN shuttles would collect them as promised if they were too drained to return to the *Ottawa*. They had only tried this briefly— Mesrra stopped that thought; now was not the time for doubt.

When she arrived at the far end of the line of Urigan ships a short while later, she knew the others had spread out as they had been told to. They were small, so on their own they were an almost impossible target for the Urigans; in a cluster, they gave the enemy a target. When the Lismarians were in place, the Urigans were in front and the FWN behind them.

For a moment everything was still, both sides unsure what was happening.

Mesrra wished she knew what the Urigans were thinking; she could sense them but could not understand their minds. Did they not consider the Lismarians a threat? How wrong they were.

Mesrra let out the first burst of energy, though not as powerful as the first time. Now she had a better understanding of the level of energy needed and this fight was going to last longer.

She guessed the shields went down on the second blast as she watched, relieved, as the Urigan ship broke apart. She shared with the others the amount of energy she had expended, hoping that, as the fight progressed, they would understand the information better and become proficient in their energy use.

The Urigans did not sit complacently for long. As soon as the first ship was attacked, they started firing back. The size of the Lismarians made it difficult for them to be locked onto but Mesrra was still worried as the enemy fire went past her. She realised that the Urigans didn't need to be accurate, they just needed to fire a lot and chance that they would hit her people and kill them. It was a sentiment that her people shared, and they started to speed up their attack on the Urigans.

As if realising that trying to kill this new threat was pointless, the Urigans started firing past them and at the FWN fleet instead. The order to the FWN fleet to power down weapons made them vulnerable but if they fired on the Urigans, they risked the Lismarians being caught in the cross-fire.

Mesrra stopped being conservative about the amount of power she used – now she just wanted this over. She increased the strength and power in each blast and shared why she was doing it. They needed to protect the humans.

She felt the others following her lead. They would have to trust Amber and the crew on the *Ottawa* to bring them home safely if they drained themselves too much.

❁

'Captain, I don't fully understand what's happening but a Urigan ship has just been destroyed.'

'I'd say the admiral definitely has a plan. Keep me updated. I want to know everything that is happening,' Captain Wilhelm said.

'Yes, sir. It looks as if they have split up and more shots have been fired. They're attacking multiple locations across the enemy line. It appears that every shot is accurate. They're inflicting significant damage.'

'Are the Urigans not retaliating?'

'They are starting to fire at the energy sources.'

'Any direct hits?'

'Impossible to say, sir. Do you want me to re-engage our weapons?'

'No, we await further orders.' Alex could feel the crew about to object, wanting to get in on the fight, just as the telepath relayed a message from the admiral for everyone to hold their positions with shields up and weapons down.

Like his crew, he didn't like it but, not knowing what was happening for sure out there, he had to trust his orders.

❁

The retaliation from the Urigans did not stop the Lismarians. When the Urigans attack on the FWN fleet prompted a vicious retaliation from Mesrra and her people, they stopped and again tried to take them out instead. As Amber had suggested though, it just made it a bit more interesting for the Lismarians because, alone in space, they were too small a target.

Ship after ship sustained direct hits, the Urigans shields unable to hold for long against the power of the blasts. This resulted in severe losses very quickly; every blast saw the Urigan ships at best disabled, at worst destroyed.

❁

'Sir, it looks like the Urigans are retreating. What do you want us to do?'

'Let them go,' Admiral Yoland said.

'We could finish this today,' the captain said.

'There may be many more Urigans. I'm not prepared to risk our ships, or the Lismarians, in case they're trying and lead us into a trap. If they come back, we must be ready to fight.'

'Admiral, Captain Yoland is asking for shuttles to be deployed to pick up the Lismarians and bring them back to the *Ottawa*. They're asking for at least one telepath per shuttle,' Mary cut in, after receiving the message from the *Ottawa*'s telepaths.

'Pass the order to the other ships. Let's bring them in safely.'

⚛

'Captain, we're being asked to deploy as many shuttles as possible to collect the Lismarians who are too drained to return to the *Ottawa*. They need a telepath on board to assist with communication.'

'I'm looking forward to reading a report about what exactly just happened. But for now, let's get those shuttles out,' Alex Wilhelm responded.

'Sir, may I go?' asked Emily Wilson, the UTA telepath, taking him by surprise. He'd been about to order one of the telepaths on his crew to go.

'I don't know what you'll encounter out there. We can't guarantee your safety.'

'I know, but my safety wasn't guaranteed when I agreed to come on board for this war. I felt the Lismarians out there and I can still feel them. I think I can help your officers locate them and bring them safely on board.'

'Then report to the shuttle bay. I want a full debrief when you return.'

'Yes, sir,' she said and left the bridge.

He wondered what his aunt would say about him sending one of her UTA telepaths instead of an FWN one.

⚛

Emily climbed onto a shuttle and was handed an environmental suit. 'Do you know how to put it on?'

'Yes,' she replied. She'd travelled enough in her role in the UTA that putting on one of these suits had become part of her annual assessment.

'Get it on. We'll have to open the shuttle's doors. The shielding is not as strong as on the ships, and we'll lose enough of the life support to make it very unpleasant.'

Emily nodded and pulled on the suit as quickly as she could. She could feel the Lismarians, could feel their fear and despair. They were so drained that they were struggling in space.

✢

Now the fight was over, and the overwhelming emotions associated with the battle had started to subside, Mesrra began to feel a different fear. While she still had some energy left, others were dangerously drained because they had moved further away from the sun during the fight. She didn't know if they were near enough, especially the older Protectors like Gilcan whose ability to absorb energy had started to fail. Though Mesrra knew she would be fine, she wasn't sure about all of her people. Yes, they were close to a sun but surviving in space took considerable energy in itself.

'Those of you who can, get close to those who are drained. I don't want to risk the shuttles not finding everyone because some are too weak. Being close together will make it easier for them to pick us up,' Mesrra instructed.

She felt the acknowledgement, and the Lismarians clustered together. She saw a couple who were almost unconscious and propelled herself to them. She pulled them to where she could sense others trying to move. Slowly small groups emerged.

'Can you let me know who is in each group? I want to know if we are missing anyone,' Mesrra ordered.

One person from each group gave the names. She was relieved when her mother updated her group. She had not felt anyone die during the fight but, with the amount of energy expended, a death could have been missed. To lose someone now because they were too weak to help themselves was not an option.

As the last group checked in, Mesrra knew everyone was accounted for. They did not have to wait for long for the shuttles to appear, more shuttles than Mesrra had expected. She closed her eyes in relief, realising that Amber must have asked other ships for help. Her people had a chance.

❁

'They're moving,' Emily informed the shuttle pilot as they started to approach.

'I thought they knew to hold position and not to try to return to the *Ottawa*. If they spread out further, we may not find them all,' the pilot said.

'They're not returning to the *Ottawa*, they're grouping together to make it easier for us to find them.'

'Understood.' A communication went out to the other shuttles; they'd noticed the same thing and they coordinated the groups each shuttle would cover. They spread themselves evenly so no group was left without help.

As their shuttle approached a group, Emily checked to make sure her suit was on correctly and she was hooked in when the doors opened. That happened almost immediately. As the hatch opened, she was glad she was secure; so close to open space, Emily felt that if she took a wrong step she would fall forever.

Outside she saw a cluster of bodies and another shuttle on the other side of them. 'Stay on board to receive them,' she was told.

The other crew members went into space. The stronger Lismarians passed the weaker ones over, making sure they were safe before getting on board themselves. With the other shuttles, they were able to take them back to the *Ottawa* where it held its orbit in the sun.

Chapter 43

AMBER sighed with relief when Mesrra reported that all the Lismarians were accounted for. Some were so weak that it was decided to leave the shuttle bay hatch open for a short period of time to let them absorb what they needed from the sun.

Amber was going to the shuttle bay to meet them when Cal called her, a worried look on his face. 'Captain, we may have a problem,' he said.

'Are more Urigans coming?'

'No, not that I'm aware of. But I'm getting an alert. The sensor net around Lismar appears to be down.'

'Do you know for sure? Could it just be a fault with the net?'

'Without going there and checking, I don't know. I've tried to run some diagnostic checks from here and nothing is coming back. If it were a technical fault, I'd expect something but it's as if the net is no longer there.'

'I can guess what you're going to say but I'm going to ask anyway. What could cause this?'

'Something – or someone – has taken it down. I believe it's deliberate. I don't believe for a moment that the Lismarians fired on it by accident.'

Cursing, Amber went back to her office with Cal following. She put a call through to her father, hoping that communications would have returned now the Urigans had left. The call went through but it took a while for him to respond; he probably had a lot to deal with.

'Amber, it's good to hear from you. Your arrival was very timely – but now is not a good time.'

'I know, but Cal has just told me the sensor net around Lismar has gone down. He doesn't believe it's a fault,' she said, getting straight to the point.

'Damn. I'll get back to you.'

With a sinking heart, Amber left Cal in her office while she returned to the bridge. Not wanting the Lismarians to be without support, Amber asked Conner to stay there and keep her updated until she could talk to Mesrra and her parents. Reports from engineering were coming in, which kept her occupied until her father called her back. She returned to her office to take the call.

'I've just confirmed what Cal told you,' Gareth said. 'I want you to get back to Lismar now and report. I'm sending Alex and the *London* with you.'

'If the Lismarians have been attacked, I don't think two ships will be much use. The only people who can help are the Lismarians I have on board.'

'If the Urigans are in space when you get there, yes. If they're on the surface of the planet, it's a different matter. And you don't have many shuttles. We don't know what has happened yet. I don't want you assuming that you're invincible because the Lismarians are with you. Your ship is in an awful state. Don't take unnecessary risks.'

'Understood. What will the other admirals and the head chairman say about us returning to Lismar?'

'You're returning because the Lismarians are under attack. Who better to send?'

'Thank you.'

❄

With a heavy heart, Amber went down to the shuttle bay to talk to Mesrra and her parents. As she walked in, she could see that they were ecstatic at what they had achieved. Except for Lovoa and Solvan, it was the first time the Lismarians had been able to strike against the people who had caused them so much pain – and they wanted to inflict more on them. Their success made them think that they had the chance to be free of fear.

Mesrra saw Amber when she walked in and quickly realised that something was wrong.

'Can I talk to you and your parents alone?' Amber asked.

'Of course.'

Amber assumed Mesrra called them mentally because Lovoa and Solvan came over immediately. Together, they left the shuttle bay.

'What is wrong, Amber?' Mesrra asked as the doors closed behind them.

'I'm sorry to have to tell you this, but the sensor net we placed around your planet has failed.'

'What does that mean?' Lovoa asked.

'We don't believe it was a technical failure.'

'You think our planet has been attacked?'

'It's a definite possibility,' Amber admitted. 'We're heading back now with the FWN *London* to find out.'

'Last time it did not take the Urigans long to get the skins they wanted. We won't get back in time,' Lovoa pointed out.

'They took advantage of our attention being focused on the battle. They knew there wasn't anything we could do until it was too late,' Mesrra realised.

'We won't know for sure, but that is likely,' Amber said. 'I'm sorry, I never expected this would happen.'

'It is not your fault. Kelvic is on Lismar and he has a new machine. We made sure that none of the collectives were unprotected. It is unlikely that our being there would have made much of a difference,' Solvan said. 'Thank you for letting us know. We'll inform the others. Can you tell us if you learn anything new?'

'Of course.'

❃

The news of what had happened at home quickly changed the celebratory mood among the Lismarians to one of fear and worry. They knew what an attack meant: people would have been skinned alive, and they were too far away to tell if any of their families had died.

'He was too young. I should not have left him to manage the collective with his mate,' Isslac said, referring to his son.

'We made the decision together. He and his mate wanted the chance to prove themselves. He is very sensible and level headed. They are as strong as us, even though they are younger.' Erle tried to reassure him and herself at the same time.

'I would not have left if I had thought...' Isslac broke off, unable to continue.

'None of us did. But they are better equipped than we were last time. They have been running through the drills with you. They know what is needed.'

Brelsa heard her brother and Erle talking. They could not hide their fear for their children. Even though they had travelled together for days, she had avoided them – avoided most of her people, if she were honest. She'd kept mainly to herself and only talked to Mesrra and the First Protectors. Her brother had tried to engage with her but she had rejected him. Now she regretted it. The thought that their children might be dead, her nephew and niece, and that she knew nothing about them filled her with sorrow.

For the first time, she sat on the floor next to them. 'I'm sorry,' she said, not sure what else to say.

'Thank you. We worry about them, but they are strong and better than us,' Isslac said, alluding to their father's behaviour. 'Would you like to know about our children?'

'Yes, please.'

Isslac took Brelsa's hand as he showed her everything.

Chapter 44

AMBER dreaded what they would find as they approached Lismar. They had travelled as quickly as possible but their engines would not let them go at maximum speed. She had tried to get other ships to go ahead of them but most of the fleet had sustained damage; if the Urigans were in orbit, then the Lismarians would be the best line of defence. Even if another ship could be used, it would take too long to fit it out with the specialist shielding the *Ottawa* had in place.

Amber understood, but it still seemed so slow. She visited the shuttle bay every day to talk to the Lismarians but she never had any news that would ease their worry. There were no FWN ships nearer than the *Ottawa*, so they would be the first to arrive.

As they approached sensor range, Amber found herself holding her breath. If it had been the Urigans, were they still there? And if not, what destruction had they left behind?

'Captain, long-range sensors are detecting debris around the planet.'

'That's to be expected with the net down,' Amber replied.

'No, Captain, there is extensive debris. Most of it appears to be Urigan.'

Tired of going through Conner, Amber tried reaching out. *'Mesrra, can you and your parents join me on the bridge?'* She felt Mesrra's acknowledgement and waited for them to arrive. She was worried that the Urigans had slipped past them, but was also relieved that the Lismarians had defended themselves – though to what extent was still to be discovered.

When Mesrra and her parents arrived, Amber filled them in. 'Are you near enough for communication?' she wanted to know.

'We will try,' Lovoa replied.

Everyone was tense as they waited, Amber kept telling herself they weren't in Brelsa's proven range from past trips – but Mesrra and her parents? She so hoped for some indication of what they were approaching. They did not have to wait for long.

'We can just reach Kelvic. He said everything is alright.'

'That's good news. Let's get closer and update the FWN *London*,' Amber ordered.

Both ships approached Lismar cautiously. There was a growing feeling of hope among the crew and among the Lismarians. As the FWN *Ottawa* got closer, Mesrra reassured Amber that there was no threat on the planet. Their own sensors were detecting nothing near in space.

'Kelvic is glad we are returning,' Lovoa informed Amber. 'He says they were attacked but there is no threat now. We can land on the plateau.'

'Thank you, Lovoa. Open communication to the *London*.' Once the other ship had acknowledged, she continued. 'Alex, we've had an update from the planet. It appears safe to take a shuttle down.'

'Amber, I hope you're not suggesting going down to the planet yourself.'

'We can't take all the Lismarians down in one go. Most of them will have to stay on board. Our ships will be well protected while I'm on the planet. Alex, with everything that's happened, I can't hand this off to someone else. My crew are competent and they have you, though you're on a different ship this time.'

'I want regular updates from both your crew and yourself.'

'Of course. Thank you, Alex.'

❄

Mesrra boarded the shuttle with her parents and Amber, and Conner as the pilot. Isslac was left in charge of the Lismarians, with Brelsa to help him liaise with the humans. He had been reassured by the information from Kelvic; there had been a few fatalities but none on his collective. His children were alive.

They made the trip down to Lismar in silence. It was not long before Conner landed. The Lismarians unstrapped themselves and waited as the shuttle door opened.

The first person Mesrra saw was her brother. She ran out with her parents beside her, their minds reaching out and sharing, reassuring themselves that all was well.

Kelvic was going to share what had happened on the planet, but Lovoa stopped him. 'The humans are with us.'

Kelvic saw Amber and Conner standing by the shuttle, giving the family space for their reunion. 'I'm sorry. Please come in and I will explain everything that happened here.'

Once they had all settled inside, Kelvic started to explain. 'We did not feel them in the same way as before. There were no nightmares, no fear, only a feeling of something not quite right.'

Mesrra remembered that feeling when the *Ottawa* had been attacked.

'Knowing these Urigans were different, Derla and I started to contact the other Protectors, just in case. The first we knew of the attack was when I was contacted by Protector Hika, informing me that shuttles were landing on his collective and that he needed help. We sent energy over to them and they destroyed the shuttles before anyone was killed. Protector Jivok's collective was not so lucky – they lost a few of their workers before we could send over the energy to him.'

'What about the ships in orbit?' Lovoa asked.

'Not knowing how many more shuttles might come, and because of the risk of losing more people, I wanted to stop them coming down to the planet. I remembered what you had both shared,' Kelvic indicated his parents, 'and how you felt the threat from space. This time the minds were not as open and we could feel a mental barrier. We knew something was there and it was not human, so we took the decision to fire. There were no further attacks and we could not feel anything any more. Did we do wrong?'

'No. We analysed the debris in orbit and it was Urigan. If you hadn't fought back, they would have kept on attacking you,' Amber told him.

'Can you tell Cal thank you? From what I know from my parents' memories, this machine worked much better than the one they had.'

'I will. In what way was it better?' Amber asked.

'We did not experience the power drain that my parents did after sending energy over to a collective. And it allowed us to get several blasts into space. We are not as strong, but it helped us do more.'

'I'm relieved that Cal built it for you. He'll be very proud to know it worked so well.' That was an understatement; Cal had not been happy to be left off the shuttle, but Amber hadn't wanted all the conversation to be about him and his machine.

'Now it is your turn. What happened when you left?' Kelvic asked. They told him everything.

'So are the Urigans gone?' Kelvic asked.

Amber suspected it was a question that all the Lismarians were afraid to ask. 'I don't know. We caused them a lot of damage but only time will tell if it was enough,' she admitted.

'So what happens now?' Mesrra asked.

'That's something both our peoples are going to have to work out.' Amber could only guess at the ramifications of her actions. Though there had been two sanctioned visits to Hannoki's Peak, the other visits broke so many laws.

Amber knew what the Lismarians wanted to know: would those who had left the planet to fight be allowed to return home to their families?

Chapter 45

AMBER was saying her goodbyes to the First Protectors. Mesrra was next to her, having declared her intention to return to the FWN with Amber, much to her parents' disappointment.

Brelsa had asked to stay on Lismar; she wanted to get to know her brother and his family again. Amber had agreed, though she had no idea what her superiors would say. The arguments for not allowing Brelsa to return to Lismar were now redundant, especially as the other Lismarians were staying as well.

Shuttles had been ferrying the Lismarians to the plateau for the last hour or so. Cal had come down and gone straight to 'his' machine. He told Amber he wanted to run some diagnostics on it and spent time quizzing Kelvic on how he felt it had worked. He wanted more detail than Amber could give him.

Both the *Ottawa* and *London* stayed in orbit for a few days after the Lismarians left. The engineering team wanted to try and improve the ship's systems before starting the return journey. Amber was happy to agree as it also gave the Lismarians a chance to settle back with their people. She'd said that if anyone wanted to remain on the *Ottawa* she would be happy to take them.

Before leaving Lismar, Amber called her father and told him all that had happened, including about the machine that Cal had made. She thought her father would order her to bring it back but he did not.

'We've failed to protect the Lismarians on more than one occasion,' Gareth said. 'Without the machine, I hate to think how many of them would have killed. They can keep it until a decision is made about how best to proceed. If it's there, we won't need to worry about maintaining ships in orbit. For now, I want you and Alex back at Europa.'

As Amber turned towards the shuttle, Lovoa asked, 'I am curious. There was a symbol on the bridge wall. Was it ever different?'

Amber knew the symbol she was talking about: it was the FWN emblem that was displayed throughout the ship but most prominently on the bridge. 'It's changed over time. The current emblem has been in place for about ten years. The old one was very similar, though. Why do you ask?'

'I have seen something like it before. I had no idea what it meant but I think you might know. Can I show you?'

Curiously, Amber followed Lovoa. Solvan and Mesrra went with them. They didn't go far, just to the corner of the plateau where a wall protected a steep drop. Lovoa pointed to small markings on a rock. Amber recognised them as symbols for both the FWN and UTA. These could only have been made by her grandfather – but why on a wall?

She couldn't see their purpose until she realised that she was not looking at a wall. It stopped before the steep drop and was oblong in shape. Was her grandfather trying to give a signal should humans return there? Was this mark his way of saying he'd been there? Then she realised that 'the wall' was the right shape to take a body.

Amber contacted the *Ottawa* and asked for a detailed local scan at her exact location, looking specifically for human remains. She didn't have to be on the ship to know that her request confused the crew. Though the ships were capable of these scans, it was rare to use them unless on a rescue or retrieve mission.

'Captain.' The call came in.

'Go ahead.'

'We have detected human remains. The DNA is in our systems.'

'Is it David Wilhelm?'

'Yes, Captain.'

Amber placed her hand against the burial stone, her feelings mixed. She was not used to people burying their dead; the dead were cremated or sent into space. She didn't know what her mother would say about this.

'Captain, the scan showed something else as well – trace elements that shouldn't be there.'

'What does that mean?'

'I don't know if this is technology, operational or otherwise. The scans show elements that don't exist on Lismar. The quantity is minimal, so they wouldn't have been picked up by a general scan. I'm sending the information down to you.'

Looking at the reading that came up on her suit computer pad, Amber saw the materials were at the end of the burial area. There was a separate area, like a small step with a loose top. Underneath was a compartment with a small solar recording device.

Picking it up, Amber thought it looked intact and she wondered what was on it. The technology was too out of date for anything on the *Ottawa* to download and play it. She had to hope that Jane and Cal had something they could use.

'You know what this is,' Lovoa stated.

'Yes, the body of my grandfather. He was the one who built the original machine. After his wife – mate – died, he came back here. Until recently, we thought he'd died in an accident, then we discovered that he'd let us think that so no one would look for him here. Can I take this?' Amber indicated the device. 'And leave him as he is?' She pointed at the burial place.

'Of course. This is a sacred place for the First Protectors. We would not dream of touching it.'

Which may, Amber thought, cause problems if her family wanted to bring her grandfather's remains home. With a sudden, surprising reluctance she turned back to the shuttle.

Mesrra and her parents followed. As the hatch opened, Mesrra turned to say farewell. 'Hopefully, I can return here to Lismar,' Mesrra said.

'I hope so,' Lovoa replied. 'You will always have a place here should you come home.'

'Remember what I showed you,' Mesrra instructed her brother.

He nodded; he had been amazed at the information his sister had learnt in what she called the hydroponics bay. He was keen to see what he could use to improve their farming methods.

'I will,' he promised. 'I will miss you.'

'I know, and I will miss you all very much. But I know I can do so much more with the humans than I ever could here.'

'We understand,' he said, referring not just to himself but his mate and their parents.

As they boarded the ship ready to leave Lismar, Amber wondered briefly what that had been about but decided she really didn't want to know.

Epilogue

BOTH the *Ottawa* and *London* returned to Europa without incident. Amber and Alex received orders to disembark immediately and report to the admirals' conference room. The crews were to remain on board for the time being.

Alex transferred to the *Ottawa* and Amber had Conner fly them both down in a shuttle, telling the ensign to wait in the craft for further orders. Neither of the captains knew how long they would be.

When they entered, they saw Admirals Yoland and Johnson. Amber had kept her father informed of everything that had occurred, and it had been agreed that the Lismarians should be left on their planet. Gareth Yoland did not want others in the FWN to try and make them return to a culture that could not support them properly. He also feared that the medical community would renew their efforts to examine them. Gareth could see that, now there were several Lismarians, the previous rejection of the medical exams would be overturned.

To get support, he had briefed Admiral Simon Johnson and revealed his and Amber's plan. Simon's initial reaction been one of anger that Gareth had not trusted him. 'I could have helped you,' he'd argued.

'Not knowing how this was going to work out, I couldn't take the chance,' Gareth explained. 'If my actions ended my career, I needed someone I trusted to take over.'

Simon couldn't argue against that.

Amber and Alex were now standing in front of them. 'Stop looking so worried, both of you,' Admiral Yoland said. 'We asked you here so we could get your view on the best way forward with the Lismarians.'

'I think they will progress as normal if we leave them in peace. They are so short-lived that it won't take long for these events to pass into their history and then become legends. From what I understood from Mesrra, the attacks from seventy-five years ago have started to be seen by many as a boogieman story to scare the people. When the attacks started again, a lot of people thought they were part of a power play, which is why so many died at the start.'

'That's interesting. You said that only the First Protectors knew about the machine. Is this still the case?'

'Yes. Though Cal made two, only one was used. Both remain on Hannoki's Peak and they don't plan to share the knowledge with anyone else.'

'Good.' Yoland paused. Amber felt so frustrated as she waited for him to continue. 'Also, I understand Mesrra returned with you. She didn't want to stay with her people?'

'She wants to work with us around the Urigan threat. She's not convinced that they won't be back and she didn't want to sit on Lismar and wait.'

'Though we dealt the Urigans a significant blow, I fear she is right. We have no intelligence about the size of their fleet. She is more than welcome, and it could benefit us greatly to have her with us – especially if we need to maintain communications with her people.'

'They won't be left alone now?'

'By us, yes; by the Urigans, I have no idea. Everyone knows what the Lismarians can do. The Urigans were dealt a significant defeat. I don't think they'll forget recent events as quickly as the Lismarians.'

'What's likely to happen now?' Amber asked.

'I don't know. There is a lot that has to be assessed but I'll make it clear that you were acting on my orders when you left for Lismar.'

'That won't cover the major breaches in law.'

'Those breaches in law are why we are all still alive. If you hadn't arrived when you did, I'd have given the fleet half an hour before we lost. A lot of people know that.'

Amber and Alex were dismissed after finishing their report.

'I worry that they're right. The Lismarians were too effective, and no Urigan ships remained,' Johnson said.

'Including those that went to their planet.'

'The Urigans may now want more than just their wings.'

'I know – but hopefully they won't try anything again soon.'

Amber asked all of her family who were on Europa to meet her the following night. She had something she wanted to show them.

'Thank you all for coming,' she said as they settled in her mother's sitting room. Amber had not explained why she wanted to talk to them, just that it was important. 'As you know, I've just returned from Lismar. When I was there, I found something that I want to show you.'

'Why did you not mention this in the debrief?' her father asked. She had promised that she had disclosed everything.

'This is personal and to do with our past. When it was created, the Urigans were not known to us.' Amber put the small device on the table in front of her. On the trip back, Jane had downloaded the contents into a readable format so the contents could be played. Amber had decided not to see what was stored on the device. 'This was hidden next to a grave, a human grave on Lismar.'

'My father?' Mary asked.

'Yes. The Lismarians didn't know it was a grave, just a sacred place for the First Protectors.'

'What's on it?'

'I don't know. Jane converted the file so it can be played but I haven't seen it yet. That's why I asked you all here, so we could see it together.'

Amber pressed play. Her grandfather's face came up

onto the screen.

'If any of my family ever see this, I'm sorry. I thought it easier to let you think I had died in a shuttle accident. If you have found this, I'm assuming my worst fears have come to pass and the Lismarians have been attacked again. I came here as I did not trust the FWN to keep them safe. I wanted to prepare them as best I could. I hope you understand why I did what I did. This will be a log of my time here.'

If you have enjoyed this series, please remember to leave a review.

You can also follow me on Facebook and Instagram at @emmakblacker

Link to my newsletter https://landing.mailerlite.com/webforms/landing/i7n8z6